SPECIAL MESSAGE TO READERS

Jim Eldridge was born in central London towards the end of World War II, and was blown up (but survived) during attacks by V2 rockets on the area where he lived. He left school at sixteen and did a variety of jobs before training as a teacher. In 1971, he sold his first sitcom (starring Arthur Lowe) to the BBC, and had his first book commissioned. Since then, he has had over one hundred books published. He lives in Kent with his wife.

You can discover more about the author at jimeldridge.com

MURDER AT THE ASHMOLEAN

Oxford, 1895: A senior executive at the Ashmolean Museum is found in his office with a bullet hole between his eyes, a pistol discarded close by. The death has been ruled as suicide, but the museum's administrator suspects foul play. With his cast-iron reputation for shrewdness, private enquiry agent Daniel Wilson is a natural choice to discreetly explore the situation, ably assisted by his partner, archaeologist-cum-detective Abigail Fenton. Yet their enquiries are hindered by an interfering lone agent from Special Branch, ever secretive and intimidating in his methods. With rumours of political ructions from South Africa, mislaid artefacts and a lost Shakespeare play, the pair soon find themselves tangled in bureaucracy, facing players who live by a different set of rules. They will need their intellect and ingenuity to reveal the secrets of the aristocracy.

Books by Jim Eldridge
Published by Ulverscroft:

BLOOD ON THE WALL
MURDER AT THE FITZWILLIAM
MURDER AT THE BRITISH MUSEUM

JIM ELDRIDGE

MURDER AT THE ASHMOLEAN

Complete and Unabridged

CHARNWOOD
Leicester

First published in Great Britain in 2019 by
Allison & Busby
London

First Charnwood Edition
published 2019
by arrangement with
Allison & Busby Limited
London

A catalogue record for this book is available
from the British Library.

ISBN 978–1–4448–4314–9

Published by
F. A. Thorpe (Publishing)
Anstey, Leicestershire

Set by Words & Graphics Ltd.
Anstey, Leicestershire
Printed and bound in Great Britain by
T. J. International Ltd., Padstow, Cornwall

This book is printed on acid-free paper

For Lynne, for ever, as always

1

Oxford, 1895

Daniel Wilson and Abigail Fenton stood in the book-lined office and studied the walnut desk and the empty leather chair behind it.

'And this is where Mr Everett's body was discovered?' Daniel asked Gladstone Marriott.

'Yes,' said Marriott. 'Sitting in that chair, his head thrown back, with a bullet hole in the middle of his forehead. The pistol was on the floor beside the chair. The police believe it fell from his hand after he'd shot himself.'

The three of them were in the office of the recently deceased Gavin Everett, a senior executive at the Ashmolean Museum in Oxford. Daniel and Abigail had travelled to Oxford to investigate the death of Everett after receiving a telegram from Marriott requesting their help.

'The Ashmolean is possibly the most famous museum in Oxford,' Abigail had informed Daniel on their train journey from London. 'It's also very old.'

'Older than the Fitzwilliam in Cambridge?' asked Daniel, referring to the place where the couple had first met.

'Much older,' said Abigail. 'Although it's only been at its present location in Beaumont Street since 1845, about the same time the Fitzwilliam moved to its current site on Trumpington Street.

But the Ashmolean was originally established as a museum in 1683. It's actually the oldest university museum in the world.'

'You are a mine of information,' said Daniel.

Abigail looked again at the wording of the telegram they'd received. *Strange death at museum. Your help needed. Please come. Marriott, Ashmolean.*

'He doesn't mention the name of the dead person,' said Abigail.

'He doesn't need to,' said Daniel. He handed her the copy of *The Times* he'd been reading, pointing at a news item.

TRAGIC SUICIDE OF PROMISING MUSEUM
CURATOR IN OXFORD

We have received reports of the tragic death by his own hand of one Gavin Everett, a senior executive at the Ashmolean Museum in Oxford. At this time, details of his death are sketchy, with no apparent reason for him to take his own life, according to the museum's administrator, Gladstone Marriott.

'That's all there is,' said Daniel.

'When did it happen?'

'The day before yesterday.'

'If it's a suicide, why has he asked us to look into it? It's not as if there's been a crime committed.'

'Legally, suicide is a crime,' Daniel reminded her.

'Yes, but not one where the criminal can be arrested and brought to justice.'

'I'm sure all will be revealed once we get to Oxford,' said Daniel.

When they disembarked at Oxford railway station, Daniel began to head towards the line of waiting hansom cabs, but Abigail stopped him.

'It's only a short distance to the city centre,' she said. 'The walk will do us good after sitting down all the way from London.'

'Yes, good idea,' agreed Daniel. 'It will give me a chance to see these famous university buildings up close.'

'Later,' advised Abigail. 'This way takes us straight to the Ashmolean before we get to the historic colleges.'

'You should set up as a tour guide,' commented Daniel as they set off. 'I'm sure there's money to be made taking visitors around the university towns and cities.'

'Thank you, but I have enough to keep me busy,' replied Abigail.

'Indeed you have,' agreed Daniel. 'An archaeologist and a detective, while I have just the one job.'

'If you're looking for flattery from me, you're wasting your time,' said Abigail. 'You already know you are the best at what you do. That's why people like Gladstone Marriott at the Ashmolean ask for you.'

Daniel smiled. 'Yes, but I do like to hear you say it.'

'I'm not sure if that's because of your vanity, or a lack of confidence in your own abilities,' commented Abigail.

'Let me guess: you're quoting one of these newfangled psychiatrists?' said Daniel.

'No, my own observation,' retorted Abigail. She grinned at him. 'I'm just using the techniques you've taught me about being a detective: study the subject's demeanour in order to work out their motivation.'

'So I'm a subject for scientific observation?' queried Daniel.

'Of course,' said Abigail. 'Admit it, you do it all the time with me, trying to work out whether I'm happy, or upset with something.' She gestured at a very large white-and-sandstone-coloured building they were nearing on their left. 'Here we are. The Ashmolean.'

Daniel followed her as she mounted the wide stone steps towards the main entrance.

'I see the architect has gone for the same kind of columns they've got at the front of the Fitzwilliam and the British Museum,' he noted. 'Is it some kind of legal requirement that all museums have to look like Roman temples from the outside?'

'I believe it's to show that inside is a place of classical education.'

A man in a steward's uniform was standing just inside the entrance, and Daniel and Abigail approached him.

'Good afternoon,' said Daniel. 'Mr Daniel Wilson and Miss Abigail Fenton, here to see Mr Gladstone Marriott.'

The man's face broke into a smile.

'Ah yes! Mr Marriott asked me to keep watch

for you and to let him know as soon as you arrived.' He pointed at the bags Daniel and Abigail each were carrying and offered: 'Would you like me to have those put in the cloakroom? It'll be less cumbersome for you while you see Mr Marriott.'

'Yes, thank you,' said Daniel.

The man gestured for another uniformed steward who was standing at the foot of a flight of sandstone stairs to join them. 'George, these are the visitors Mr Marriott has been expecting. Will you take their bags to the cloakroom, and then take over here at the main entrance while I show them to Mr Marriott?'

George nodded and took their bags, leaving Daniel and Abigail free to walk unencumbered up the wide stone steps behind their guide.

'I'm so glad you've arrived,' said the man. 'I'm Hugh Thomas, the head steward here at the Ashmolean, and I can tell you this dreadful event has upset us all greatly, and none more so than Mr Marriott.' He shook his head to show his bewilderment. 'It was so unlike Mr Everett. But I'm sure Mr Marriott will give you all the details.'

They came to an area at the top of the stairs containing many glass cases laden with a variety of exhibits. Thomas led them past the exhibits and into a short corridor. He stopped at a door, knocked, and at the command from inside of 'Enter!', opened the door and announced, 'Mr Wilson and Miss Fenton have arrived, Mr Marriott.'

Gladstone Marriott, a short, round man in his

5

fifties with a bush of unruly white hair adorning his head, leapt up from behind his desk and came towards them, hand outstretched in greeting.

'Mr Wilson! Miss Fenton!'

He shook them both by the hand heartily. There was no mistaking the expression of obvious relief on his face. He was smartly dressed in a pinstripe suit of dark material that would have suited a banker, although it was offset by a silk waistcoat in a garish collection of motley colours and ornate, almost oriental, patterns.

'I'm so glad you could come!' he said. 'I've heard about the brilliant work you did at both the Fitzwilliam and the British Museum, and I'm hoping you can do the same for us.'

'I'm not sure what there is for us to do,' said Abigail. 'According to the newspaper reports, Mr Everett killed himself.'

'Yes, that's the official story,' said Marriott.

'But you're not sure?' asked Daniel.

Marriott hesitated, then said, 'Perhaps it would be best if you examined the place where it happened, and hopefully you can come to your own conclusion.' As he led them along the corridor towards Everett's office, he informed them, 'Because we — that is, the Board of Trustees — feel that this might take a day or two, we've booked you rooms at the Wilton Hotel. I do hope that's acceptable to you?'

Daniel shot an enquiring glance at Abigail, who nodded to show she knew the Wilton and it was acceptable to her. Although, Daniel

6

reflected, as Abigail had spent time in tents while on digs in Egypt and elsewhere and seemed happy in his small cold-water terraced house in Camden Town, one of the poorest districts of London, he was sure it would prove acceptable whatever the conditions.

They entered the office of the late Gavin Everett and Marriott showed them the scene of the tragedy: the desk, the chair, the spot where the pistol had been found on the carpet.

'Was the door locked?' asked Daniel, spotting the damage to the thick oak door close to the door handle.

Marriott nodded. 'From the inside. The lock had to be forced in order to gain access. The key was on the floor, just inside the door. Again, the police believe the key fell from the lock onto the carpet when force was used.'

'So, suicide,' said Abigail.

'That is what the police say. However, I have serious doubts, which is why I contacted you.' He gestured for them to sit in two of the chairs in the room and took the third for himself. Daniel noticed that he avoided seating himself in the leather chair where the body of Everett had been found. 'Everett had been working here for the past two years, and in that time, I have never known him to show any signs of low spirits or worry. On the contrary, he was a cheerful young man, full of life and always looking for new innovations to improve the museum.'

'Did he have money worries that you might know of?' asked Daniel.

'None!' said Marriott firmly. 'He was a single

man with no dependents. He had lodgings in a house in Oxford which were comfortable but not ostentatious. I believe he must have had a private income as well as his salary from the museum, because he never seemed to have any concerns about money.'

'His health?'

'He was fit and well. He was the kind of man who used to run up a flight of stairs rather than walk up them. He'd never taken a day off for sickness in the time he was here.'

'How old was he?'

'In his early thirties.'

'Local to Oxford?' asked Abigail.

Marriott shook his head.

'I believe he came from Bedfordshire originally because he once mentioned having family there. But he'd been a traveller, somewhat of an adventurer, from what I could gather. Just before he joined us at the Ashmolean, he'd spent two years in South Africa, prospecting for gold in the Transvaal.'

'And was he successful?'

'I do believe that was where his private income came from, as a result of investments he made following some success in the goldfields.'

'But not a major success, I would guess, otherwise he'd hardly want to take a job, however worthy.'

'I must admit that did puzzle me,' agreed Marriott. 'But Gavin explained that his mind needed stimulation. He could never just loaf around and rest on the money he'd made in the goldfields. He did say it wasn't a great deal of money, he told me it was sufficient to support him comfortably, but he wanted a new adventure, and the Ashmolean seemed to supply that. As I hinted, he was a very energetic young man, and certainly his contacts in the Transvaal and Cape Colony have been very useful to us. The material he sourced through them has resulted in our African collection becoming noteworthy.'

'Did you see him on the day he died?'

'I did, and that's another reason why I cannot believe he committed suicide. He came to my office full of excitement and told me he'd had a most unusual proposition which he wanted me to consider.

'He told me he'd been offered the prologue and first act of an unfinished play by Shakespeare, in Shakespeare's own hand. The man who offered it to him told him it had come into his hands through a lady — a titled lady. It had been kept, and in great secrecy, according to her, by her husband's family. His ancestor, an earl in the sixteenth century, being the one who commissioned the play from Shakespeare before he became well known and paid him a small advance. But when Shakespeare was informed his first play was to be performed, and he was getting paid for it, he abandoned the other play — especially as he was told that the earl had run out of money and couldn't afford to pay for the rest of it.

'Gavin told me the man had asked for five hundred pounds for the document. He added that he'd asked the man for provenance to prove

9

the authenticity of the piece of work, and the man said he'd be returning with the proof. He'd arranged to see him the evening he died.'

'What was the proof?' asked Abigail.

'Apparently, a letter from the lady herself verifying that the work had come from her husband's family's private collection, and its genesis. Under normal circumstances I'd have taken the matter to the keeper of the Ashmolean for guidance, but in the current circum-stances . . . ' And he gave them a look that showed his great concern.

'I understand,' said Abigail sympathetically. 'What was your decision?'

'I asked him to let me see the documents, and if they seemed genuine, I could see no reason why the museum wouldn't agree to fund the purchase. As I'm sure you'll agree, anything by Shakespeare would be a bargain at just five hundred pounds.'

'Which makes me wonder why the price was so low?' asked Abigail.

'The same thought occurred to me,' said Marriott. 'According to Gavin, the lady in question was selling the manuscript as . . . well . . . to take some sort of revenge against her husband rather than making a lot of money from it.'

'But was it hers to sell?' asked Daniel.

'According to the intermediary, it was. He said she had a letter from her husband to prove it.'

'I wonder how she'd managed to get such a letter?' wondered Daniel. 'And if it was genuine?'

'That was one of the aspects that Gavin said

he'd look into before completing the deal.' Marriott gave a heavy sigh as he looked at them. 'You see why I have grave doubts about the idea that Gavin killed himself, with this new project going on.'

'Did the pistol belong to him?' asked Daniel.

'To my knowledge, Gavin never owned a pistol of any sort,' said Marriott.

'Do you know at what time Mr Everett was due to meet this intermediary?' asked Daniel.

'At six o'clock. The museum closes at five-thirty.'

'And no one saw this intermediary go into Mr Everett's office?'

'No. In fact, we didn't discover Everett's body until the next day. When the cleaning staff arrived, his office was locked. Although that wasn't usual, the staff just assumed he'd locked it for security of something inside.

'I went to his office soon after I arrived at the Ashmolean because I was keen to discover the outcome of his meeting the previous evening, but found it locked. That was rare, because Gavin was always at the museum by nine, but I thought that perhaps he'd decided to come in late for some reason.

'When there was still no sign of him by eleven, I sent a messenger to his lodgings to check that all was well with him, but the messenger returned and said that his landlady had seen no sign of him since he left for work the morning before. It was then that I decided to have the door forced.'

'You felt that something bad might have

happened during his meeting with the intermediary?'

'I did, but I was puzzled why the door should
still be locked. Was his visitor locked in there
with him? There had been no sounds from the
office. Anyway, I got one of the stewards, who
also works as a general handyman, to force the
lock so that we could gain access, and that was
when we found poor Everett.'

'Who was the police inspector in charge of the
investigation?' asked Daniel.

'An Inspector Pitt from Oxford Central,' said
Marriott. He frowned, puzzled. 'It's odd. At first
Inspector Pitt appeared to view the death as
suspicious, but then suddenly he announced the
official verdict was suicide and declared the case
closed.'

'I'm sure he had his reasons,' said Daniel.
'One last thing, Mr Marriott: it would help us
enormously to talk to people who Everett was
particularly friendly with to get an idea of his life
outside work. Was there anyone here at the
Ashmolean he confided in, or had a sort of
friendship with?'

Marriott frowned thoughtfully, then shook his
head.

'No one in particular,' he said at last. 'Now I
come to think of it, in spite of the fact that he
was always cheerful and friendly to everyone, full
of bonhomie, I can't think of anyone here that he
spent time with outside the museum. It might be
worth talking to Hugh Thomas, the man who
brought you up to my office. He's our chief
steward and he knows most of what goes on with

12

the staff, certainly better than I do. I leave that sort of thing to him while I concentrate on the administrative side.'

2

After their meeting with Gladstone Marriott, Daniel and Abigail left the museum and made for a coffee house not far from there, where they could discuss the case away from the very concerned looks of Gladstone Marriott.

'What do you think?' asked Daniel as he spooned sugar into his coffee. 'About this Shakespeare play?'

'Absolute nonsense,' said Abigail. 'If anyone really did have anything of Shakespeare's, and in his own hand, they'd take it to the Bodleian, not the Ashmolean.'

'Who or what is the Bodleian?' asked Daniel.

She stared at him.

'Surely you've heard of Oxford's famous Bodleian Library?'

'No,' he said. 'As I said on the train, this is my first visit to Oxford, and I know as little about it as I did Cambridge the first time I went there. Except that Oxford is the oldest university in the world.'

'Second oldest,' Abigail corrected him.

'You mean Cambridge is the oldest?'

'Cambridge is the second oldest in Britain and fourth oldest in the world. The world's oldest university is Bologna in Italy.'

This time it was Daniel's turn to stare.

'How do you know these things?' he asked.

'Because it's what university graduates do,

find out about other universities and exchange information. All it means is you and I each have different areas of knowledge. For example, I wouldn't know how to pick a lock, or understand any of the language most common criminals use, all of which you are very well versed in.'

'Can we get back to the Bodleian,' said Daniel. 'Why would this mysterious person have offered it to them instead of the Ashmolean?'

'Because the Bodleian is one of the oldest and most respected libraries in the world. It was accumulating books before printing was invented. It already holds copies of Shakespeare's works. Whereas the Ashmolean is mainly about artefacts: sculptures, pottery, articles of clothing. So, which one would be the natural choice to take this alleged Shakespeare to?'

'Unless it was too obviously a forgery,' mused Daniel.

'Exactly,' said Abigail. 'Someone is always claiming they've discovered a supposedly lost play or poem of Shakespeare, or other writers such as Chaucer. It's quite an industry among the literary criminal fraternity. The documents — if they exist — are nearly always faked, and often badly. It will be interesting to actually lay eyes on this alleged Shakespeare and see what standard of forgery it is.'

'You're convinced it's a fake?'

'If it exists at all,' said Abigail. 'So, what's our next move? Talk to Hugh Thomas and see if he can give us any information about who Everett socialised with?'

'I think my next move is to pay a call on this

Inspector Pitt,' said Daniel.

'Without me?'

Daniel smiled. 'You must have learnt by now that most police forces are notoriously unhappy about private enquiry agents being involved in their area, and they are even more suspicious of women detectives. If not downright hostile. This Inspector Pitt may be the same, in which case I shall be evicted from the police station, but there's no need for us both to suffer that indignity. If I find that, on the contrary, Inspector Pitt is welcoming then my visit will break the ice for both of us.'

'You're being overprotective,' sniffed Abigail disapprovingly.

'I can't see the point of you suffering sarcastic comments and being ejected from a building, if that's how it might turn out,' said Daniel. 'Life's hard enough without creating unnecessary troubles.'

She smiled. 'Very well. But I shall be making the acquaintance of this Inspector Pitt at some time or other.'

'I know you will,' he said. 'I'm just trying to make things easier. What will you do? Go to the hotel?'

'Good heavens, no! I shall go back to the Ashmolean and avail myself of the opportunity to immerse myself in the museum's wonders. For example, have you ever seen the Alfred Jewel?' She shook her head. 'No, that's a silly question as you haven't been to Oxford before.'

'The Alfred Jewel?' he asked.

'An ornate piece of jewellery made for Alfred

the Great. It's quite superb, and it's been one of the Ashmolean's greatest prizes for two hundred years. So, while you're having an awkward confrontation with this Inspector Pitt, I shall be rejoicing in the Ashmolean's treasures.'

'Yes, that was another thing that came up during our conversation with Mr Marriott,' said Daniel, puzzled. 'What was that business about not being able to take the matter to the keeper of the Ashmolean? The 'current circumstances' he talked about.'

'The keeper of the Ashmolean is Arthur Evans, a very distinguished archaeologist,' explained Abigail. 'He was appointed in 1884 and he's done a superb job. Before him the Ashmolean was in a bit of a parlous state; artefacts had been loaned out to other museums, the upper floor was being used for social functions, but Evans reversed all that, brought the artefacts back, instigated a proper collections policy, and returned its academic credibility. Sadly, a couple of years ago, he suffered two terrible tragedies. First his father-in-law, Edward Freeman, died. Freeman was more than just his father-in-law, he was his mentor in so many ways. And then a year later, Evans' wife, Margaret, Freeman's eldest daughter, also died while the couple were in Greece.

'Since that, Evans has stayed abroad, immersing himself in archaeological digs. He's rarely seen in Oxford any longer, leaving the running of the museum to people like Gladstone Marriott.'

'So, one tragedy after another,' mused Daniel. 'All fatal, and all connected to the Ashmolean.

17

Let's hope that's not an omen for us.'

'The deaths of Edward Freeman and Margaret Evans were from natural causes,' Abigail pointed out.

'But not that of Gavin Everett,' said Daniel. 'Let's hope we don't encounter more deaths before this case is over.'

3

Abigail stood before the glass case that housed the Alfred Jewel, rapt. She'd seen the jewel before, but she never failed to feel excited by items such as this, real objects that stretched back in time and gave a solid connection between then and now. It was one of the reasons she'd become an archaeologist, to be able to hold in her hands things that had been wrought hundreds of years before. Or, in her case, with Egyptian, Roman and Greek antiquities being her speciality, many thousands of years. The Alfred Jewel was almost modern when compared to those ancient treasures, having been made, it was believed, in the late ninth century, but that was still a thousand years ago, and the piece itself was exquisite: the image of a man — assumed to be Jesus Christ — made of painted enamel, with the green of his clothes predominant, surrounded by a gold circle, on which the engraved words '*Aelfred mec heht gewyrcan*' were clear, Old English for 'Alfred ordered me made'. It had been dug up in 1693 on land in Somerset, Alfred's old Kingdom of Wessex, and the restoration that had taken place filled Abigail with admiration, to restore something to such original beauty after it had lain for many hundreds of years in soil showed a very special talent.

'Miss Fenton? Abigail Fenton?'

Abigail, jolted out of her reverie over the jewel, turned and saw a young blonde woman smiling, albeit slightly apprehensively, at her. The young woman held out her hand. 'Esther Maris. I'm a reporter for the *Oxford Messenger*.'

'A woman reporter,' commented Abigail approvingly, shaking the young woman's hand. 'The *Oxford Messenger* is to be congratulated on its progressiveness.'

'I heard that you and Mr Daniel Wilson are here to investigate Mr Everett's death.'

'We've been asked to look into the circumstances,' replied Abigail guardedly. 'But at the moment we don't have anything that's for publication. We've only just arrived.'

'That doesn't matter,' said Esther. 'I wonder if it would be possible to have an interview with you.'

'I'm afraid Mr Wilson isn't here at the moment.'

'No, I meant an interview with *you*.'

'Me?' said Abigail, surprised.

Esther's expression took on an apologetic look.

'When I said I was a reporter, the truth is I'm trying to be one. At the moment they've given me the women's page.'

'That's still a step forward from most newspapers,' said Abigail. 'Mostly, women tend to be avoided in their pages unless they're celebrities, murderesses, or political agitators.'

Esther gave an awkward grimace. 'Yes, and to be honest I only really got this job because my uncle is the proprietor of the newspaper and he persuaded the editor to employ me, and the editor has restricted me to what he calls 'women's issues'. But I intend to prove to him that I can be a proper journalist, so I'm using my column to expand what most people think of as 'women's issues'. For example, you. A woman detective!'

'I'm not sure if it's accurate to describe me as a detective,' said Abigail doubtfully. 'I work with Mr Wilson, who is a former detective with Scotland Yard, and I'm learning from him. So, I suppose you could call me a trainee.'

'In the same way that you could call me a trainee journalist,' said Esther enthusiastically. 'Please, my readers would love to hear about you. Can we talk? I promise I'll let you see what I write before I put my copy in.'

'Very well,' said Abigail. She looked towards an attendant, who was glaring at the two women with an expression of disapproval. 'But somewhere else. I don't think the Ashmolean would approve of us disturbing the rather reverential air here with a stream of chatter.'

'Why don't we go to the Randolph Hotel across the road,' suggested Esther. 'They do a lovely afternoon tea there. And the *Oxford Messenger* will foot the bill.'

★ ★ ★

Daniel had made his way to Oxford's central police station at Kemp Hall, an ancient timbered building from days long gone by, possibly Elizabethan to Daniel's eye. It was set in a yard just to the south of the high street. He was told that Inspector Pitt was on site and was escorted by a uniformed constable to a small office at the back of the police station, where Inspector Pitt was sitting at his desk, studying some papers. Pitt looked up unsmiling and wary at Daniel as he entered the office.

'Good afternoon, Inspector. My name's Daniel Wilson and I'm a private enquiry agent. Out of courtesy, I've come to let you know that Miss Abigail Fenton and I have been asked by the Ashmolean to look into the events surrounding the death of Mr Everett there.'

'It's suicide,' said Pitt curtly.

'I know,' said Daniel. 'We've been asked to look into why he may have committed suicide, in case there might be any adverse reflection on the Ashmolean.'

The inspector studied Daniel thoughtfully for a moment, then he said, 'You were one of Abberline's crew.'

'I was,' said Daniel. 'But that was some time ago. I left the force shortly after he did.'

'Your name came up when I was talking to one of your old colleagues recently. John Feather of the Met.'

Daniel's face broke into a smile.

'John! How is he? I haven't seen him . . . '

'Since that business at the British Museum,' finished Pitt. 'Yes, he told me about that. And how you never got the credit for cracking the case. You and your partner, this Miss Fenton.'

'Credit would be nice, but that's not why we do it,' said Daniel. 'John's a great detective, and an even better person.'

'Yes, he said the same about you,' said Pitt. He cast a look around to make sure they weren't being overheard, then got to his feet and said in almost a whisper, 'That's why I'm going to tell you something.' He jerked his head towards the door. 'Let's go out the back. Less chance of wagging ears.'

Intrigued, Daniel followed the inspector out of his office, down a corridor, and then through a door and into a cobbled courtyard that smelt strongly of horse manure.

'The stables,' said Pitt.

Daniel smiled and gave a sniff. 'Yes. I picked up the clue.'

A row of four half-doors ran along one side of the yard. All were shut, so Daniel assumed the horses were out.

'This Everett business,' said Pitt. 'I didn't like it, and I said so to my guv'nor, Superintendent Clare. For one thing there were no powder marks around the wound, and if the pistol had been fired with the end against his forehead, you'd have expected powder marks at least.'

'So, the indication was that the shot came from a longer distance.'

'That was my thinking.'

'And the business of the door being locked?'

'Did you examine the door?'

'Yes. There was space at the bottom for a key to be pushed under it.'

'Exactly. The way I see it, someone aims a pistol at Everett and shoots him in the forehead, then drops the pistol by his hand. They go out, lock the door from the outside, then push the key under the door back into the room so that when the door's opened it looks as if the key fell out of the lock.'

'How did your super react when you told him this?'

'At first he was all for starting an investigation. And then the telegram arrived. 'No investigation into Everett death. Suicide.' The super showed it to me, but with strict instructions not to say anything to anyone else. I'm only telling you based on what John Feather told me about you, and to warn you that if you carry on with this you'll be moving into dangerous territory.'

'Who was the telegram from?'

'The War Office.'

Daniel frowned. 'The War Office? What would they have to do with an executive of a museum in Oxford?'

'It suggests to me he was more than just that.'

'Was he ever involved with the military? In the armed forces, for example?'

'Not that we could discover.'

'Did Superintendent Clare question the instructions in the telegram?'

Pitt shook his head. 'The super's a good bloke, but like all supers I've ever known, he doesn't like to upset the powers that be. So, officially, that's it. But remember what I said: I haven't said anything to you about the case, and especially not about the telegram.' He saw the look of doubt darken Daniel's face, and asked, 'Is that a problem?'

'No,' said Daniel hesitantly, 'but I don't feel

comfortable about keeping that from Gladstone Marriott at the Ashmolean. They're the ones paying us, and we're supposed to keep him informed. And, of course, there's my partner, Miss Fenton.'

Pitt deliberated on this for a brief moment, then nodded.

'Understood,' he said. 'Your partner, yes. But as far as the Ashmolean is concerned, can I ask you to only keep it to Marriott? And to persuade him to keep this to himself. If it gets out, the super will know it came from me, and he's a good bloke. I don't want him to feel I've let him down.'

'Trust me,' Daniel promised him. 'Miss Fenton and Mr Marriott, and no further. And I'll impress on Marriott the need to keep it to himself, and no one else.'

⋆　⋆　⋆

Abigail and Esther sat in the elegant tea room in the opulent surroundings of the Randolph Hotel. Abigail had been here before when visiting a friend in Oxford. It seemed to her that the Randolph was where people brought other people to impress them. Was that the case here with Esther Maris? If so, Abigail had been tempted to tell the young woman it wasn't necessary; for Abigail it was people who impressed her, or didn't, not their surroundings. But she had to admit, the pastries they served at the Randolph were particularly good.

'I've been doing some research into you and

Mr Wilson, and I learnt that you used to be an archaeologist before you became a detective,' said Esther.

'I still am an archaeologist,' said Abigail. 'Mr Wilson brings me into the detective work when there might be a historical aspect.'

'I found some articles you wrote about your work in Egypt, unearthing ancient relics at the site of the pyramids. How hard was that for you as a woman? Mostly it seems that sort of archaeology is done by men.'

'In fact, there are quite a few women archaeologists, but most prominence is given to men because they tend to lead the expeditions. I suppose I'm unusual in that I also write articles about the digs, and in that aspect, I've been fortunate in the fact that the men who led the expeditions and digs I've been on encouraged me to do that.'

'You were involved in digs in Egypt and Mesopotamia, and Greece and Turkey. Were there any problems for you as a woman while you were there?'

'No, I was accepted by the locals as a person doing a job. Don't forget, there have been many other women doing such work before me. Hester Stanhope, for example, who in the last century was the first to carry out an archaeological dig in the Holy Land.'

'You got your degree in history at Cambridge, didn't you? At Girton?'

'You have been doing your homework,' Abigail complimented her.

'Again, that's unusual for a woman.'

'Not that unusual,' said Abigail. 'Here at Oxford you have Somerville College, which is a women's college. I accept these may be early days in society accepting that women deserve an equal education to men, but Girton and Somerville are just the start.'

'But has your success been at the expense of romance?'

'What do you mean?' asked Abigail, warily.

'Most women expect to fall in love and marry and have children — '

'No. *Society* expects women to marry and have children,' Abigail interrupted her. 'Women have a choice.'

'But how about you? Do you want to marry and have children?'

Abigail hesitated.

'At the moment it's not something I'm thinking about,' she said.

'So you're putting your career before romance?'

'Would you ask that same question of a man?' queried Abigail. 'A politician? A man archaeologist? A male detective?'

'Yes, but it's different, isn't it,' insisted Esther.

'Only because society considers it to be,' said Abigail. 'And I would point out that we have a woman on the throne as Queen. And not just Queen, but Empress of the British Empire, which covers a third of the world's population. Yet it hasn't stopped her marrying and having children.'

★   ★   ★

There'd been something evasive about Abigail Fenton, Esther decided as she left the Randolph. It had happened when Esther had asked about romance. From her experience, most women she'd interviewed had either waxed lyrical about their other half or laughed and said they were just waiting for Mr Right to appear. Abigail Fenton had done neither. So — was there a romance in her life? If so, who? Could it be this Daniel Wilson? She certainly seemed to have formed some kind of partnership with him. And as far as she'd been able to find out, Daniel Wilson was a single man. That made them ideal for a coupling. Even though their social backgrounds were so different.

Or was Abigail Fenton being defensive because there was something else happening romantically, something less orthodox? Esther thought of some of the women she'd met who'd been at university and had thrown themselves into a society of brilliant — and *single* — women, often to the exclusion of men. Quite a few of them had been quite masculine in their attitudes, although not all of them in appearance. There had been quite a few who were very attractive, but who seemed to reserve their favours for their own sex. Was that what Abigail Fenton was hiding, that her thoughts of romance were for other women, not for men?

But Esther had to admit that if that was so, there'd been no hint of it during their conversation. No lingering looks from her. Instead, Fenton had been . . . careful. Secretive. What was she hiding? Whatever it was, it would certainly add spice to the story she was planning. The sudden death of a prominent executive of the Ashmolean, alleged to be suicide, although there seemed to be no reason why he would take his own life. She smiled to herself. More secrets to be uncovered. This could be the story that finally saw her throw off the 'women's page' tag.

4

Abigail was crossing the street from the Randolph to the Ashmolean when she saw Daniel approaching from the other direction.

'Well?' she demanded. 'Did you get thrown out of the police station?'

'No,' Daniel told her. 'In fact, Inspector Pitt was very welcoming. And he also gave me some information which confirms Mr Marriott's suspicions about Gavin Everett's death.'

'It was murder?' asked Abigail.

'Definitely,' said Daniel.

Briefly, he filled her in on what Pitt had told him, then said, 'So now we take this to Mr Marriott. Though we wait to see whether he'll be pleased at the revelation that his suspicions were correct, or more worried as a result.'

They headed up the stairs to Marriott's office, where Daniel made his report.

'It now transpires that the police still believe that Mr Everett was murdered, and his death made to look like suicide.'

'But they told me that they were viewing it as suicide, and the case was closed,' said Marriott.

'Because they were instructed to do so by certain political powers in government.'

Marriott stared at them. 'The police told you this?'

'In confidence,' said Daniel. 'The information is not to be revealed. In fact, they were reluctant to admit it to me and only did so because of certain contacts I still have inside Scotland Yard. But they have insisted it must remain a secret. As far as the public are concerned, and everyone here, Gavin Everett committed suicide. So, officially, Miss Fenton and I will be looking for reasons why he took such an action. But in reality, that will mean us trying to find out who murdered him, and why. Providing you agree to us continuing with our investigation, of course.'

'Most certainly!' said Marriott. 'My concern is that what happened to Everett could happen to any one of us here at the Ashmolean.'

'Depending on the motive,' said Daniel. 'We may find his death was nothing to do with the museum, but for more personal reasons.' He frowned, and added thoughtfully, 'Although, from what I picked up from the police — and this is in the strictest confidence and mustn't be repeated outside this room . . . '

'I understand,' said Marriott.

'The fact that the investigation was halted due to intervention by a senior government official in London suggests there may well be a political motive.'

'But Everett wasn't involved in politics!' burst out Marriott.

⋆   ⋆   ⋆

'So, we are investigating a murder which may have political associations,' said Abigail as they left Marriott's office.

'It may indeed,' said Daniel. 'Although,

31

according to Marriott, that seems unlikely. For my part, it seems a great coincidence that he's killed while supposedly having this meeting to talk about this piece by Shakespeare.'

'*Alleged* piece by Shakespeare,' Abigail corrected him. 'If such a work does exist, and if the story about it being in this mysterious titled woman's family is true, then if her husband found out that she planned to sell it, one way to stop that would be to kill Everett.'

'Simpler, surely, to kill his wife,' said Daniel.

'Yes, true,' admitted Abigail. 'Perhaps he already has. Perhaps some aristocratic establishment in Oxford is currently holding a wake for the recently deceased lady of the house.'

'The whole thing could be a dead end,' said Daniel. 'The story may be true, someone may have offered it for sale to Everett, but it may be nothing to do with his death. And the only way we can decide is by finding out who the titled lady is, and the identity of her husband, and then dig into that situation.'

'That's not going to be easy,' said Abigail. 'The aristocracy can be very protective of their reputations; most of them have had long experience in hiding unpleasant family secrets.'

'So, the weak link here is the intermediary who Everett was dealing with. If we can find out who that was, that's our way in. Which means our first thought about finding out who Everett was known to be associated with, either through business dealings, or socially, was the right one. Because, as you rightly pointed out, if someone really had a genuine Shakespeare piece to sell, they'd take it to the Bodleian. Or, if not the Bodleian, to one of the very many literary scholars in Oxford. If they brought it to Everett, it's because they knew him personally.'

'So, it's back to finding out who Everett was particularly friendly with,' said Abigail.

'Which is why we are going to talk to Hugh Thomas and see what he can tell us,' said Daniel.

Unfortunately for them, the head steward wasn't able to offer any clues as to who Everett's close friends had been, either inside the museum or outside.

'He was always very friendly, not stuck-up or patronising at all, not like some people would be in his position. Always a good word for everybody. But as for forming any particular friendships, I must admit I can't think of any.'

They received the same response from everyone else they spoke to at the museum; everyone liked him, but no one was particularly close to him. No one socialised with him outside of work, and no one knew of any social circle he might have been involved with.

'In short,' summed up Daniel as they carried their luggage to the nearby Wilton Hotel, 'we have a good-natured chap who, despite being very friendly to everyone, actually keeps himself to himself. Frankly, a bit of an enigma.'

'A mystery to unravel,' agreed Abigail.

At the hotel, they were shown to their adjoining rooms, and once the porter had left, they both went into Abigail's room.

'This will do for us,' announced Abigail. 'It has

a better view. But the idea that we have to have separate rooms at all is ridiculous!'

'We're not married,' said Daniel. 'The hotel has a reputation to maintain.'

'That's nonsense!' said Abigail. 'I bet there are many men staying here with women who aren't their wives, and the hotel knows it but turns a blind eye.'

'That may well be true, but our stay here is being paid for by the Ashmolean, and they have booked us a room each, because we are two single people, a man and a woman. They haven't asked about our living arrangements, and we haven't told them we live together. We can confront the issue and tell everyone — the Ashmolean, the hotel — that we are a couple and insist on sharing a room, but if we do that, I'm sure that certain people will raise the question of morality with the Ashmolean, the hotel, and potential future clients of ours. Or we can do what everyone else does, play out the charade of having two rooms while we only use the one, and rumple the bedclothes of the one in the room we're not using to pretend we're occupying both.'

'It's so hypocritical!' groaned Abigail.

'I agree,' said Daniel. 'We could always get married, of course. You said you'd marry me.'

'And I will. When the time is right.'

'When I'm old and grey?' asked Daniel with a smile.

5

Next morning, their first call was to Everett's lodgings.

'Hopefully we'll find out from his landlady the names of his friends outside of work,' said Daniel. 'Or at least what sort of social life he led.'

Mrs Persimmons was a tall, austere-looking woman, who regarded them with suspicion until they explained the reason for their call.

'We're here on behalf of the Ashmolean,' Daniel explained. 'We're trying to find out why your lodger, Mr Everett, tragically did what he did, and to that extent it would help us enormously if we could find out as much as we can about his life outside of the museum.'

'He was a lovely man! An absolute gentleman!' Mrs Persimmons told them.

'So we have been told, but in order to understand what happened we need to find out what was going on in his life. Did he express to you any worries he may have had, for example?'

She shook her head. 'Absolutely not. In fact, he was the perfect tenant. He kept himself to himself, never interfered with the rest of the house, and was always prompt with his rent.'

'Do you have any other lodgers?' asked Abigail.

'No, Mr Everett was the only one,' said Mrs Persimmons. 'One's enough for me. I can only

35

hope the tenant I get to replace him will be as considerate.'

'What sort of people did he socialise with?' asked Daniel.

'That's difficult to say, sir. He didn't socialise with them here. He knew how careful I am keeping my house neat and tidy. Mr Everett was no problem at all, but some young gentlemen I've had before have been known to have untidy habits, especially when drink's been taken.'

'Was Mr Everett a great drinker?'

'Good heavens, no! In fact, I never saw him touch a drop. I thought at one time he might be temperance, or one of them sort, but I never heard of him attending any sort of meetings like that.'

'What about women friends?' asked Abigail.

Mrs Persimmons looked at her, shocked.

'There was nothing of that sort!' she said firmly. 'I run a decent house!'

'I meant women — or men — he may have seen relatively frequently. Not necessarily here, but . . . '

'In which case I wouldn't know anything about it,' said Mrs Persimmons curtly. 'I don't pry into people's private affairs. And neither should other people, either.'

'But Mr Everett has died by his own hand . . . ' insisted Abigail.

'And in my opinion, he should be left to rest in peace,' said Mrs Persimmons, looking more indignant. 'I've said what I had to say. He was a decent man who never gave me a moment's trouble and I'm sorry to lose him. And now, I'll

36

thank you to let me get on.'

With that she closed the door.

'I don't think I have your skill in charming people,' sighed Abigail as they walked away.

'I think we learnt enough to know that whatever kind of life Mr Everett lived, it wasn't at Mrs Persimmons' house,' said Daniel.

'Nor, by all accounts, did it include anyone at the Ashmolean,' said Abigail. 'Don't you find that strange?' She looked questioningly at Daniel. 'Where to now?'

'I think,' said Daniel, 'it's time you made the acquaintance of Inspector Pitt.'

*   *   *

Inspector Pitt's face broke into a welcoming smile as Daniel ushered Abigail into his small office.

'Miss Fenton!' he said, coming from behind his desk and holding out his hand to shake hers. 'It's a pleasure to meet you! Especially after I've heard such good things about you.'

Abigail shot an amused glance towards Daniel.

'You don't need to believe everything that Mr Wilson tells you,' she said.

'Not Mr Wilson, Inspector Feather at Scotland Yard. I met him at a conference recently, and your names came up about the recent case at the British Museum. Do I take it that you specialise in cases where murders occur in well-known museums?'

'I hope not,' said Abigail. 'It makes me sound like a harbinger of doom, and if word gets

37

around some museums will view my arrival with trepidation and wondering who will die next.'

'Miss Fenton is the historical expert of our team,' explained Daniel.

'Yes, so John Feather said. He outlined your career as an archaeologist. I must say, it sounds more exciting than detective work.'

'The locations may be less exotic, but the work can be a lot more interesting,' said Abigail.

Pitt lifted a pile of papers off a chair and gestured for Abigail to sit.

'I'm afraid my office is rather cramped,' he apologised. 'This may be the main police station for Oxford, but space is at a premium.'

'We've come because we're trying to get an idea of Everett's friends,' said Daniel. 'People he associated with outside work.'

'Looking for a personal motive?' asked Pitt.

'Possibly. At the moment we're hitting blank walls. He didn't seem to have any close friends among the staff at the Ashmolean, no one he socialised with outside of work, anyway. And his landlady wasn't very helpful.'

'No, she wasn't when I spoke to her,' agreed Pitt. 'She seemed more intent on letting me know how clean her house was, and what a delight it was to have such a tidy man as Everett lodging there. I got the impression I was a bit too shabby for her taste.'

'Did you find anyone he associated with? Friends? Romantic involvements?'

Pitt shook his head. 'We didn't have the time. We'd barely begun before we got told to back off. Not that we found much to begin with. He worked at the Ashmolean, he lodged at Mrs Persimmons' house. That was it. We might have discovered more if we hadn't been told the investigation was over.' He regarded them quizzically. 'Have you got any ideas yet?'

'No,' admitted Daniel. 'As you said, it's early days yet, and at the moment Mr Everett seems to be an enigma. We have had a report that he might have been negotiating to buy an alleged Shakespeare play.'

'From Mr Marriott.' Pitt nodded. 'Yes, he told me the same. If we'd been allowed to continue, I'd have tried to find out who the person was he was supposed to meet at the Ashmolean to do the deal, because it certainly seems to me that's the person we're looking for. But once we were ordered to stop, that was it.'

'When you heard about the play, you didn't have any ideas as to who might be selling it?'

Pitt shook his head. 'I'm afraid I don't move in those exalted circles involving titled families, nor where literary types mix. But if you get any ideas, and you think I can help, you're welcome to call in at any time and I'll see what I can do.'

★ ★ ★

'What a nice man,' commented Abigail as they walked away from the police station heading back towards the museum.

'Indeed,' said Daniel. 'It makes such a difference not to be obstructed by the local police force. I'm glad he's on our side.' He thought for a moment, then said, 'I think I'm

39

going to ask Mr Marriott if we can use Everett's office, as long as he hasn't got plans to use it himself. That way we have a base to work from and where people can contact us.'

'Good idea,' said Abigail. 'I can't see that Marriott will need the office for himself. At least, not immediately. Assuming they replace Everett, it will take a week or so for them to find a suitable person.'

'Tell me about the Ashmolean,' said Daniel.

'There's not much to tell,' said Abigail. 'It's the oldest university museum in the world, but I've already told you that.'

'Where does it get its name from?'

'From Elias Ashmole. He was an astrologer and alchemist, but with a variety of other interests. He gave the museum his own collection of antique coins, books, engravings, along with geological and zoological specimens gathered from across the world.'

'So, he was also an explorer?'

'No, he got most of the specimens from a father-and-son team of collectors, John Tradescant and his son, also called John. They were gardeners and one of their major interests was in bringing seeds back from America, such as the magnolia and aster plants to create gardens for the rich in England. In fact, both father and son were head gardener to Charles I. But they also brought back from America various other items, such as the ceremonial cloak of Chief Powhatan. By some means which is still not entirely clear, Ashmole inherited the Tradescant collection, and that became the basis for the museum.' She gestured towards the large white building which they were almost at. 'So, by rights, it should really be called the Tradescant Museum.'

To her surprise she found herself being pulled back by Daniel grabbing her arm.

'Wait!' he whispered urgently.

'What? Why?' asked Abigail, puzzled.

Daniel released her arm. 'Did you see that man leaving the Ashmolean just now? He's walking away from us, wearing a brown overcoat and a trilby hat.'

Abigail followed his look. 'Yes, I see him. Who is he?'

'His name's Walter Grafton. He's an inspector with Special Branch. I knew him when he was with the detective division. What puzzles me is what he's doing in Oxford, and especially what he was doing at the Ashmolean.'

'Could it be to do with the murder?'

'It must be. But why? Special Branch don't get involved in criminal cases, they're about politics and terrorism. Especially Irish terrorism. But so far there have been no whispers of any Irish involvement in Everett's murder.'

'We should ask Mr Marriott if he knows.' She frowned. 'Although if he knows why this Inspector Grafton is here, surely he'd have told us.'

'Not if he'd been warned not to,' said Daniel. 'And that's Special Branch's way, keeping their involvement secret and warning people off.'

6

'I understand that Special Branch have taken an interest in the case,' said Daniel. 'I saw Inspector Grafton leaving just now.'

Marriott looked up at Daniel and Abigail, and shifted uncomfortably in his chair.

'Their presence is supposed to be a secret,' he said awkwardly.

'I think we may have the answer as to why the government got involved and stopped the police investigating,' commented Daniel. 'Special Branch have a tie-up with the Secret Intelligence Service.' He looked quizzically at Marriott. 'Did Grafton say what in particular they're looking for?'

'It seems it's the South African connection.'

'What South African connection?' asked Abigail.

'You remember I told you Everett had been in South Africa for a few years before he joined us. He had lots of contacts with people in the Transvaal and Cape Colony, which was very useful when it came to adding to our collection. Our African collection is noteworthy, thanks to him. Inspector Grafton was interested in finding out who those contacts were, and how many of them might be in Britain.'

'What did you tell him?'

'That I had no idea if he had any connections in Oxford with anyone from South Africa. As I told you, Everett seemed to keep himself to himself socially.'

'Is there a South African community in Oxford?' asked Daniel.

'Not to my knowledge,' said Marriott. 'There may be a few individuals, but I'm guessing they have just assimilated into the overall Oxford community.'

'I assume Inspector Grafton made a search of Everett's office while he was here?' said Daniel.

'I believe he did,' said Marriott. 'He was in there for a long time.'

'Do you know if he found anything of interest to the case?' asked Abigail.

'If he did, I'm afraid he didn't share that with me.'

'No, Special Branch like to play everything close to their chest,' said Daniel. 'I assume you told him you had engaged us?'

'Yes,' said Marriott. 'It seemed wise.'

'How did he take it?'

'He was not happy. He asked that we end your employment on the case. However, I told him that our concern was the protection of the Ashmolean, that was why you had been engaged, and we intended to honour our agreement with you.'

'Thank you, Mr Marriott,' said Daniel. 'I promise you, we will do our very best to uncover the reasons for Mr Everett's death. In fact, we have a request to make. As this case seems to be becoming more complicated at every turn, I think it would be a good idea if Miss Fenton and I had a base where we can be easily contacted by

43

anyone with information that might be useful. Do you have any immediate plans to use Mr Everett's office for anything?'

'Well . . . no,' said Marriott.

'Would you allow us to use it as our base of operations? We'll have access to everything associated with Everett, and also be easily available to all interested parties. Especially yourself. You won't have to go looking for us if anything happens, we'll be just along the corridor.'

Marriott frowned as he thought it over, then he nodded.

'Yes,' he said. 'That might be a good idea.'

They left Marriott's office and headed along the corridor to Everett's.

'At least now we have a base to operate from,' said Daniel, as they entered the room.

'I wonder if Grafton found anything when he searched it?' mused Abigail, standing and surveying the office.

'I'm not sure if there was much to find,' said Daniel. 'I believe Inspector Pitt made a search, before he got warned off.' He walked to Everett's desk and sat down in the big leather chair, studying the desk. 'I'm intrigued at Grafton's asking about the South African connection. Special Branch only investigate murder if there's a serious political aspect to it.'

'So, what's the political aspect here?'

'I don't know,' admitted Daniel. 'If it involves South Africa, that suggests something to do with the Boers.'

'But the Boer War was fifteen years ago,' said

Abigail. 'Everything there has settled down.'

'Does anything ever settle down?' commented Daniel. 'After any war there are always resentments bubbling. The anger of those who lost, and also the anger of the victors at the losses they suffered.'

'So now we have two possible motives for his death,' said Abigail. 'The alleged Shakespeare play, or hostilities surfacing with the Boers.'

'And we've only just begun,' said Daniel.

★　★　★

Mrs Persimmons returned home from shopping filled with determination to take control of her house again. At the police's request she'd left Everett's rooms as they'd stood, but now the conclusion had been reached that he'd taken his own life, it was time to clear the rooms of his possessions and prepare it for letting again. Those rooms were her income, and as a widow the money was vital. Yes, she'd been able to put money aside by being careful, but any such savings would soon disappear. She needed a new tenant, and hopefully one as quiet, tidy and as little trouble as Mr Everett had been.

With that in mind, as soon as she entered her house, she put the shopping bags in the kitchen, then headed upstairs to her late tenant's rooms to take stock of the situation. She pushed open the door and entered, and then stopped, shocked at what she saw.

Someone had been in here! The drawers in the dressing table were open, where before she knew for certain they'd been shut. Similarly, the wardrobe door was now ajar. And the bed! She knew she'd left it neatly made up, just in case a potential tenant should arrive and ask to see the room. But now, the blanket had been pulled to one side and the pillows were on the floor.

A sense of rage filled her. It wasn't just that an intruder had been in here, but the sheer and deliberate untidiness of it was an insult that felt like a knife in her heart.

And then another thought filled her with horror. Had the intruder been into the rest of the house? Into *her* own private rooms?

Her hand flew to her mouth and she almost screamed, but then she controlled herself.

Someone would pay for this outrage!

★ ★ ★

Inspector Pitt walked into the main reception area of the police station, just as Mrs Persimmons stomped in from the street.

'Ah, Inspector Pitt! Just the man I was hoping to see!'

'Yes, Mrs Persimmons?'

'Something terrible has happened. I have been burgled!'

'Burgled?'

'I only discovered it when I went into Mr Everett's old rooms after I returned home from shopping. I decided it was time to remove his belongings and prepare the rooms for letting. The intruder had been in Mr Everett's rooms. Things had been disturbed.'

46

'Do you know what was taken?'

'Nothing, as far as I can make out. But, of course, I didn't examine Mr Everett's personal possessions, so I'm not sure.'

'What about the rest of the house?' asked Pitt. 'Anything taken or disturbed?'

She shook her head. 'No. I checked the rest of the house very carefully. It looks as if the intruder only went into Mr Everett's rooms.'

'Had the door been broken into? Or a window broken?'

'No. It's as if someone had a key. But I know that the only key is the one I have!'

Pitt nodded. 'Very well. I'll get my coat, Mrs Persimmons, and accompany you. Hopefully, we'll find out what's going on and who's behind it.'

★ ★ ★

Daniel and Abigail were methodically going through the books on the shelves of what had been Everett's office in the hope of finding something that might give a clue to his character, his likes and dislikes.

'This is pointless,' announced Daniel with a groan. 'All of these books are just practical guides to historical artefacts, and by the look of them they've been here for some years. Long before Everett was here, I suspect.'

'I think you're right,' agreed Abigail. She replaced a book on South American costumes back on the shelf. 'I'm thinking I might have a word with Esther Maris.'

'The reporter you told me about?'

'Yes. She writes the women's page, so it's likely she'll be in touch with all the local gossip, who's engaged to who, that sort of thing.'

'You think she might give us a lead on any women Everett might have been involved with?' asked Daniel.

'If there were any women. He might have been of another persuasion.'

'Men?'

'It's possible.'

'If he was, I can't see this Esther Maris being very helpful. Men of that predilection tend to keep their activities secret.'

'Except for Mr Oscar Wilde,' observed Abigail. 'In his case he positively flaunts it.'

'Yes, and I hope his true friends try to dissuade him,' commented Daniel. 'I was told by some friends of mine at Scotland Yard that the Marquess of Queensberry seems determined to bring him down. More, he seems set on having Wilde imprisoned.'

'Surely he's taking a big risk,' said Abigail. 'As I understand it, Queensberry's own son, Lord Alfred Douglas, is Wilde's current paramour. If he persists, his son could also end up in jail.'

'You'd think so, but Queensberry has friends in high places, many of them sympathetic to him in view of what happened to Francis, Lord Drumlanrig, Lord Alfred Douglas's eldest brother and heir to the Queensberry title.'

Abigail frowned. 'I'm sorry, this is foreign to me. I know about Wilde and Lord Alfred, as does almost everyone, because Wilde seems intent on making a scandal and relishing it. What happened to this Lord Drumlanrig?'

'He shot himself last year, following what was rumoured to be a sexual relationship between him and the Prime Minister, Lord Rosebery.'

'I saw nothing about that in the newspapers.'

'You wouldn't have. Rosebery's people were quick to make sure it was hushed up.'

'So how do you know about it?'

'If you remember, Fred Abberline and I were involved in the Cleveland Street Scandal.'

'Ah yes, the homosexual brothel. Telegraph boys and members of the aristocracy.'

'Exactly. They thought, as it was the same area, that I might have some light to throw on the subject.'

'And had you?'

'No. And I had no wish to be involved. Political intrigue can be very dangerous. As I understand it, the official verdict on Drumlanrig's death was that he died as a result of a hunting accident. But all the talk in London's social circles was of the real cause.'

'His relationship with Lord Rosebery.'

Daniel nodded. 'Whether it was true or not, Queensberry evidently believed the rumours, because when stories about Wilde and Lord Alfred began to surface, he was heard to say that he was determined to rescue his son 'from the clutches of that damned predator, Wilde. I will not let the same fate befall Alfred as befell poor Francis.''

A gentle tap at the open door made them both

turn, and they saw the figure of Inspector Pitt in the doorway.

'Inspector, do come in!' welcomed Daniel. 'Take a seat.'

'Thank you,' said Pitt, settling himself into a chair. 'I've come to tell you that there was a burglary at Everett's lodgings, either last night or this morning while the landlady was out shopping. By all accounts, they only went into his rooms, not the rest of the house.'

'What did they take?'

'According to Mrs Persimmons, nothing as far as she could see. I went to the house with her and took a look. The drawers in the bureau and the sideboard had been turned over, and the mattress had been disturbed, suggesting someone was looking for something that Everett had hidden, but she couldn't tell if anything had actually been taken.'

'Any signs of an actual break-in?' asked Daniel. 'Window broken? Door lock interfered with?'

'No,' said Pitt. 'It was very neat. As if they had a key.'

'Or a lock-pick,' said Daniel. He frowned thoughtfully. 'The entry was neat and tidy, yet the intruder left signs of a mess. Why?'

'A message,' said Pitt. 'To tell us that he'd been in.'

'But why?' asked Daniel again.

'I think whoever did it wants to stir thing up,' suggested Pitt. 'And deliberately point the finger at Everett.'

'I'm guessing that whoever did it also searched

50

his office first,' murmured Daniel. 'The fact they've burgled his rooms suggests they didn't find what they were looking for at the museum.'

'Do you think it was the person who shot him?' asked Pitt.

'I'm not sure,' said Daniel. 'I wonder when Inspector Grafton arrived in the city?'

'Who?' asked Pitt.

'Inspector Walter Grafton. He's with Special Branch in London. We saw him earlier today leaving the Ashmolean. Mr Marriott confirms he was here asking questions about Everett, and he also took the time to search his office.'

'If he's here on official business then by rights he's supposed to report to the local police superintendent,' said Pitt. 'And Superintendent Clare hasn't mentioned anything to me about Special Branch being here.'

'I'm sure Grafton will check in, in his own good time and when it suits him,' said Daniel. 'Regardless of the rules and police protocol, I've found that Special Branch tend to work to their own set of rules.'

'Do you think it was this Grafton who burgled Mrs Persimmons?' asked Pitt.

'He's certainly capable of it,' said Daniel. 'But if he did, it's not his style to deliberately leave a mess announcing he was there. Unless, as you say, he did it to stir things up.'

'And what was he looking for?' asked Abigail.

'Something flat, if he looked under the mattress,' said Daniel.

'Papers of some sort?' suggested Pitt.

'The Shakespeare play?' wondered Abigail.

'It's possible,' said Pitt. He rose to his feet. 'Anyway, I'd better get back to the station and see if I can come up with something that will satisfy Mrs Persimmons, although I doubt it. In the immortal words of Mr W. S. Gilbert, a policeman's lot is not a happy one.'

7

Abigail entered the reception at the offices of the *Oxford Messenger* and went straight to a woman sitting at a desk with 'Enquiries' written on it.

'Good afternoon,' she said. 'My name's Abigail Fenton. I wonder if it might be possible to speak to Esther Maris. She does know me.'

The woman wrote a message on a notepad on her desk, tore it off and summoned a uniformed man standing guard by the double doors that Abigail assumed led to the reporters' area.

'Please take this to Miss Maris,' she said.

The man nodded, took the note and disappeared through the double doors. Abigail thanked the woman and went to look at the recent editions of the *Messenger's* front pages displayed on one wall. The death of Gavin Everett featured, although the report was suitably vague: *The sad and tragic death of Mr Gavin Everett, assistant curator at the Ashmolean Museum, has been reported. According to official police reports, Mr Everett took his own life by means of a gunshot wound. There seems to have been no obvious reason for his action. It is not known whether Mr Everett has any relatives. The museum says it is not aware of any, and has asked that if anyone knows of any family he may have had, or any other person who was close to him, to get in touch with the museum director, Gladstone Marriott, at the*

Ashmolean Museum in Beaumont Street, Oxford.

'Looking at our work?' came Esther's voice behind Abigail.

Abigail turned and smiled at the young woman.

'Just while I was waiting for you. I hope I'm not disturbing you.'

'Not at all,' said Esther. 'At the moment I'm writing about knitting patterns, so this is a welcome break.' She lowered her voice as she asked hopefully, 'Is this to do with Mr Everett?'

'Yes,' said Abigail. 'As you know, we're trying to find out what made him do such a thing, but the problem is we can't find anyone who knew him outside of work. And the people at the museum didn't know him very well, not socially, anyhow. So, I wondered if you might have known anything about him, even from local gossip. You know, was he involved with anyone, for example.'

'A romance?'

'Even rumours of a romance would help,' said Abigail.

'Not that I know of.' Esther frowned. 'I must admit, I did a bit of nosing around after he died in case there might be a story there. You know, a tragic love affair, or something. That would be a great story! But I didn't get far. Mr Pinker, the editor, heard me asking one of the other reporters if there might be a woman involved, and he told me to leave that particular story alone and concentrate on 'less salacious items' for my women's page, as he termed them.' She gave Abigail a conspiratorial smile. 'But now I'll start asking around, however this time I'll talk to people outside the newspaper and won't let Mr Pinker know.'

'I don't want to get you into trouble,' said Abigail, concerned.

'Don't worry,' Esther assured her. 'This is what I want to do, proper reporting on a proper story. I intend to be taken seriously as a real journalist, so this will be the start.'

★   ★   ★

Daniel sat at the desk, going through the papers he'd found in the drawers. Nothing in them gave any clue as to Everett's personal life; everything here was about the Ashmolean. There were copies of letters to collectors tentatively sounding them out about the Ashmolean acquiring — either permanently or on loan — some of their collection for display at the museum. There was correspondence between Everett and different firms who carried out restoration work on some of the museum's exhibits. There were provisional dates for a schedule of specialist exhibitions that Everett was planning. But nothing of a personal nature at all.

The sound of a grunt made Daniel look up, and he saw the stocky figure of Inspector Grafton entering the office.

'Inspector Grafton. What a surprise to see you here,' said Daniel.

'Not that much of a surprise, Wilson,' said Grafton sourly. 'Marriott told me you'd asked about me and the investigation. So, I'm here to tell you that there is no investigation.'

'No?'

'No. Everett's death was suicide. That's it.'

'And yet you're here. You're trying to tell me that Special Branch investigates suicides? Is this a new departure?'

Grafton scowled, put his hands on the desk and leant in towards Daniel. 'My advice to you, Wilson, is just walk away, or else things might get difficult for you.'

'Difficult?'

'You know what I mean. There are some powerful people who don't like others poking their noses into things that don't concern them.'

'But Gavin Everett's death *does* concern me. The Ashmolean has hired me and Miss Fenton to look into it.'

Grafton gave Daniel an icy smile.

'Yes, that's another thing you ought to think about,' he said. 'Miss Fenton's safety. Ruffians and all sorts seem to be on the loose in this city. These are dangerous times for a woman.'

At these words, Daniel wanted to crash his fist into Grafton's face and wipe the smug look off it. Instead, he rose to his feet and leant towards Grafton, then said, firmly and deliberately, 'Let me tell you something, Grafton. If anything happens to Miss Fenton — *anything at all* — I'll kill you.'

Grafton stopped smiling and swallowed as he saw the intensity of the look of anger in Daniel's eyes.

'Are you threatening me?' he demanded, his voice hoarse.

'No, I'm making you a promise,' said Daniel.

Grafton stepped back from the desk and glowered at Daniel.

'You'd better be careful, Wilson,' he said. 'I'm warning you, you're out of your depth with this one. You're treading on dangerous ground. Take my advice and clear out. Leave Oxford before you find yourself in big trouble.'

With that, he stormed out.

Daniel watched him go, then sat down at the desk again. What did Grafton know? What was so special about this case that it brought a detective from Special Branch in? Inspector Pitt had said he didn't know about Grafton being here in Oxford. So, was the Special Branch man here in an unofficial capacity? In which case, what was going on?

He got up and pulled on his coat. It was time to call on Inspector Pitt and see if he was able to throw any light on it. Pitt hadn't been able to before, but in a case like this, things could change by the hour. Just before he went out, he left a note for Abigail on the desk: *Gone to see Inspector Pitt. Back soon.*

★　★　★

Daniel Wilson was a problem that needed to be dealt with, reflected Walter Grafton angrily as he left the Ashmolean. His mind went back to when he'd been called in by Superintendent Mason and given the brief: 'You're to go to the War Office and see a Commander Atkinson. A difficult case has arisen in Oxford which may have implications for national security.'

'Terrorists?' asked Grafton.

'Possibly,' said Mason. 'A man has been killed who had links to foreign forces opposed to Britain. According to the War Office he was a double agent. Our side didn't kill him, so we want to find out if it was the other side who did.'

'The Irish Brotherhood?'

'No, there's no Irish connection with this one, Inspector. At least, not as far as we know. Commander Atkinson will give you the details.' And then Mason had added pointedly: 'A result here will be very good for your career prospects, Inspector.'

Promotion, thought Grafton. *Chief inspector.* This could be the making of him.

Commander Atkinson was a soldier in every way: tall, ramrod stiff, and who spoke in clipped military tones.

'Your superintendent recommended you because you've shown initiative in dealing with terrorists and people who wish to overthrow the British order,' he said to Grafton once he had taken a seat in Atkinson's office. The walls were decorated with memorabilia from various military encounters. 'You didn't serve in the army, did you?'

'No, sir. I joined the police and worked my way from uniform through to the detective division, and then to Special Branch.'

'Where I understand you've had success in preventing terrorist plots from being carried out on the mainland against certain targets, including Her Majesty herself.'

'Yes, sir.'

Atkinson nodded in thoughtful approval, then asked, 'How much do you know about the Boers?'

'I know we fought a war against them, but that was about fifteen years ago.'

'You know the outcome of that war?'

Grafton hesitated before replying awkwardly, 'The Boers won. Britain lost.'

'It was lunacy!' growled Atkinson. 'The whole campaign, from start to finish! Britain had the whole of South Africa under its control and because of the sheer stupidity of its commanders, threw it away. We ended up signing a treaty that gave the Boers control of two of the four republics in South Africa, the Orange Free State and the Transvaal, while Britain retained control of the other two colonies, Cape Colony and Natal. At first it seemed a reasonable deal; the Boer colonies were just scrub and poor land. But then in 1884 gold was discovered in the Transvaal, followed by the discovery of the biggest goldfield ever at Witwatersrand two years later, and that changed everything.

'British miners went out there in their hundreds and were welcomed by the Boers because they had the skill and the labour to mine the gold. Many of them made money. But most of the wealth, and certainly the power, went to the Boer government.

'About nine months ago we were approached by a man called Gavin Everett. He'd been one of those British miners in the Transvaal — Huit-landers, the Boers called them — and he'd returned to Britain and had been working as some sort of executive at the Ashmolean Museum in Oxford. He told us that in Oxford he'd met up with someone he'd known in the Transvaal, a Boer. This Boer, while in his cups apparently, and mistakenly thinking that Everett was an old friend, told him of a plot that was being hatched in the Transvaal by the Boers, now they had this huge wealth, to take over the two British colonies in South Africa, starting with Cape Colony. The plan, according to Everett, involves a military incursion.

'Everett offered to find out more by cultivating this Boer and pretending to be on their side, and even offered his help in passing on information to the Boers about the British aspect, garnered from people he'd known in Cape Colony. Unfortunately, he wasn't motivated by patriotism but money. He wanted paying for acting as a double agent because, as he said, he was putting his life in danger by pretending to spy for the Boers, and if he was discovered, they'd kill him.

'We investigated and found out that he had spent two years in the goldfields of the Transvaal, and also spent some of that time in Cape Colony. By all accounts he was the sort of person who made acquaintances easily in both communities, Boer and the Cape, so his story had enough of the ring of truth to enlist him.

'To be honest, although he kept us informed of the development of the proposed raid, he didn't pass on any details such as the names of the conspirators, or even the Boer he'd met in

Oxford. This Boer, it appears, was just one of a group of Boers who'd relocated to Oxford. According to Everett, they were cultivating support for the Boers from certain British politicians. We can only assume he was keeping the names to himself because he was worried that once we knew those, we'd deal with the matter ourselves and his income from us would stop.

'Then, last week, we heard that Everett had been found dead in his office at the Ashmolean, shot through the head. It had the appearance of suicide, but certain things didn't add up. However, we sent a telegram to the local police in Oxford ordering them to accept suicide as the verdict and stop any further investigations.

'It's possible that Everett's death was for some other reason, but there is the possibility that this group of Boers discovered that he was a double agent and killed him. In which case, we need to know who they are so that we can arrest and interrogate them. That's your job. Find out if there is any truth to this group of Boer conspirators or if it was some kind of fraud that Everett was perpetuating, and report back.'

'Yes, sir,' said Grafton. 'Can I ask if you had any confirmation from your sources in South Africa about Everett's story?'

'We passed the initial information to the governor of the Cape and his people have been looking into it.'

'So, it's possible there could have been a leak there which filtered back to the group in Oxford.'

'It's possible,' agreed Atkinson. 'If so, you'll need to be on your guard. But remember, all of this is top secret. If you find anything, telegraph me here and I'll send you support. But, until then, we don't want to alert the opposition by putting in too large a force, so you'll be on your own.'

'That's fine by me, sir,' Grafton assured him. 'If there is anything to find, I'll find it.'

And he would. But first he had to find a way of getting rid of Daniel Wilson, because he couldn't afford to have Wilson dogging his steps and getting in the way of his investigation. No, Wilson had to be got out of the way. Along with that Fenton woman.

8

Abigail picked up the note Daniel had left for her on the desk. She wondered why he'd gone to see Inspector Pitt. Had there been a development? If so, she'd find out soon enough, when he returned. In the meantime, this would give her a proper opportunity to do what she'd been hoping for since she arrived at the Ashmolean: to explore the exhibits in the Egyptian Rooms. It would be interesting to see what new additions had been made to the collection since she was last here, and to compare the treasures from ancient Egypt owned by the Ashmolean with the ones she'd curated when she'd been at the Fitzwilliam Museum in Cambridge.

She made her way down to the basement area where the Egyptian collection resided. She passed the large statues which had been there before and made her way to the display cases. While most people were in awe of the pyramids and the large statues that guarded them, for Abigail it had always been the smaller statuary, the pottery, the small and often wonderfully ornate items left in the pyramid to accompany the dead pharaoh to the Other World that fascinated her. The collection looked much as she remembered it; she certainly wasn't aware of any new additions being present, but she remembered Marriott telling them Everett had spent a lot of time extending the African collection through his contacts, so that had obviously been his priority.

Her eye was caught by one of the decorated plates on display in one of the glass cases and she remembered she'd seen it before, but this time there was something not quite right about it. She bent down and peered closer at it.

It was the blue. It was . . . different. Less luminescent, somehow.

She gestured at the attendant on duty in the room, who'd been watching her, and he came over to join her.

'Yes, Miss Fenton?' he asked. 'Can I help you?'

She pointed at the display case.

'Do you have a key to this case?' she asked. 'I'm curious to see that plate up close, without the glass between us.'

'I'm sorry, only Mr Marriott and Mr Thomas have keys to the display cases,' said the attendant apologetically. 'But I can go and fetch Mr Thomas. He's just in the next room.'

'Thank you,' said Abigail.

She peered even closer at the plate through the glass. Yes, although the rest of the colours seemed fine, the blue was definitely wrong. Could it have faded? Surely not. Not this particular material.

'Yes, Miss Fenton?'

Abigail looked and saw that Hugh Thomas, the head steward, had arrived, accompanied by the attendant.

'I wonder if you'd mind opening the case so that I can get a proper look at that plate,' she said.

'Not at all,' said Thomas. 'It will be my pleasure.'

He reached for the bunch of keys suspended by a small chain from his belt, selected one, and unlocked the case.

Carefully, Abigail reached in and lifted the plate out. She turned it over, then back so that its decorated side was showing once more.

'Beautiful, isn't it,' said Thomas.

'Yes,' said Abigail. 'But I'm afraid it's also a fake.'

★   ★   ★

Inspector Grafton entered the main police station and strode meaningfully to the desk, where a uniformed sergeant stood on duty.

'Who's the senior officer in charge?' he demanded.

The sergeant, taken aback and offended by his hectoring tone, asked, 'Why do you want to know?'

For answer, Grafton produced his warrant card and held it under the sergeant's nose.

'Special Branch,' he said curtly.

The sergeant swallowed.

'That'll be Superintendent Clare, sir,' he said.

Grafton handed him his visiting card.

'Tell him I'm here and want to see him,' he said brusquely.

★   ★   ★

Abigail was returning to the office when she saw Gladstone Marriott heading along the corridor for the same place. He was carrying a small brown paper bag.

'Ah, Miss Fenton,' said Marriott. 'I was just coming to see you.'

'And I was just coming to see you,' said Abigail. She gestured at the bag. 'Is this related to the case?'

'It is indeed,' said Marriott. 'I'll tell you all when we're in the office.'

She followed him in and closed the door, while he put the bag on the desk.

'Is Mr Wilson around?' he asked.

'He's gone to see Inspector Pitt about something,' said Abigail. 'But I'll pass on anything he needs to know.'

Marriott pointed at the bag.

'The undertakers delivered this to me today. It's Everett's possessions that were found on him. They've now been given permission by the authorities to release his effects, but as there's no next of kin as far as we know, they brought them to me.' He upended the bag and the contents fell on the desk's surface.

'It's not much, is it,' said Marriott. 'But I assume he had more at his lodgings.'

Abigail looked. It wasn't much. A few coins. A silk handkerchief. And a leather wallet.

'I had to take a look at the wallet's contents because I had to sign for them,' explained Marriott. 'But there's not much there. A few notes. Some business cards.'

Abigail opened the wallet and examined the contents. As Marriott had said, nothing that might be of help. She flicked through the

66

business cards, then picked one out and held it out towards Marriott.

'This one's unusual,' she said.

The card was engraved with the drawing of a quill feather and had the number 3471 written on it in black ink.

'Yes,' said Marriott. 'I have no idea what it means. It's a puzzle.'

'It's a puzzle we'll let Mr Wilson examine when he returns,' said Abigail. 'In the meantime, I'm afraid we have a big problem.'

★ ★ ★

Superintendent Clare studied the words on the pasteboard card. Detective Inspector Walter Grafton — SB. The address was Scotland Yard in London.

Special Branch. Clare hated Special Branch, throwing their weight about and upsetting everyone. They acted as if they were a law unto themselves. Ruefully, he reflected that they *were* a law unto themselves. And now one of them was here on his patch, which meant trouble.

There was a knock at his door, then Sergeant Edmonds opened it and looked in.

'The inspector from London, sir,' he announced.

Inspector Grafton thrust Edmonds to one side as he entered the office and stood glowering.

'That'll be all, thank you, Sergeant,' said Clare.

Edmonds saluted, then left, pulling the door shut. Clare handed Grafton his visiting card back.

'Welcome to Oxford, Inspector,' he said. 'How can we be of help?'

'You can arrest Daniel Wilson,' grunted Grafton sourly.

'I assume you're referring to the Daniel Wilson who's been engaged by the Ashmolean to find out why Mr Everett killed himself?' asked Clare politely.

'How many other Daniel Wilsons are there in Oxford?' snapped Grafton.

'I would imagine quite a few,' said Clare. 'It's not an uncommon name. Although there are no others I can think of who are ex-Scotland-Yard detective inspectors, with a long and distinguished career while working under Inspector Abberline.'

'That's irrelevant,' snorted Grafton. 'He's no longer on the force and I want him arrested.'

'On what charge?'

'On any charge. He's interfering with a Special Branch investigation.'

Clare fixed Grafton with a firm look, then said levelly, 'Mr Wilson is a private citizen going about his lawful business. I've not heard of any crime he may have committed.'

Grafton glared at the superintendent. 'He threatened to kill me,' he said. 'That's a serious charge.'

'It is,' said Clare. 'Do you have witnesses to this threat?'

Grafton hesitated. 'No,' he admitted.

'So it would be your word against his.'

'The word of a Special Branch inspector.'

'Do you wish to press charges?' asked Clare. 'Making the case, and your name, public?'

Grafton glowered at him, doing his best to contain his temper.

'Are you deliberately obstructing a Special Branch investigation?' he demanded.

'Not at all,' replied Clare. 'I'm doing what I'm paid to do, which is to uphold the law in Oxford and protect its citizens.' He looked coldly at Grafton, then said, 'Perhaps you'd enlighten me on the investigation you are carrying out here in the city. It cannot be to do with the death of Mr Everett because I was informed by telegram from the War Office that the verdict of suicide was sound and there was to be no further investigation. Or do you have contrary information that would mean us reopening the case?'

'Listen — ' snarled Grafton, but he was cut short by Clare grating at him, 'No, you listen. You may be from Special Branch, but you are an inspector, and as a superintendent, I outrank you. You do not come here and give me orders as if I was just some lackey. If you have an official request to make for action by my men, backed by evidence, then tell me what it is and we'll do our best to comply. Otherwise, get the hell out of my police station.'

Grafton swallowed hard, glaring at Clare.

'You have just made a very big mistake, Superintendent,' he hissed. 'You'll be hearing from my superiors.'

'And they'll be hearing from me with a complaint about a rude, ill-mannered lout of an inspector who doesn't know how to conduct himself when addressing a superior officer. I wish you good day.'

9

Abigail stood by the open display case, the plate in her hands, watched by Gladstone Marriott and Hugh Thomas with expressions of horror on their faces. An attendant stood guard at the temporary barrier that had been set up to stop the public from coming into the Egyptian Rooms.

'A f-fake?' stammered Marriott hoarsely.

'Or, more exactly, a copy of the original, I suspect. But not an old one, and not Egyptian. It's recent and made in this country. Which means, yes, I'm afraid it's a fake.'

Marriott stared at the plate, then at her.

'But . . . but . . . ' he stammered. He gulped hard. 'Are you sure?'

'Absolutely certain,' said Abigail. She pointed at the areas of blue paint in the design. 'It was the blue that first caught my attention. The ancient Egyptians used lapis lazuli for decoration, which gives a very intense ultramarine blue. It was highly prized and very expensive. Only the highest classes in Egyptian society could afford it, so it was a statement of wealth. I've observed many examples of lapis lazuli decoration both when I was in Egypt, and also in some of the pieces we received when I was curating Egyptian relics at the Fitzwilliam. This blue, however, is just an ordinary commercial blue paint, the sort that can be found in any

70

modern hardware store.'

She turned the plate over and showed the underside to Marriott and Thomas. 'What's worse, and the final incontrovertible proof, is this.' She tapped a patch in the middle of the underside where the white surface had been scratched to reveal long gouges in the clay beneath. 'I hate to say it, but this is just an ordinary commercial plate available in many shops. The mark here is where the maker's stamp had been removed.' She turned it over to show the decorated side again. 'This is a modern copy of an ancient Egyptian design. Locked behind a glass case, there's no reason for anyone to examine it closely; unless, like me, they have made a study of ancient Egyptian lapis lazuli decoration.'

Marriott's face wore an expression of horror. 'But . . . but . . . Are you sure it couldn't have been sent, even as a copy, with a consignment from Egypt?'

'No,' said Abigail. 'I have seen copies being illegally added to consignments in Egypt that are to be sent out to museums abroad, but even those can be identified as having been produced in Egypt by hand. I'm certain this kind of earthenware is the product of the potteries here in England. Which would suggest it was introduced into the glass case once the original ancient Egyptian plate had been removed. In other words, a switch.'

Marriott's face was ashen.

'I'm sorry,' he apologised. 'I'm having difficulty working out how it can have happened.

71

The items in the glass case are under lock and key. How could someone make a copy of the original and then swap them over?'

'I'm afraid it can only have been done with the connivance of someone with the key,' said Abigail.

'But only three of us have keys to the cases!' burst out Marriott. 'Myself, Mr Thomas, and Gavin Everett, when he was alive.'

Abigail looked at the bewildered and horrified expression on the faces of the museum director and his chief steward, then said, 'I think we may have stumbled upon a possible motive for Mr Everett's death.'

'You mean, he was involved in swapping original artefacts and replacing them with copies?' said Marriott, shocked.

'Well, if it wasn't either of you who put it in the glass display case, that does only leave Everett.'

'But . . . I'd have trusted him with everything here!' He looked at her aghast, and then, clutching at straws, said imploringly, 'Perhaps he did it unwittingly. He sent a piece for restoration, and when the criminal sent back a copy instead of the original, he put it into the glass case in good faith?'

'Highly unlikely,' said Abigail. 'In daylight, no longer obscured by glass, any curator familiar with the items would have been suspicious about the blue and would have spotted that it wasn't lapis lazuli on further inspection. Not to mention the fact that this is not an ancient piece of pottery but a modern plate. I can't believe that someone like Mr Everett, with his museum experience, wouldn't have noticed.'

'But . . . but what can we do?'

'I suggest the first thing is to examine the other items in this case and see if there are any other copies that have been introduced,' said Abigail.

'Others?' echoed Marriott, and this time he went visibly pale and began to sway, and if Hugh Thomas hadn't grabbed him quickly, he'd have fainted to the floor.

★ ★ ★

Daniel left Kemp Hall police station with a feeling of frustration. Pitt hadn't been available, the desk sergeant informing him that the inspector was out on an investigation. Daniel had left a note for Pitt asking him to call at the Ashmolean when it was convenient but adding 'Not urgent' at the end of his note. He knew from experience how busy the job of a police inspector was and he didn't want to add to his burden unnecessarily. He was just leaving the yard and about to walk up the high street towards the Ashmolean, when he saw the familiar figure of Inspector Grafton leaving the police station.

Immediately, Daniel was alert. He withdrew into the cover of a black police van and watched the inspector. There was no mistaking the very unhappy scowl on Grafton's face as he stomped across the cobbled yard. So, whatever his mission had been, it had come to naught. But what had been his mission? There were two options, both connected to the death of Everett. The first was that Grafton was trying to find out information about Everett. The second was that he'd come to Kemp Hall to try and get Daniel and Abigail stopped from continuing their investigation, especially after what he'd said to Daniel at the Ashmolean. But he obviously hadn't been successful.

One thing that puzzled Daniel was why Grafton seemed to be acting on his own. There had been no sign of a sergeant accompanying him, and the usual practice for any Scotland Yard detective inspector on an official investigation was to have a detective sergeant with him. Again, the thought occurred to him that perhaps Grafton was acting unofficially. If so, who was he working for? The War Office seemed the most likely, in view of the telegram the Oxford police had received warning them off. But even so, Daniel would have expected Grafton to have a sergeant with him. But then, Special Branch often made up its own rules.

Intrigued, Daniel set off in slow pursuit of the inspector, curious to see where he would go next. Fortunately, Grafton seemed deep in thought, so he didn't look around to see if he was being followed. But then, Daniel supposed that Grafton didn't consider the possibility that he might be followed here in Oxford.

Daniel followed the inspector as he walked along the wide street that took him past the ancient sandstone university buildings, past the Bodleian, past the circular building that housed

74

the Radcliffe Camera — thanks to Abigail he now had a basic grasp of the locations and purposes of some of the city's ancient buildings — and then down a narrow street. At the end of the street, Grafton disappeared into an old building, going up the steps and past the high columns.

Daniel arrived at the building, where a red and gold sign outside informed him it was the Swan Inn.

Daniel mounted the steps and went in. There was a bustle of people inside, well-dressed men and women, some sitting at tables with pots of tea or coffee in front of them, some with alcoholic drinks. So, not so much an inn but a hotel.

Daniel kept by the main door, his gaze sweeping the area, and only when he was certain that Grafton was not to be seen did he approach the reception desk.

'Excuse me.' He smiled at the clerk on duty. 'I'm just checking if I have the right place. A friend of mine, Walter Grafton, told me he was coming to Oxford and would be staying at the Swan, but I forgot to ask him for the address, and I've discovered there are at least three establishments called the Swan in Oxford: yourselves, then there's the Swan Hotel, and the Old Swan. I was wondering if he might be staying with you.'

'Why yes, we do have a Mr Grafton staying with us,' said the clerk. 'In fact, he's just arrived back and gone to his room. Would you like me to send a message up to him?'

Daniel smiled again. 'No, that's fine. I don't want to disturb him now. I said I'd see him later, and at least I now know I've got the right place. Which room is he in?'

'Room 7, sir.'

So now I know where he's staying, thought Daniel with satisfaction as he left the inn.

10

Abigail was sitting at the desk in their temporary office when Daniel returned.

'Ah, you're back,' she said. 'How did it go with Inspector Pitt?'

'It didn't,' he said. 'Pitt was out, but I did find out where Inspector Grafton is staying.'

'Will that help us?' asked Abigail.

'I'm not sure,' admitted Daniel. 'But it's always a good thing to know where your enemy is based.'

'And Inspector Grafton is our enemy?'

'Absolutely,' said Daniel firmly. 'How did you get on with Esther Maris?'

'She's going to look into Everett's social life and see what she can uncover. But more importantly, I may have found a motive for Everett's death.'

'Oh?'

Abigail told him about the fake ancient Egyptian plate she'd discovered.

'I then found another three copies, one in the Egyptian Rooms and two in the Greek collection — all decorated plates. As you can imagine, Mr Marriott is petrified there's even worse to come, that huge numbers of the items on display have been copied and the originals replaced. Sculptures. Costumes. Jewellery. I hope I was able to reassure him I think that's unlikely. Most people who make fakes keep to one type of subject or style. What we found suggests it's the decorated plates that might be suspect, rather than more ornate ceramics.'

'Because it's easier to paint a design on a plate than recreate a three-dimensional piece.' Daniel nodded.

'And cheaper,' said Abigail.

'Yes, we found that was the case with fakes and forgeries we uncovered when I was at Scotland Yard. There was one artist we caught doing his own versions of George Stubbs' paintings of horses, and they weren't bad. But horses were all he could do. He got caught because he tried to do a kangaroo, and it looked awful. He might have got away with it if he hadn't put Stubbs' signature on the painting. In this case, I wonder what's happened to the originals?'

'Sold, I expect,' said Abigail. 'To private collectors.'

'By Gavin Everett?'

'It couldn't have been done without his involvement,' said Abigail.

'But how did he get them copied without anyone noticing?' asked Daniel.

'Restorers,' said Abigail. 'All museums use restorers to bring a piece that may be damaged, or faded, back to life. It's then replaced. But in this case, the restorer made a copy and it was the copy that was put back into the display case and the original sold. Which makes me think that some of the artefacts were stolen to order.'

'Someone comes in, sees a piece they like, and approaches Gavin Everett about buying it.'

Abigail nodded. 'That's the size of it, which means they have to know he's corrupt.'

'And perhaps one of his clients took umbrage at something that Everett did over one of these pieces. Perhaps Everett may have slipped him a fake rather than the genuine article, and — with no recourse to law — the angry client kills him.'

'That's one possibility,' said Abigail. 'But with fakery like this, there could be many other motives. Thieves falling out.'

'That explains why this person with the alleged Shakespeare came to him, because word had spread that he's in the market for fakes,' said Daniel. 'But how was he able to get away with it without being caught?'

'By keeping his business small, only a very few trusted clients. And as for the copies not being spotted, why should they be? Behind glass, they look fine to the layperson's eyes.'

'So, what's the next move?'

'I asked Mr Marriott for the name of the restorer they use so that we could talk to him, but he wasn't sure if Everett was still using the same one. Anyway, the restorer he mentioned is a Mr Ephraim Wardle, so I suggest we go and talk to him. If he did the work, he may have made the copies in all innocence.'

'Unlikely,' said Daniel.

'Not necessarily. Everett asks him to make a copy of the original for — I don't know — so they have a copy in case the original gets broken. The restorer doesn't know the copy will be used as part of a scam to cheat the museum.'

'I still think it's unlikely,' said Daniel. 'The

restorer would surely wonder why he was only asked to make copies of certain items and not others.'

'I'm trying to give whoever the restorer was the benefit of the doubt. Innocent until proven guilty, remember.'

'I think we'll get an indication of guilty or innocent when we start asking him questions.' He gave her an approving look 'Well, out of the pair of us you've been the busiest and most successful today.'

'And there's more,' she said.

'More?'

Abigail produced the small card with the engraving of the quill pen on it and handed it to Daniel.

'The undertakers returned the few possessions that were on Everett's body. This was in his wallet.'

Daniel studied the small card.

'What's it mean?' he asked, puzzled.

'I have no idea, and neither does Mr Marriott.'

There was a tap at the door and they turned to see Inspector Pitt in the doorway.

'I got your note when I got back to Kemp Hall,' he said.

'Yes, I'm sorry about that,' said Daniel. 'I'd had a visit from Inspector Grafton, the Special Branch detective I told you about, which annoyed me. He tried to warn us off, so I came to tell you about it.'

Pitt grinned. 'Yes, he came to Kemp Hall and tried the same on my guv'nor. He wanted you arrested.'

'Arrested!' said Abigail, shocked. 'On what charge?'

'Threatening behaviour,' said Pitt. 'He said you threatened to kill him.'

Abigail turned to Daniel and demanded angrily, 'Daniel, what have you been up to?'

'Nothing,' said Daniel defensively. 'It was just a bit of a shouting match, that's all.'

'Anyway, Superintendent Clare told him to sling his hook.'

'I'm grateful to your superintendent,' said Daniel. He held out the small white card to Pitt. 'Any idea what this is?'

Pitt took the card and looked at it.

'Where did it come from?' he asked.

'It was in Gavin Everett's wallet,' said Abigail. 'It turned up today when the undertakers brought his personal possessions here to give to Mr Marriott.'

'Have you seen anything like it before?' asked Daniel, catching the look of recognition on the inspector's face.

'Yes,' said Pitt. 'It's a membership card for the Quill Club, which is a very private gentlemen's club here in Oxford.'

'So private that they don't put its name on the card,' observed Daniel.

'Nor that of the member,' added Abigail.

'That's about the size of it,' said Pitt, handing the card back to Daniel. 'On the surface it appears respectable, professional types and a few academics from the university, but we had a complaint from a young woman who worked there, an Eve Lachelle, that she'd been attacked by some of the men while they were drunk.'

'How attacked?'

'Raped. Her clothes torn. We went to investigate, but of course they denied any such attack had ever taken place. We spoke to the women who worked there as waitresses, and they also said there'd been no attack. What made me suspicious was that at first these other women denied even knowing Eve Lachelle. It was only after we pressed them that they admitted she had worked there, but they insisted there'd been no attack that they knew of, and that she had left of her own volition. But it was their denial of even knowing her at first that made me suspicious.'

'When did all this happen?' asked Daniel.

Pitt searched his memory, then said, 'About four months ago.'

'Did the girl name Gavin Everett as one of her attackers?'

'No,' said Pitt. 'His name didn't come into it at all. In fact, until you showed me that card, I'd no idea he was even a member of the Quill Club.'

'And since that complaint from Eve Lachelle? Has there been any other trouble reported?' asked Abigail.

'Nothing. No disturbances, nothing apparently out of order. Although I'm fairly sure that some of the alleged waitresses are actually prostitutes there to service the members. The club certainly seemed to have a larger contingent of waitresses than were needed just to serve drinks.'

'Have you ever raided it?' asked Abigail.

'On what grounds? It's a private members'

club, and unless we get some complaint — such as we had with Eve Lachelle — we can't touch them without an order from a magistrate. Which, as the members include some very eminent citizens, isn't that easy.'

'I assume gambling goes on there?' said Daniel.

'Cards, mostly.'

'And does it have a licence?'

Pitt smiled. 'It's a private members' club.'

'So, an upmarket brothel and gambling den that people turn a blind eye to.'

Pitt shrugged. 'You know how things work when you're dealing with the upper strata of society. As I recall, you and Abberline had the same problem with the Clarence Street brothel due to the fact that most of its clients were lords, and some even in the royal circle.'

'But we still busted them,' said Daniel.

'Most of them fled abroad, from what I remember, and found safe haven on the Continent until they were able to return to England.'

'Are we talking the same level of society here? Titled people?'

'No, because we don't have as many titled people as London, a few dukes and earls and lords, but in a place like Oxford the gentry is often made up of academics, as I mentioned, and other apparent pillars of the Establishment. And the prostitutes at Clarence Street were mainly telegraph boys, as I remember. The Quill Club is careful to vet the kind of people they employ. No telegraph boys, or servant girls, just women of a certain type working officially as waitresses.'

'Who owns it?'

'The property is owned by a consortium of local businessmen. The building houses offices. The Quill Club is located in the basement.'

'Who runs it?' asked Daniel.

'A man called Vance de Witt.'

'What's he like?' asked Abigail.

'I only met him that once when we called to investigate the complaint from Miss Lachelle. He's in his early forties. Smooth. Smug. Confident.'

'Vance de Witt?' mused Daniel. 'Dutch?'

Pitt frowned. 'I don't think so. He's got an accent, but it's not like that of Dutch people I've met. And we get a few visiting Oxford who invariably find their way to the police station, either because they're lost, or they've had their pocket picked or something.' He thought for a bit, then said, 'If I was asked to describe his accent, I'd say it was similar to Australian, but flatter.'

Daniel remembered Marriott's report of his conversation with Inspector Grafton about Everett, looking for an African connection.

'Could it be South African?' he ventured.

Pitt thought it over, then nodded. 'Yes, it could well be,' he said. 'So, will you be talking to Mr de Witt?'

'I think I will,' said Daniel.

Pitt looked at the clock on the wall. 'I'd better be getting back to Kemp Hall,' he said. 'Is there anything else I should know about?'

'Actually — ' began Daniel.

84

'No,' interrupted Abigail, with a smile. 'Nothing, except to let you know I've asked a young woman reporter at the *Oxford Messenger* to do some digging for us into Everett's private life.'

'Good luck with that,' said Pitt. 'But hopefully you might find out something about that now through Mr de Witt and the Quill Club.'

After Pitt had gone, Daniel queried Abigail, 'You didn't want him to know about the fake plates you discovered? They're surely crucial to one reason why Everett may have been killed.'

'I think the fewer people who know about the copies the better,' said Abigail. 'It's about protecting the Ashmolean. It would be very unfair for gossip to spread and have the museum's reputation tarnished unfairly.'

'Pitt isn't the sort who spreads gossip,' countered Daniel. 'And he gave us confidential information right at the start, when he told us about that telegram from the War Office. He trusts us, and I think we should return the compliment.'

'And we will,' promised Abigail. 'But right now, our loyalty is to Mr Marriott and the Ashmolean. And Inspector Pitt, much as I like and respect him, isn't officially on this case. We are.'

11

Walter Grafton strode into the Wilton Hotel. Marriott had told him, when pressed, that this was where the Ashmolean had booked rooms for Wilson and the Fenton woman. He walked up to the man at the reception desk and produced his warrant card, which he held out for the receptionist to examine.

'Scotland Yard?' said the receptionist, worried.

'I need to look at your register,' said Grafton.

The man complied with alacrity, putting the open book on the desk. Grafton studied it. The Fenton woman was in room 14 and Wilson in 15. He pushed the register back across the desk.

'Thank you,' he said curtly.

'Is there anything we should know?' asked the receptionist, concerned. 'Anyone we should be worried about?'

'No,' said Grafton shortly. 'Except that I was never here and never asked to look at the register. Is that clear?'

The man nodded, and Grafton made for the stairs to the first floor. He'd already checked that Wilson and Fenton seemed to be tied up at the Ashmolean, so he hoped to have time to examine their rooms. And unlike his visit to Everett's rooms, this time he'd be leaving no trace. Going into Everett's lodgings had been different. Then he'd deliberately left signs he'd been there in the hope that word about the break-in and search would spread and unsettle his Boer opponents, if there were any. *Start the hares running*, they called it in Special Branch. Beat the bushes and see if anything moves.

He decided to start with Wilson's room. He took his lock-pick from his pocket and opened the door. His first impression was surprise at how tidy the room was. No clothes left draped over the back of chairs, no personal possessions spread over the dressing table. His surprise deepened as he began to open drawers, and then the wardrobe. Everything was empty. There were no clothes, no papers, no personal articles of any sort.

There was a suitcase beside the bed. Grafton picked it up, and knew immediately it was empty, but he opened it just to check. There was nothing inside it. In short, the room wasn't being used. Which could only mean that Wilson was sharing the room next door with Fenton.

So they were lovers.

He smiled to himself at this realisation. It explained why Wilson had become so enraged when Grafton had warned him that 'something bad' might happen to Fenton. Well, this was an interesting aspect. It gave him something over them, if necessary. Wilson wouldn't want this being made public, with Fenton's reputation tarnished. Maybe this was the lever he needed to get them to abandon the case, but he'd have to be careful how he approached it. Wilson had a temper, and a reputation as a brawler in rough situations. And the Fenton woman was known to sling a punch when seriously upset. He'd have to think about this. In the meantime, he'd slip into the Fenton woman's room and dig around there, see what papers and information he could come up with.

He checked to make sure that he'd left everything in the room exactly as it was when he came in, then let himself out, and was shocked to come face-to-face with a young blonde-haired woman standing outside the door of the Fenton woman's room.

Abruptly and automatically, he turned his head so his face was away from the young woman, and he hurried swiftly along the corridor to the stairs. Behind him, he heard the young woman knock at the door and call, 'Abigail! It's Esther!'

Esther who? he wondered. And where did she figure in this?

★   ★   ★

Esther knocked again at the door and waited. Still no answer.

She was puzzled by the man who'd appeared from the next-door room and hurried off in such a furtive manner. Surely that couldn't have been Daniel Wilson? But she was sure that Abigail had told her she and Mr Wilson had rooms next to one another.

She went down to reception and gave the man at the desk an apologetic smile.

'I'm sorry to trouble you, but I think I've forgotten the number of the room where my friend is staying. Miss Abigail Fenton. I thought she said she was in room 14, but I've tried the room and there was no answer.'

The receptionist looked at the open pages of the guest book.

'Yes, Miss Fenton is in room 14,' he said. 'But her key's here, so I assume she's out.'

'And her colleague, Mr Wilson?' asked Esther. 'I think she said he was in the next room, room 13.'

'We don't actually have a room 13,' said the man. 'Some people are quite superstitious.' He checked the register again. 'Mr Wilson is in room 15. But as his key's also here, I assume they're both out.'

'Has he just left?' asked Esther. 'Did I just miss him?'

'No,' said the receptionist. He indicated the hooks where the keys were hanging. 'The key to room 15 has been here since this morning.'

Esther thanked the receptionist and left, her mind in a whirl. So the man who'd come out of room 15 hadn't been Daniel Wilson. Who was he? A burglar? Whoever he'd been, this was something that Abigail and Mr Wilson needed to know about.

★   ★   ★

Inspector Grafton was angry. In London the merest sight of his Special Branch warrant card by any police officer of whatever rank, even a superintendent, brought immediate cooperation. But here, in Oxford, it hardly made any impression. Yes, it got the desired result from people like the receptionist at the Wilton Hotel, but they were low level. Even that curator at the Ashmolean, Marriott, had refused his demand to stop hiring Wilson and Fenton. It was unthinkable!

At one point he'd thought of telegraphing Commander Atkinson for assistance, but then he'd rejected the idea: that would be an admission of failure on his part, and there was no way he was going to admit to that. No, he'd been entrusted with this mission and if the Boers had killed Everett then he was going to find out who they were, and bring them in.

He needed information. Hard information, and he wasn't getting anything useful from the local police, or from the Ashmolean. So where to try next? If he'd been in London, he'd have tried the various drinking dens where informers hung out, but he wasn't in London, he was in this alien city where being a Special Branch inspector apparently had no value with the authorities.

And then it struck him. Of course, the one place in any city where all information, all gossip, gathered together.

That would be his next port of call.

12

In their office at the Ashmolean, Daniel and Abigail discussed their next course of action in the light of recent events.

'I think my next move is to pay a visit to the Quill Club and have a word with this Mr de Witt,' said Daniel.

'Without me?' queried Abigail.

'You heard what Inspector Pitt said, it's a very discreet *gentlemen's* club. I get the feeling I might have more luck doing it man-to-man, so to speak, rather than man-and-woman to man.'

'Yes, I think you're right.' Abigail nodded. 'While my next move is to check on the fakes by talking to this restorer Mr Marriott mentioned, Ephraim Wardle.'

'I think you'd better be careful,' warned Daniel. 'If he was a criminal associate of Everett's and you start asking questions, he might turn nasty. Especially if he was involved in Everett's death.'

'Don't worry,' Abigail promised him. 'I know what I'm doing. I'll just be there as an archaeologist with a long history of working with artefacts from Egypt and Greece, who's making enquiries about restoration.'

There was a knock at the door, which opened to reveal Esther Maris.

'Esther!' Abigail smiled. She gestured at Daniel, who rose to his feet and walked towards

Esther, hand extended for her to shake.

'Daniel Wilson,' he introduced himself. 'We haven't met before, but Abigail has told me an awful lot about you.'

'I knew it wasn't you!' exclaimed Esther, shaking Daniel's hand.

'What wasn't?' asked Daniel, puzzled.

'The man who came out of the room next to Abigail's at the Wilton Hotel. Room 15.' As Daniel and Abigail shot startled looks at one another, Esther enlarged on what had happened. 'I'd gone to the Wilton to see if Abigail was there to tell her what I'd found out about Mr Everett's private life ... which, unfortunately, was nothing ...'

'The man who came out of my room?' Daniel prompted.

'Yes, well, I was knocking at the door of room 14, when suddenly the door of room 15 opened and this man came out.'

'What did he look like?' asked Daniel.

'He was shorter than you. Relatively well dressed, but not very well dressed. Tidy rather than smart.'

'Hair? Beard? Moustache?'

'Dark hair, cut quite short. Possibly a military style of cut. No beard, but a moustache. Not a big bushy one, but large enough.'

'It sounds like — ' began Abigail.

'No one we recognise,' cut in Daniel. 'Well done, Esther, and thank you. And it was lucky you were there. Having tried my room, I'm sure he'd have tried Abigail's next.'

'Do you think it's connected with the case?

With Everett's death?'

'I don't know,' said Daniel. 'There's a particular breed of thief who sneaks around hotels, getting into their rooms and robbing them. Fortunately, I don't leave anything of value in my room.' He turned to Abigail. 'It might be worth checking your room, in case he went in there first before he went into mine.'

'Yes,' agreed Abigail. 'We'll get along there now.'

'Before you go, the other reason I came looking for you was to give you this,' said Esther. She opened her bag and took out two sheets of paper covered in neat handwriting. 'It's the interview I did with you. I promised I'd let you see it and get your approval before I handed it in.'

'Why thank you!' said Abigail. 'I promise I'll read it and let you have it back later today. Where will I find you?'

'If you like, I can come back here,' said Esther. 'Would two hours be enough for you? Because I promised my editor I'd let him have it this afternoon, and if there's anything that needs changing . . . '

'That'll be fine,' said Abigail. 'I'll see you back here in two hours' time.'

Esther smiled, wished them both a good day and left, while Abigail and Daniel put on their coats and made themselves ready to head to the Wilton Hotel to check if the intruder had been in their room.

'Why didn't you let me tell her about Inspector Grafton?' demanded Abigail as they headed down the stairs to the street. 'You said before you thought he was the most likely.'

'Because she's a reporter, and I'm wary about what I say to reporters.'

'But you talk to reporters and tell them things. Look at that friend of yours on the *Daily Telegraph* when we were at the British Museum.'

'That's different, I've known Joe for years, and I trust him to keep what we tell him secret and not use it until we tell him he can.'

'It could be the same with Esther,' protested Abigail.

'It could, but we don't know her well enough yet. She's ambitious, you said so yourself, so she might use things we tell her to push her own career forward without consulting us first.'

'She gave me the interview she did with me to read first before handing it in to her editor,' Abigail pointed out. 'Surely that bodes well.'

'Yes, alright,' admitted Daniel. 'But there's another thing: her safety. If it *was* Grafton at the Wilton and Esther starts poking around and investigating him, it could be dangerous for her.'

'All the more important she knows about him, so she's warned about the situation,' said Abigail.

Daniel sighed, defeated.

'Very well,' he said reluctantly. 'You tell her, but stress this is not for public consumption, not yet.'

★   ★   ★

When they arrived at the Wilton Hotel, while Abigail went upstairs to check on their room,

94

Daniel approached the receptionist, Charles.

'Good afternoon, Charles,' he said, and smiled.

'Good afternoon, Mr Wilson. Do you want the key to your room?'

'No thank you, just some information, if you don't mind. I've discovered that a Special Branch detective was in here earlier, and I assume he asked to look at the register.'

Charles looked uncomfortable and very unhappy.

'I'm afraid I was told not to say anything,' he said apologetically.

'And I won't ask you to,' Daniel assured him. 'But, as you know, Miss Fenton and I have been booked in here by the Ashmolean Museum as part of our work for them, which is to look into the circumstances surrounding the unfortunate Mr Everett's death. So, any questions I have are really coming from the Ashmolean, and I know you'd like to keep the Wilton's continuing relationship with the museum on its present very good terms. But, as I said, I won't ask you to say anything. Instead, if I ask you something, all I need you to do is nod or shake your head. That way you are exonerated because you won't have told me anything. Is that acceptable?'

Charles did not look convinced. 'The gentleman who told me not to say anything was very firm. One might also say threatening.'

'I understand, and if you're unhappy with what I've just suggested — which, I stress again — won't involve you *saying* anything, I can ask Mr Marriott to come and have the conversation

95

with you. Although, I do feel he won't be happy about being brought from the very important work he's engaged in at this moment, but hopefully that won't affect his decision-making when it comes to making booking arrangements for his visitors and guests.' He smiled reassuringly. 'Trust me, I was a detective inspector for many years at Scotland Yard, and what I'm suggesting is an old and established tradition for situations such as this. So, did this man show you a police warrant card?'

Charles hesitated, and then nodded.

'And did he ask to look at the hotel register?'

Again, after a hesitation, Charles nodded.

'Thank you.' Daniel smiled. 'Lastly, was the name on the police warrant card Inspector Grafton?'

The shock of recognition at the name was enough to give Daniel his answer.

'Thank you, Charles. You have told me nothing. And if I'm pressed, that is what I will say.'

He became aware that Abigail had joined them. She handed her room key to Charles, and then steered Daniel away from the desk.

'I don't think he was in our — my — room. Nothing has been disturbed.'

'Well, I've established it was Grafton, and he can be very careful about covering up when he wants to be.'

'Trust me, I would know. I left certain personal items which he would have had to move to get to the contents of the drawers, and they were untouched.'

96

'So, he went into my official room first, and was just about to root around in yours when he must have come upon Esther, and so he scarpered.'

'And it's thanks to Esther that we know about it,' added Abigail.

'Yes, alright,' said Daniel. 'I've already agreed with you on telling her about Grafton.'

'I thought I'd also pick her brains about which titled family might own this alleged Shakespeare play, especially if the lady in question is unhappy in her marriage. Newspaper reporters are usually in the know about that sort of gossip, especially those who write the women's page.'

'Alright but do be careful how much you tell her. As I said, we don't know her.'

'I'll be discreet,' Abigail assured him. 'And now I'd better get back to the Ashmolean and read her article on me before she arrives. And, after that, I'll go and find this restorer, Ephraim Wardle, while you seek out this Mr de Witt at this gentlemen's club.' She grinned. 'But be careful, I know what some of these gentlemen's clubs can be. Hotbeds of debauchery.'

'Oh, and how do you know that?' asked Daniel.

'My sister, Bella, used to read cheap romantic novels where the hero was always being trapped by loose women in such places.'

Daniel grinned back at her.

'I promise you I shall keep my virtue intact.'

13

Inspector Pitt had told Daniel that the Quill
Club was in the Broad, which Daniel learnt was
Oxford-speak for Broad Street. As he walked
from St Giles' along the street, passing Boswells
department store, he reflected that this, of all the
places in Oxford, showed its ancient history as a
seat of learning, and also philosophical and
religious dissent. A granite cross set into the road
outside Balliol College marked the spot where
the Protestant martyrs, Hugh Latimer, Nicholas
Ridley and Thomas Cranmer had been burned
at the stake in the middle of the sixteenth
century. The original Ashmolean Museum had
been established here in the Broad, before
moving to Beaumont Street. No one, he felt,
could fail to be impressed by the superb
architecture of the sandstone Sheldonian The-
atre, and the ancient building that housed the
Bodleian Library. There were ghosts here of
hundreds of years of erudition and thought. And
the two bookshops, Thornton's and Blackwell's,
had obviously been located here to take
advantage of the readers, writers, thinkers and
philosophers who still inhabited this part of
Oxford.

Daniel followed Pitt's directions and found the
Quill Club, although there was nothing to
indicate that it was here. A gap in the row of
metal railings gave on to stone steps that led

down to a basement area, where a door of black oak furnished with brass fittings was set into a blank wall. A bell pull was by the door, and Daniel gave it a tug. After a few moments, the door opened and a middle-aged man in shirtsleeves looked out at him, wariness and suspicion writ large on his face.

'Yes?' he snapped.

'Good day. My name's Daniel Wilson and I'd like to see Mr de Witt, if that's possible. Mr Vance de Witt.'

The man hesitated, and Daniel got the impression he was about to close the door, when another voice from inside said, 'That's alright, Albert. I'll deal with this.'

Albert moved away, and the door opened to reveal a short, well-built man, dressed in an expensively cut dark suit, with a high-collared white shirt highlighted by a blue silk tie. His longish blonde hair was immaculately coiffured, as was his pencil-thin moustache.

'Mr de Witt?' asked Daniel, although his ear had already picked up the flat tones of South Africa in the man's voice.

'You say you wish to see me?'

'Yes, with your permission. My name's Daniel Wilson and I've been asked by the Ashmolean to look into the death of Mr Gavin Everett.'

De Witt looked at Daniel warily. 'And why would your investigations bring you here?'

Daniel produced the small card Abigail had found in Everett's wallet and showed it to de Witt.

'I believe this was Gavin Everett's membership card of your club.'

'And what makes you think that?' asked de Witt.

'The quill feather.' Daniel smiled. 'Along with information received.'

'Information from whom?'

Daniel gave de Witt the smile again. 'Let's just say that'll have to remain confidential for the moment. I promise you, I'm very good at keeping secrets.'

De Witt studied Daniel, then said, 'If we're going to have a conversation, shall we do so in more comfortable surroundings? My office?'

De Witt led the way into the club. It was small, but elegant. The tables had white linen tablecloths covering them, and to one side was a bar stocked with a variety of bottles and glasses, behind which stood the man, Albert, who watched Daniel suspiciously as he followed de Witt through an avenue between the tables to a door at the rear. De Witt opened it and gestured Daniel in. The office was as elegant as the club room itself.

De Witt gestured Daniel to a leather chair and took a seat behind his desk.

'Can I get you anything to drink?'

'No thank you, I'm fine. As I said, I'm looking into the death of Mr Everett and hoping you might be able to help throw some light on it.'

De Witt pursed his lips in a thoughtful frown, then said, 'Everett was a member. But there's nothing unusual or mysterious about that. The Quill Club has a membership list drawn from the very best in Oxford.'

'Yes, so I understand,' said Daniel. 'I'm

certainly not suggesting there's any sort of skulduggery here. I'm just trying to find out why Everett should do such a thing as take his own life.'

'Who's to say why anyone does such a thing?' said de Witt with a shrug.

'What sort of man was he?'

Before de Witt could answer, there was a knock on the door, which opened and Albert appeared.

'Sorry to trouble you, Mr de Witt,' he apologised, 'but the suppliers have short-changed us on the order for champagne. Again.'

'You're sure, Albert?' asked de Witt.

Albert nodded. 'I've counted the crates twice, and there's definitely one with four bottles missing. If you remember, it happened about two months ago.'

'Yes, I do,' said de Witt. 'Very well, I'll write to the supplier telling them that this is the second time this has happened and reminding them that the first time they discovered the missing case had been left at their depot and was returned to us with fulsome apologies and a promise it would not happen again. Yet it has.'

'I don't believe it was ever just left at their depot; I reckon the driver swiped it,' said Albert.

'Yes, I believe you're right, but a warning should bring them to their heels. They'll be worried we might go to a competitor, even though we've got a good deal with them.' He smiled. 'Thank you, Albert.'

Albert nodded and withdrew, pulling the door shut.

'He's a good man,' said de Witt. 'Most bar managers aren't as tenacious as Albert in making sure we get what we pay for. He's worth his weight in gold.' He turned to Daniel. 'What were you asking before we were interrupted by Albert?'

'I was asking what sort of man Gavin Everett was.'

'Outside of the club, I've no idea,' said de Witt.

'And inside the club?'

De Witt shrugged. 'He was a member. Not particularly noticeable. He didn't cause any trouble, but then most of the people who come here don't, otherwise we'd rescind their membership. We run a very quiet, very sedate little establishment where members can relax with like-minded people, talk, drink, play cards and escape from the humdrum for a brief while. We are an oasis.'

'And a very discreet one,' said Daniel. 'For example, there's no mention of the name of the club on your membership cards.'

'There's no need,' said de Witt. 'People who hold membership know who we are and where we are. We don't advertise; we have no need to. Members who enjoy their time here introduce their friends.'

'And who introduced Gavin Everett?'

De Witt chuckled. 'Really, Mr Wilson. I think I've made clear we are very discreet about our members, and that includes who may have brought someone else in.'

'Was there anyone among your members

you'd think of as being particularly close to Everett? As a friend? Someone he spent more time with than others?'

De Witt frowned as he thought the question over.

'Not really,' he said. 'There was no one I can think of I'd say he was particularly close to. Not that he was antisocial, far from it. Always friendly, with a smile for everyone. Easy-going.'

'Did you know him before you came to Oxford?'

'No,' said de Witt, his answer coming just a little too quickly. 'Why should I?'

'I'm guessing you both had South Africa in common,' said Daniel. 'Your accent suggests you have a South African background, and Everett spent a couple of years there before coming to England.'

'South Africa is a vast place, Mr Wilson. There are thousands and thousands of people in South Africa I've never met. Among those was Gavin Everett.'

'Until you and he came to England.'

'Exactly.'

'Which part of South Africa were you in?' asked Daniel.

'Why?' asked de Witt suspiciously.

'No reason,' said Daniel. 'Just curious. I had a cousin who went out there to dig for gold and he used to write to me urging me to go out and join him and make my fortune. He used to wax lyrical about the country, saying how magnificent it was.'

'It is,' agreed de Witt. 'I assume your cousin

was in the Transvaal? That's where most of the goldfields are.'

'Indeed, although I can't remember exactly where he was. Unfortunately, he died soon after he returned to England, so I can't ask him.'

'Myself, I came to England from the Orange Free State about eighteen months ago,' said de Witt. 'There, it's mostly diamonds, rather than gold.'

'Did you prospect yourself?'

De Witt shook his head. 'Prospecting is not my kind of activity. I prefer more sedate pursuits. A hand of cards, for example. We have some enjoyable games here and I'd invite you to join, although I must warn you, the stakes can be quite high.'

Daniel smiled. 'I expect they'd be too high for me.'

'I'm sure we could extend you a line of credit. We do for most of our members. And we'd make you an honorary member for the evening.'

'Credit has to be paid off in the end,' said Daniel. 'What about Mr Everett? Did he use extended credit?'

De Witt chuckled. 'If you're asking if Everett ever got out of his depth financially here, and that may be why he ended it, I can assure you that was not the case. Everett always paid his bills. Once or twice he may have been held up for a day or two, but then any bills were always paid in full. He certainly didn't appear to have any money troubles.'

'Yes, I was told he had a private income that kept him comfortable.'

'I don't know about that,' said de Witt. 'We don't enquire where our members' money comes from, so long as it comes.' He looked at his watch. 'Is there anything more, Mr Wilson? Only I have things to do to prepare for this evening, and the afternoons are the only quiet time I have. I call it the lull before the storm.'

'Of course, and I thank you for your time,' said Daniel. He got up, as did de Witt. Daniel was about to head for the door, when he stopped and asked, 'One final question, if you don't mind, Mr de Witt. You said before that if members misbehaved, their membership would be withdrawn. Is that what happened over the matter of Eve Lachelle? I understand she complained to the police that she was attacked here by some of your members.'

De Witt gave him an apologetic smile. 'I'm afraid you've been misinformed, Mr Wilson. Yes, I believe that Miss Lachelle lodged a complaint, but on investigation it was found to be without foundation. A false accusation against some completely innocent men.'

'Why would she do such a thing?' asked Daniel.

De Witt shrugged. 'As I said about Gavin Everett shooting himself, who knows why people do the things they do. Suffice to say that the police dropped the investigation, although they did threaten to charge Miss Lachelle with wasting police time.'

'And what happened to her? I assume you sacked her.'

'There was no need to. She left of her own

accord. She simply failed to turn up for work, and no more was heard of her.'

★ ★ ★

Abigail handed the two sheets of paper to Esther with a smile of approval.

'I have to say, you've done a marvellous job with the interview,' she complimented the young woman. 'It was flattering to me, but not too effusive. And also very accurate. I wish all journalists were as correct about facts when writing.'

'Thank you,' said Esther, putting the pages into her bag. 'I'll tell Mr Pinker, my editor, you were pleased and hopefully he'll print it as it is without wanting changes.'

'Tell him if he changes anything, I shall be very upset.' Abigail smiled. 'By the way, we have some news for you, but at the moment it's for your ears only, not for publication. The man who you saw coming out of Daniel's room at the Wilton Hotel was an inspector with Special Branch at Scotland Yard, called Walter Grafton.'

'Special Branch?' repeated Esther, puzzled. 'I don't know what that is.'

'According to Daniel, they're a branch of the police that investigate terrorism and work to prevent assassinations.'

'Like the attempts that were made on the Queen's life?'

'Just so,' said Abigail.

'But why would someone like that be searching Mr Wilson's room?'

'We're not sure, but we think it might be to do with the fact that we're looking into Gavin Everett's death.'

Esther looked even more bewildered. 'But what has his death to do with terrorism and assassinations? He killed himself.'

'To be honest, we don't know. But Daniel thinks it's the only reason why a detective inspector from Scotland Yard would be in Oxford and poking around like that.'

'Does his being here mean that Mr Everett didn't kill himself, but was murdered?' asked Esther, shocked.

'It's possible,' said Abigail. 'But at the moment, this has to be between us. None of this is for publication.'

Esther nodded. 'I understand. And you have my word I'll keep it to myself until you tell me I can write it.' She gave a smile of delight. 'If it is a murder, and I write about it, this could make my name as a proper journalist!'

'Indeed, it could,' said Abigail. 'Which is why we're going to keep you informed of whatever we find, but — again — only on your promise that you keep it between us until it's ready to be made public.'

'Is there more?' asked Esther eagerly. 'I get the impression there is.'

She's quick, thought Abigail. *Whatever Daniel's reservations about her, I'm sure she could be an asset to our investigation.* Aloud, she said, 'There is. We've received information that just before he died, Everett was due to meet someone to discuss buying an alleged play by William Shakespeare, which we've been told a lady from a titled family was offering for sale.'

'And you think this could be one of the reasons why Everett died?' asked Esther. 'Why? Was it because of some sort of scandal?'

'We're not sure,' said Abigail. 'Frankly, there's a lot we don't know but which we're trying to gather information about. For example, who's the titled lady who was offering the play for sale?'

'Do you think she really had one to sell?' asked Esther. 'I know a lot of people say there are plays that Shakespeare wrote that have never been seen, but I've always been a bit suspicious of them.'

'And rightfully so,' agreed Abigail. 'Personally, I have my doubt if such a play even exists, but we have to investigate. So far, from what we've been told, the person we're looking for is a titled lady who we believe to be unhappily married. Her husband's family have had their title for many centuries, certainly since the late sixteenth century.

'As far as I know, the first play Shakespeare wrote was *The Two Gentlemen of Verona* in about 1588, so if this family really did commission a play from him, it would have been in some time during the 1580s. So, we're looking for a titled family who've been in this area since that time.'

'There are four who claim to be the oldest aristocratic family in Oxfordshire,' said Esther thoughtfully. 'The Duke of Charlbury, the Duke of Abingdon, the Earl of Eynsham and Baron

Whichford. I believe all their titles go right back to the fifteenth century.'

'All married?' asked Abigail.

'The Duke of Abingdon is a widower,' said Esther. 'His wife, Mirabelle, died two years ago. She was seventy, and he's eighty-one. The other three are all married.'

'I think we can strike Abingdon off,' said Abigail. 'With the other three, is there any gossip about them? Unhappy wives?'

'There are always unhappy wives,' said Esther. 'Except for the Earl of Eynsham and his wife. By all accounts they're a very devoted couple.'

'Have they been married long?'

'Thirty years or more.'

'So that leaves us with the Duke and Duchess of Charlbury, and Baron and Baroness Whichford. What do you know about them?'

'Nothing really,' admitted Esther. 'I don't really move in those sort of circles.' Then her face brightened as she said, 'But I could. If my editor agreed, I could do a feature on them both. Sort of 'Local aristocratic families, the women's view', which would involve interviewing them. You never know, it could give me a chance to see if either of them is particularly unhappy in her marriage. Check out if there's a possible lover in the background.'

'That's brilliant!' said Abigail.

'I could dig into the family's ancient ancestry, in the nicest and most flattering way. These old families love boasting how long they've been around. Mention the name Shakespeare and see if one of them picks up on it. Although, if she's

109

trying to sell a manuscript, it's unlikely she'll admit to that part,' she added.

'Perhaps you might be able to talk to the husband, or someone else in the family,' suggested Abigail.

'Yes, I can say I'm looking for added colour to the story and bring in famous people the family must have known in the past.'

'That's good,' said Abigail. 'I can see you have a flair for this sort of thing.'

'Being a journalist?' asked Esther.

'I was going to say, being a detective,' said Abigail. 'After all, in both it's about asking questions in a clever and oblique way.'

14

Daniel left the club and mounted the steps to the pavement. The club's bar manager, Albert, was standing beside a pile of wooden crates containing bottles which had obviously just been delivered, and he and another man, dressed in slightly shabby clothes, were stacking the crates against the metal railings.

'Excuse me,' said Daniel to Albert. 'I'm sorry to trouble you, but as you know, I was in with Mr de Witt just now because I'm making enquiries about one of your members, Mr Gavin Everett.'

'Oh yes,' said Albert suspiciously.

'Yes. His employers, the Ashmolean Museum, have hired me to see if I can find out why he may have killed himself, but I'm having difficulty in finding out the right sort of people to ask.'

'I'm not the right sort of person to ask,' said Albert. 'I just saw him when he was in the club and I served him drinks.' He scowled at the other man, who was standing, holding a crate of spirits and listening. 'Go on, Joe. Hurry up!'

Joe headed for the door of the steps leading down to the basement, carrying his precious load. Albert turned to look aggressively at Daniel and demanded, 'So? Is that it?'

'Not quite,' said Daniel. 'What I'm trying to find out is if there were any members, or other people, he spoke to more than others when he was here.'

'What did Mr de Witt say?'

'He said he couldn't recall anybody in particular. That Mr Everett was friendly to everyone. But it struck me that Mr de Witt, as the manager, is a very busy man and may not always be in the club itself. Whereas you would be in a perfect position to be able to observe if he was particularly friendly with anyone.' Hastily, he added as he saw a scowl developing on Albert's face, 'I only want to know the names of people it might be worth talking to, to give me an insight into Mr Everett's condition, if anything might have been worrying him.'

'If there was, he never showed any sign of it,' grunted Albert. 'As for special people he talked to?' He shook his head. 'No, just as Mr de Witt told you, he was the same with everyone.' He picked up a crate. 'Now if you'll excuse me, me and Joe have got to get this stuff inside. Leave it outside too long, and it vanishes. As it is, we do it one going in, one out here.'

On cue, Joe appeared from up the steps.

'You took your time,' snapped Albert, and he headed for the steps, with a last barked command back at Joe: 'And don't talk to 'im!'

As Albert disappeared through the door into the club, Joe hissed at Daniel, 'I can tell you, but not here. Albert'll be back out in seconds. Where can I find you?'

'The Ashmolean or the Wilton Hotel. The name's Daniel Wilson.'

'I'll see you at the Wilton in three hours' time,' muttered Joe. 'And I ain't doing it for free. Now

112

get off before Albert comes out and sees you still here.'

★　★　★

Abigail had found the shop belonging to Ephraim Wardle, restorer and renovator, on Woodstock Road. Ephraim Wardle was a man in his late fifties, and he didn't turn from his work as the bell above the door tinkled at Abigail's entrance. He was sitting at an easel before a painting or a portrait of a young man dressed in what looked like one of Cromwell's Parliamentarian outfits, delicately dabbing at a patch of the costume with a paintbrush whose bristles had been wrapped in a small piece of cloth. A palette daubed with paint, and pots with different coloured paints were on a small table beside him. The overwhelming smell was of oil paint and paint thinner.

'That looks like a Frans Hals,' observed Abigail. 'It's not one I've seen before, but the style looks like his.'

Wardle turned and looked at her, an expression of respect on his face.

'You've got a good eye,' he said. 'Yes, it's Frans Hals right enough, but the reason you won't have seen it is because it's in a private collection. The owner asked me to do a repair job. One of his servants spilt some stuff on it, would you believe. Needless to say, the servant was sacked.' He studied Abigail, then asked, 'So, are you a dealer or a collector?'

'Neither,' said Abigail. 'I'm an archaeologist,

113

and currently I've been hired by Mr Marriott at the Ashmolean to look into some things for him.'

'What sort of things?'

Abigail hesitated. It was obvious to her that Mr Wardle was an astute person, and — from the portrait on the easel and the skilful way he was working on it — that he was proud of his work and would be insulted if she asked him direct if he'd done the restoration on the crudely copied Egyptian plate. Instead, she said, 'I believe you used to do restoration work for the Ashmolean.'

'Used to is right,' grunted Wardle sourly. 'But that changed about a year ago. That Mr Everett told me they'd decided to go with someone else.'

'Did he say why?'

'He said the Ashmolean was having to watch its costs.' He scowled. 'As if restoring — proper restoring — can be done on the cheap! You can use substitutes for some things, but take lapis lazuli, for example, which is used to make ultramarine. D'you know how expensive the real stuff is?'

'Yes, I do, actually,' said Abigail. 'My speciality as an archaeologist is ancient Egypt, so I'm familiar with painting techniques and materials used at that time.'

Wardle looked at her warily, then asked, 'You wouldn't be Miss Abigail Fenton, by any chance, would you?'

'Yes, I am,' said Abigail.

Wardle laid down his brush and stood up, his hand outstretched. 'Will you permit me to shake your hand,' he said.

'It will be my pleasure,' said Abigail, 'to shake

114

the hand of someone who can reproduce the style and technique of Frans Hals as well as you.' As they shook hands, she added in surprise, 'But I'm surprised you've heard of me.'

'That's because I'm not just your ordinary run-of-the-mill restorer,' said Wardle, sitting down again and indicating for Abigail to sit on a wooden chair nearby. 'I read the magazines to keep up with what's happening, including those with articles about archaeological digs and the relics being found in Egypt and Greece and the like. I get them mainly for the pictures, so I can see what the originals look like, because I can't get to see them in real life. Except at a place like the Ashmolean.'

'Have you been there lately?' asked Abigail.

Wardle shook his head.

'Not since that Everett laid me off. I vowed after that I'd never set foot in that place again.' Then he added thoughtfully, 'Mind, now Everett's topped himself, I might be able to go again. I always liked the place, and I had a great deal of respect for Gladstone Marriott. It was a pity he handed over the restoration commissions to Everett.'

'Do you know who Mr Everett employed to do the restoring after you?'

'Yes, I do,' said Wardle sourly. 'But not because that Everett told me — oh no! Tried to keep it to himself, but I made a point of asking around. We restorers all know one another, and we know who's good and who's bad. And it was no surprise to me that the name that came up was a right rascal, in my opinion. Not worth the name of restorer. A charlatan! A hack!'

'And his name?' asked Abigail.

'Josiah Goddard.'

'And where would I find him?'

Wardle looked at her suspiciously. 'And what would someone like you be wanting with a rascal like Josiah Goddard? Surely not to do some restoring work on an Egyptian piece?'

'Oh no!' Abigail assured him quickly. 'I just want to talk to him about his association with Mr Everett.'

'His association!' said Wardle, his voice full of scorn. 'Whatever it was, it wouldn't have been honest. There was something rotten about Everett. I could tell when he was talking to me about my price, trying to force it down.'

'Did he ever ask you about copying any article?' asked Abigail. 'Pieces of ancient pottery, for example?'

Wardle let out a cackling laugh.

'So that's what this is about!' he chuckled. 'Him and Josiah Goddard working crafty!'

'No,' said Abigail hastily, keen not to reveal the secret of the copied artefacts. 'It's just part of our investigation.'

'Our?' asked Wardle.

'My partner and I,' said Abigail. 'Daniel Wilson.'

'Wilson. Wilson,' muttered Wardle thoughtfully. Then his face brightened. 'Got him! Used to be at Scotland Yard! Part of Inspector Abberline's team. Did the Ripper case. Went private, so I remember. That's what it said in the papers.'

116

'Yes,' said Abigail. 'That's him.'

'And now he's here, with you, looking into Everett and Josiah Goddard.' He chuckled. 'I was right! He was crooked.'

'Did he ever ask you to copy anything?' asked Abigail again.

Wardle nodded. 'He did,' he said. 'I told him no, I don't do copying. I do restoration. Repair work. Because I know where copying leads. Fakery.'

'Did Everett say that's what he was after?'

'He didn't need to. I've got a reputation to keep. I don't take chances.'

'But Josiah Goddard would do copies?'

'Is that what's happened at the Ashmolean?' asked Wardle.

'No,' replied Abigail firmly. 'But I have a feeling he might have been considering it.'

'That wouldn't surprise me. And if he was, Goddard would be his man. Not that I've seen any of his work, but then I don't associate with him and that low level of so-called 'restorer'.' He scowled, then gave her a very proud smile. 'I'm an artist.'

15

Esther was walking along the corridor towards Mr Pinker's office, when she heard a man's voice from the stairwell growl gruffly, 'Where's the editor?'

'Just along the corridor, third door on the left,' came the answer.

The next moment the man that Esther had seen coming out of Mr Wilson's room at the Wilton Hotel — Inspector Grafton, according to Abigail — appeared from the stairwell. Immediately, Esther ducked into an empty office and pushed the door half closed, then watched through the crack as Grafton stomped along the corridor and arrived at Pinker's office. He rapped hard at the door and was already reaching for the door handle as Pinker called, 'Come in!'

As Grafton went into the editor's office, Esther slipped out from her hiding place and moved to Pinker's door, gently placing her foot against the frame as it closed to prevent it shutting completely and listened to the conversation.

'Mr Pinker?' asked Grafton.

'Yes,' said Pinker, a tone of puzzlement in his voice.

'I'm Inspector Grafton from Special Branch at Scotland Yard. This is my warrant card.'

'Scotland Yard?' echoed Pinker, the puzzlement now replaced by worry.

'My visit here is secret,' said Grafton. 'You must not tell anyone I was here or what we talked about. Is that clear?'

'Yes, but what's this about?' asked Pinker, sounding even more worried.

'It's about national security,' said Grafton curtly. 'Did you know Gavin Everett?'

'From the Ashmolean? The one who killed himself?'

'Yes.'

'Well, I knew him to meet on a social level if anything was happening at the Ashmolean. I wouldn't say I knew him on a personal level.'

'Do you know who did? And I'm looking for someone with a South African connection. In particular, someone who might have Boer sympathies.'

'Boer sympathies?' echoed Pinker, bewildered.

'That's what I said. Anyone who might be sympathetic to the Boer side rather than the British.'

Pinker's voice took on an indignant tone. 'I'll have you know that Oxford is a very patriotic city. To the best of my knowledge we've never had any reports of anyone in Oxford, or even the outlying areas, who expressed support for the Boers during the war in South Africa.'

'And what about since the war?'

'Well . . . no. There'd have been no need. The war's over, and everyone's working together. In fact, lots of Brits have gone to South Africa to work in the goldfields in the Boer areas. I believe that Gavin Everett did so himself.'

'So how about anyone who went to the

119

Transvaal to work in the Boer goldfields and came back having made good money?'

'Again, that could describe Gavin Everett, though I'm not sure if he actually made a great deal of money there. If he had, he wouldn't have been working at the Ashmolean.' He thought for a moment, then said, 'There's Lord Chessington, of course.'

'Lord Chessington?'

'He went out there as a part of a business venture rather than working digging for gold.' He laughed. 'In fact, I can't imagine Lord Chessington ever getting his hands dirty. But he did come back very rich, and by all accounts the money's still rolling in. That's where the money is, Inspector, in business speculation, not in using a shovel.'

'Where is his mine?'

'*Mines*, Inspector. Plural. As I understand it, he partners with some businessmen in the Transvaal.'

'Boers?'

'I would expect so. I don't think Brits have ownership rights out there, so they go into partnerships with locals.'

'Do you know who his partners are?'

'You'll have to ask Lord Chessington himself,' said Pinker. 'Though whether he'll tell you is another matter. He keeps his business affairs very close to his chest.' He chuckled. 'The very rich don't like paying taxes if they can avoid it.'

'There's no one else you can think of in Oxford with a South African Boer connection?' pressed Grafton.

'Well, there's Professor Vorster. He's from South Africa, and Vorster's a Boer name, isn't it.'

'Who's he?' asked Grafton.

'He lectures at Exeter College. I've only met him a couple of times, at social dos the university holds. I must admit he didn't come across as in any way being involved in politics of any sort. A very pleasant man, although with a slightly abstracted air about him, like a lot of these academics. So many of them only seem to come alive when they're talking about their particular subject.'

'And what's this Professor Vorster's particular subject?'

'The development of early Christian religion. You know, stemming from the Jewish faith in Israel and north Africa, and reaching Rome. He'll talk about that for hours.'

'Anyone else?' asked Grafton.

'There's a man called Vance de Witt,' said Pinker thoughtfully. 'I've never met him, but I know people who have.'

'What sort of people?'

'Mostly academics, some businessmen, the local gentry. All very respectable.'

'And what's this de Witt do?'

'He manages a gentlemen's club in Oxford. It's called the Quill Club. Very respectable, and very discreet.'

'In what way?'

'Well, it doesn't advertise itself. Membership is by recommendation only.'

'You're not a member?'

'No, no, it's too rich for my tastes,' said

121

Pinker. 'Card games with high stakes. That sort of thing.'

'And what's his connection with South Africa?'

'I'm told he comes from there,' said Pinker. 'But which part, I have no idea. As I say, I've never met the man.'

'Where do I find this Quill Club?'

'It's in the Broad. Or Broad Street, to give it its proper name. I believe it's opposite Blackwell's bookshop.'

'You believe?'

'Well, as I said, I've never been there, but I'm told there's no sign outside identifying it, just a gap in some railings and steps down to a black door in the basement area.'

'Well that's three names worth looking at,' grunted Grafton. 'Anyone else you can think of?'

'No,' said Pinker. 'That's it for South Africans in Oxford, as far as I know. And Lord Chessington's English, anyway.'

'If you do think of anyone else, you can leave a note for me at the Swan Inn. Do you know it?'

'Just off the Broad.'

'Good. Thank you for your assistance, Mr Pinker. And remember, not a word to anyone.'

Esther darted back from the door and once again took refuge in the empty office opposite. She waited until Grafton had gone before emerging, then she knocked at the door.

'Come in!' called Pinker.

Esther went in, taking the two pages of her interview with Abigail from her bag as she did so.

'Here you are, Mr Pinker,' she said. 'The interview with Miss Fenton, the eminent archaeologist I mentioned to you.'

'Oh yes, thank you,' he said, taking the pages. She could tell he was distracted, not giving her his usual full concentration.

'Miss Fenton has read it and approved it,' she said. 'So, there'll be no legal problems.'

'Very good,' said Pinker.

'Is everything alright, Mr Pinker?' she asked.

'Alright? Why shouldn't it be?'

'You seem a bit . . . distracted.'

'No, no, just things to think about, as always.'

'Well actually, Mr Pinker, I've got something I'd be grateful if you'd think about. It's for the women's page.'

'Oh?'

'Yes. I was thinking about doing a couple of interviews with titled ladies from local aristocratic families. You know, get them to talk about their clothes, the decor of their houses, their gardens, their families, that sort of thing.'

'An excellent idea!' said Pinker enthusiastically, suddenly ceasing to appear distracted. 'That's the sort of thing our women readers love! Had you got anyone in mind?'

'I was thinking of the Duchess of Charlbury and Baroness Whichford,' said Esther.

'Even better!' Pinker beamed. 'Both claim to be the oldest family around, and if you get one you're sure to get the other. Both families are great rivals, always trying to outdo the other.'

'The only problem is I don't know either of the ladies, so they may not believe I'm interviewing them for the *Messenger*,' began Esther.

'No problem!' Pinker smiled. 'I'll send them both a letter from me, telling them what's planned. This is the sort of thing we need for the women's column if we're going to get them to persuade their menfolk to buy the *Messenger* regularly!'

16

'How did you get on with your restorer?' asked Daniel.

He and Abigail had met up again in the office at the Ashmolean to bring each other up to date with the latest developments.

'Ephraim Wardle,' said Abigail. 'And he was a really nice man. Very talented, and very honest. I'm absolutely sure that he wasn't involved in any way in Everett's skulduggery. But he gave me the name of the man who was: Josiah Goddard. He has a place on the edge of town where he works, and, according to Mr Wardle, Josiah Goddard is a crook of the first water. As well as not being very good at what he does. Which is why I suspect it was this Goddard who copied the plate I showed you, using a commercial blue paint instead of the more expensive lapis lazuli.'

'You've got his address?'

'I have,' said Abigail. 'And in this case, I think it might be a good idea if we both visit him, just in case it might be difficult. I know I can handle myself . . . '

Daniel nodded. 'But if things got awkward and he produced a pistol . . . And what about Esther?'

'Oh, that's very promising!' said Abigail. 'She's going to talk to her editor about conducting interviews with the two titled ladies most likely to have the so-called Shakespeare play for sale.

The Duchess of Charlbury and Baroness Whichford. Both of them fit the bill, according to her.'

'It sounds very successful,' said Daniel. He let out a rueful sigh. 'I have to admit you certainly had more luck today than I did. I hit a brick wall at the Quill Club.'

'Did you see this man, Vance de Witt?'

'I did. And there is definitely a South African connection there. He's from the Orange Free State, which is Boer territory. But he says he didn't really know Everett outside of the Quill Club. Nor did he have any knowledge of the whereabouts of Eve Lachelle. In fact, in the smoothest and politest of ways, he told me absolutely nothing. Although a man called Joe who works at the club has promised to call later at the Wilton to sell me some information about people close to Everett. But I'm not sure how dependable it will be. I suspect he'll only be telling me stories for the money he expects to earn from it.'

'When's this Joe coming?'

Daniel looked at his watch. 'In about an hour. I'd better get off so I can be there when he calls.'

'Perhaps if *I* tried asking questions at the Quill Club?' suggested Abigail.

'Use your feminine wiles on de Witt?' Daniel smiled.

'No, I was thinking of the women who work there.'

'The waitresses who are also possibly prosti-tutes?'

126

'They might talk to another woman.'

Daniel thought it over.

'It's possible,' he said. 'Although, as soon as you say who you are and why you're asking questions . . . '

'Then I won't. I'll use a ruse of some sort.'

'What sort of ruse?'

'I'll pretend I'm looking for Eve Lachelle for some other reason. An inheritance.'

Daniel looked at her, doubt on his face.

'You'd need something to back it up,' he said. 'An inheritance is no small thing.'

'But it could be,' she said. 'Say Everett had left Eve Lachelle a small sum in his will. Twenty-five pounds, say. And it has to be delivered to her personally by me, in cash. I'm sure once we explain to Mr Marriott what we're doing, he'd agree to put up twenty-five pounds if it finds us this Eve Lachelle and throws some light on the case.'

'That's assuming she's still in Oxford, and that she's connected to Everett in some way.'

'We won't know if we don't try,' said Abigail.

'True.' Daniel nodded. He looked at her in some surprise. 'This is a new aspect of you, Abigail. I've always thought of you as not being able to tell a lie, yet here you are coming up with this fabrication.'

'It won't be a complete fabrication,' said Abigail. 'I'll say I'm a private enquiry agent and I'm representing the people who are handling Mr Everett's estate. Which is true, in a way.'

Daniel laughed. 'Only in a very twisted sort of way.'

Daniel was sitting in the reception area of the Wilton when Joe arrived. Daniel gestured him to the empty chair next to him, but Joe stood, looking reluctant to sit down.

'I'm not sure if this is the right place to talk,' he said. 'I'm taking a risk talking to you.'

'Would you feel happier somewhere else?' asked Daniel.

'Your room?' suggested Joe. 'There's less chance of me being seen with you.'

Daniel nodded, then led the way up the stairs to the first floor and to his room. Once they were inside, Joe seemed to relax slightly.

'If Mr de Witt and Albert knew I was here talking to you, I'd be in big trouble,' he said. 'So it's gotta be worth my while.'

Daniel produced two florins.

'The first one of these is for you to start talking,' he said, handing one of the coins to Joe. 'You get the second if what you tell me is of value.'

Joe hesitated, as if reluctant to take the deal, then he nodded and slipped the florin into his pocket.

'Like Albert and Mr de Witt told you, mostly Everett kept himself to himself. No particular special friends. But that changed about three months ago. Suddenly he's bosom pals with one of the other members, Piers Stevens, whereas before they hardly seemed to know one another. But suddenly they sit together, play cards together, and they leave the club together, sometimes with Everett with his arm around Stevens' shoulders like they're the very best of pals.'

'Everett's arm around Stevens' shoulders?' asked Daniel. 'What about the other way round?'

Joe shook his head. 'If you ask me, Stevens didn't appear to like this being so friendly. Not that he says anything against Everett. He laughs and smiles when Everett's with him, and I notice that Stevens puts his hand in his pocket when it comes to buying the drinks much more than Everett does. And a couple of times when it comes to settling up at the end of a card game, and Everett says he'll pay what he owes in a day or two, I was sure I noticed an unhappy look on Stevens' face when he said it. Like that's where the money was going to come from.'

'So you think that Everett might have had something on this Piers Stevens?'

'I don't know for certain, I'm just going by how things sort of changed. The two of them suddenly being best buddies. Or rather, Everett being Stevens' best friend, when there was nothing like that between 'em before.'

'And this change happened about three months ago?'

'Right.'

'Any idea what might have brought about the change?'

'No,' said Joe.

Daniel remembered what Inspector Pitt had told them about the attack on Eve Lachelle, which had been four months ago, and asked,

'Was it anything to do with what happened to Eve Lachelle?'

Joe frowned. 'Why? What did happen to Eve Lachelle?'

'She claimed she was attacked at the club. Raped. Four months ago, which is the month before Everett and Stevens became such good pals.'

'That was just before I started working there,' said Joe. 'I'd been there about three weeks when Everett and Stevens suddenly got pally. Like I say, before that neither of them had the time of day for each other.'

'Did you know Eve Lachelle?' asked Daniel.

Joe shook his head. 'She left just before I started. I only know about her because I heard some of the girls asking what had happened to her, and where she'd gone all of a sudden.'

'And where did she go?'

'No one seemed to know,' said Joe. 'Is that worth that other florin?'

'Yes, I believe it is,' said Daniel. He handed the coin to Joe. 'And there's more if you can find out what happened to Eve Lachelle.'

★ ★ ★

Abigail loitered outside Blackwell's bookshop, ostensibly studying the display in the window but, in reality, her attention was on the gap in the metal railings on the other side of the Broad, the entrance to the Quill Club. The sight of two women walking towards the club at a determined pace, showing they weren't just tourists or casual visitors, piqued her interest. So far very few women had been in evidence in the Broad. She walked across the wide road and caught up with the two women, just as they reached the gap in the railings and looked as if they were about to walk through and descend the stone steps to the basement.

'Excuse me!' she called.

The two women stopped and looked at her quizzically.

'I apologise for troubling you. My name's Abigail Fenton and I'm a private enquiry agent. I've been hired by a firm of solicitors who are administering the will of a Mr Gavin Everett, and one of his bequests is the sum of twenty-five pounds to be paid to a Miss Eve Lachelle of the Quill Club of Oxford.'

At the mention of the name, Abigail saw that the two immediately grew more wary.

'Unfortunately, I've been informed she's no longer at the Quill Club, and I don't have an address for her,' continued Abigail. 'I saw you going in, so I wondered whether you know where I might find her, so I can give her the money. It's only a small amount, but it is in Mr Everett's will, and we do our best to comply with a client's wishes.'

As the two women leant into one another and began to whisper together, Abigail was aware that the door in the basement area had opened, and a man had come out carrying a rag and a tin of polish. He stopped and looked up at the three women, then turned his attention to polishing the door's brass ornamentation.

'Twenty-five quid?' asked one of the women.

'Yes,' confirmed Abigail.

The two women exchanged conspiratorial looks, then the one who'd asked about the money said, 'We're not sure, but if we can get a message to her, where can she find you?'

'I'm staying at the Wilton Hotel in Broad Street. Just ask for Miss Abigail Fenton. And your names are . . . ?'

'I'm Colette and she's Deirdre,' said the woman.

'Thank you,' said Abigail.

* * *

The two women watched Abigail walk away, then descended the steps.

'Who was that woman you were talking to?' demanded Albert, stopping his polishing work.

'She says she works for some firm of solicitors,' said Colette.

'Oh? And what does she want?'

Colette hesitated, then said, 'She was asking about Eve Lachelle.'

'What about her?'

'She says that the bloke who died — Everett — left her some money in his will. She's trying to trace her to give it to her.'

'How much?' asked Albert.

The two women exchanged looks, then Deirdre said, 'Twenty-five quid.'

Albert's face grew grim. 'Don't have anything to do with her. It's a con.'

'How do you know?' demanded Colette.

132

'Trust me, I know,' said Albert. 'Did she say who she was?'

'Yes. She said her name was Abigail Fenton and she's staying at the Wilton Hotel.'

'She said she's a private enquiry agent working for these solicitors.'

Albert nodded. 'Alright. But remember what I said, don't have anything to do with her.'

Albert returned to polishing the brass of the door, while the two women went into the club. Once they were in and out of earshot of Albert, Colette whispered, 'Twenty-five quid. That's not to be sniffed at.'

Deirdre nodded. 'I was thinking the same thing.'

'Trouble is, she's seen us both now, and she knows it's neither of us.'

Deirdre shook her head. 'If we bring in one of the other girls, we'll have to share it with her.'

'So, what do we do?'

'One of us goes along there and tells her she's Eve, but we say we were wary about saying it at first, because the club had told us not to say anything about her, if anyone asked.'

'Yeah, that could work,' agreed Colette. 'So, who goes?'

'You,' said Deirdre. 'You can carry that sort of thing off better than me.'

⋆　⋆　⋆

Vance de Witt studied the accounts ledger with a quiet smile of satisfaction. The club was in good profit, and once again he thought about the possibility of opening another branch where they could capitalise on the well-heeled local clientele who appreciated the discretion the club offered. London was the obvious choice, but there were already many similar clubs operating there. Possibly Cambridge?

There was a tap at his door, which opened, and Albert entered.

'A problem,' he announced, closing the door behind him.

'Oh?'

'This woman was just asking questions about Eve Lachelle.'

'What? To you?'

'No, I saw her talking to Deirdre and Colette by the railings, so I asked them what she wanted. They said she told them she was a private enquiry agent acting for the solicitors handling Everett's estate, and he'd left twenty-five pounds for Eve Lachelle, and she was trying to find her.'

De Witt gave a snort of derision. 'What absolute nonsense!'

'Yeah, that's what I thought,' said Albert.

'Who is this woman? Did she give a name?'

'She said she was Abigail Fenton, and she was staying at the Wilton Hotel.'

De Witt frowned thoughtfully, then said, 'I think she needs to be dissuaded from asking any further questions about Eve Lachelle. Can you arrange that, Albert?'

'Leave it to me,' said Albert with a grim smile.

'But without involving the club,' said de Witt. 'So I'd rather you got someone else to — er — talk to her. We don't want to run the risk of her recognising you at some point.'

'As I said, Mr de Witt, you can leave that to me. I know the very person.'

17

Daniel reread the notes he'd made of his conversation with Joe. The suggestion was that Everett had some kind of hold over Piers Stevens and was blackmailing him. But what was that hold? It seemed to be connected to the attack on Eve Lachelle. So, was it that simple? Had Stevens been one of the men who'd raped Lachelle? But the charges against the men had been dropped, so Stevens had nothing to fear there. Inspector Pitt had said there were *men* involved in the attack, plural. So why had Stevens been singled out by Everett?

He was just running these thoughts through his mind when there was a tap at the door, which opened, and Esther Maris looked in.

'Excuse me,' she said. 'Am I interrupting?'

'No, no,' said Daniel. 'Please, come in.'

Esther entered and asked, 'Is Abigail around?'

'No, she's out on the case,' said Daniel. 'But she told me about the idea of interviewing titled ladies who might be trying to sell the Shakespeare play. I think it's a clever idea.'

'So does my editor.' Esther smiled, sitting down. 'He's sending letters of introduction about me to the two we're going to concentrate on: the Duchess of Charlbury and Baroness Whichford, so we'll see what happens there. But I wanted to tell her — and you — about what happened at the newspaper offices. That man who was in your room at the Wilton Hotel — Abigail said his name was Inspector Grafton . . . '

'That's right,' said Daniel. ' 'That's who we think it was.'

'It most definitely was, because he came to see Mr Pinker, the editor, today and he introduced himself.'

'Interesting,' said Daniel. 'Did you happen to discover what he wanted?'

'I did,' said Esther proudly. 'I listened at the door.'

'That was very shrewd of you,' Daniel complimented her. 'What did you hear?'

'This Inspector Grafton was after the names of people in Oxford who might be sympathetic to the Boer cause in Africa. He was especially interested in anyone who might have associated with Mr Everett.'

So, I was right, Daniel told himself, satisfied. *Special Branch see a Boer connection.*

'Mr Pinker gave him the names of three men: Lord Chessington, Professor Vorster and a man called Vance de Witt, who manages a place called the Quill Club.'

'Yes, I met Mr de Witt,' said Daniel. 'The other two are unfamiliar to me.'

'I don't know any of them,' said Esther. 'Lord Chessington is a very rich businessman, and according to Mr Pinker his wealth comes from gold mines he owns in the Transvaal, which is a part of South Africa run by the Boers, he says. Professor Vorster is also said to be a Boer from South Africa. He lectures at Exeter College on the early Christian religion.'

'I have to admit, Esther, when Abigail suggested we bring you in to help us with the investigation, I was doubtful. But I take all my reservations back.'

'And if there is a story about Mr Everett's death . . . ?'

'I promise you, you'll have the exclusive on it from us. But at the moment we're still scrabbling in the dark.'

'But he was murdered?' pressed Esther.

Daniel hesitated before saying, 'Let's just say we're keeping an open mind on it.'

'Oh, I hope it does turn out to be a murder!' exclaimed Esther. 'Crime reporting is what I want to do, and this could be my big break!'

★   ★   ★

Walter Grafton headed back to his room at the Swan, weighing up his next course of action. Now he had three names: Lord Chessington, Professor Vorster and Vance de Witt. But this wouldn't be a case of going to see them and flashing his Special Branch card at them, as it had been with Gladstone Marriott, and Pinker at the *Oxford Messenger*. These were suspects. If Grafton showed his hand to them and one of them was guilty, he'd just vanish. No, he needed to dig into them, collect evidence, and when he'd got enough to point to one of them, then he'd hook him: take him into custody for questioning. And not here, not in Oxford, but in London, where he was on his home ground.

Abigail made her way to Kemp Hall police
station where she asked for Inspector Pitt, and a
few moments later was shown to his office.

'Good afternoon, Miss Fenton,' Pitt greeted
her. 'Do you have news for me?'

'Abigail,' she insisted, 'and actually, I'm
hoping that you'll be able to help us. You met
Eve Lachelle, didn't you?'

Pitt nodded. 'Yes.'

'Could you give me a description of her?'

'Why?' asked Pitt.

'Because I have a feeling that I'm going to
receive a call from someone claiming to be Eve
Lachelle, and I don't think it will be.'

'What's going on?'

'We're not sure, but there's something not
quite right about the Quill Club. Daniel talked to
Mr de Witt but got nowhere. So, we're trying a
ruse to see if we can shake things up.'

'What sort of ruse?'

'We'll tell you if it gets a result.' Abigail smiled.
'We don't want to implicate you if it turns out
that what we're doing might cross the line.'

'Miss Fenton — ' said Pitt firmly.

'Abigail, please.'

'Miss Fenton,' repeated Pitt, looking grim.
'I'm an officer of the law. I uphold the law. So,
I'm warning you that if you're thinking of doing
anything illegal . . .'

'No, no!' Abigail assured him. 'We'd never do
anything against the law.'

'Then what is going on?' demanded Pitt.

Abigail hesitated, then told him their plan. 'We feel that this Eve Lachelle might have information about Everett, but she seems to have vanished. So, I told a couple of the women who work at the Quill Club that I was a private enquiry agent — which is true — but I embroidered it by telling them that I was acting for a firm of solicitors handling Everett's estate and he had left the sum of twenty-five pounds to Eve Lachelle, which I would like to give her.'

'A lie,' said Pitt flatly.

'Not exactly a lie,' defended Abigail. 'If Eve Lachelle turns up, I'll certainly give her the money. And at the same time ask her questions about the Quill Club and Gavin Everett.'

'It's still duplicitous,' said Pitt.

'Yes, it is, but it's a way to get at the truth,' insisted Abigail. 'Don't you want to find out who killed Everett, and why?'

Pitt sighed. 'Yes, well, based on what you've told me, it doesn't sound like any laws are being broken.'

'So, will you tell me what this Eve Lachelle looked like when you saw her?'

Pitt cast his mind back, then said, 'She was tall. Tall for a woman, that is.'

'My height?'

'Possibly a bit taller. And she was very thin. Most of the waitresses at the Quill appear quite buxom.'

'Hair?'

'Black. And it struck me that she had an exotic look about her. Arab, possibly, or a southern European ancestry.' He looked at her with concern. 'I do hope you're not going to get involved in something that will cause me trouble.'

'I hope so too, Inspector,' said Abigail. 'I'll certainly do my best to avoid it.'

★ ★ ★

After Esther had gone, Daniel walked along to Gladstone Marriott's office, and found the museum director poring over some papers.

'I wonder if I could pick your brains, Mr Marriott?' he asked.

'About Everett's death?'

'Yes. We're starting to get a picture of Everett's activities outside of the Ashmolean, and there are aspects of his behaviour which raise concern.'

'Absolutely!' groaned Marriott. 'I assume Miss Fenton has told you about the . . . the . . . copies she discovered in our collection. She's convinced they could only have been put there with Everett's connivance.' He shuddered. 'And I trusted him!'

'There's something else that has come to light: the suspicion that he may have been blackmailing someone.'

'Blackmail!' gasped Marriott, horrified. 'This gets worse and worse!'

'We're not absolutely sure yet,' Daniel reassured him. 'But it does seem to be a strong possibility.'

'Who?'

'A man called Piers Stevens.'

Marriott looked at Daniel, bewildered. 'Who?'

'Piers Stevens,' repeated Daniel.

'I've never heard of him,' said Marriott.

'Apparently he's a member of the Quill Club. You remember, the gentlemen's club you found the membership card for.'

'But . . . but what was he blackmailing him about?'

'We don't know, and that's what we're trying to find out.'

'Something unsavoury?' hazarded Marriott, again with a shudder.

'I would assume so,' said Daniel. 'Also, we've learnt that Inspector Grafton, the Special Branch inspector, is looking at three men with Boer connections who might be involved in Everett's death.'

'Yes, he mentioned about the Boers when he saw me,' said Marriott. 'I told him I had no idea of anyone in Oxford with Boer sympathies. Who are the three men?'

'The manager at the Quill Club, a man called Vance de Witt. A Professor Vorster who lectures on religion at Exeter College. And Lord Chessington.'

'Lord Chessington!' burst out Marriott, appalled at the idea. 'Lord Chessington is a pillar of local society. A great patron of the arts.'

'I understand he has gold mines in the Transvaal.'

'He is certainly a partner in such enterprises, and he makes no secret of the fact,' said Marriott. 'But the idea that he may have had a part to play in Everett's death is preposterous.'

'Did he know Everett?'

'They certainly met, because Chessington was always one of the first to be invited whenever there was a new piece being displayed at the museum. As I said, he was a great patron of the arts and donated some fine pieces to the Ashmolean himself.'

'And what about this Professor Vorster?' asked Daniel.

Marriott shook his head. 'I don't know the man. The name's unfamiliar to me.'

'Do you think he might have known Everett?'

'It's possible. If he's a professor at the university he may well have come here to look at some particular exhibit or display, but I certainly have never been aware of him.' He gave a heavy sigh. 'This case is becoming ever more complicated. I just hope the outcome doesn't taint the reputation of this wonderful museum!'

★   ★   ★

Abigail sat in the reception lounge at the Wilton Hotel. She'd been sitting here for an hour, waiting to see if there might be any result from her conversation with the two women outside the Quill Club, but so far there'd been no joy. *Ah well*, she told herself resignedly, *it was always a long shot.*

She was just getting up and preparing to return to the Ashmolean, when she saw one of the two women she'd spoken to enter the hotel. The woman looked about her, and when she spotted Abigail, she came over to her.

'I didn't say anything before because I didn't

know what it was about and if I could trust you,' said the woman. 'I'm Eve Lachelle, the woman you were looking for.'

'Oh?' said Abigail. 'I was told you'd left the Quill Club some time ago, and that was why you couldn't be found.'

'That was deliberate,' said Colette. 'There was this man who was hounding me, so me and the other girls and the management decided to let it be known I'd left and no one knew where I was.'

'Did it work?' asked Abigail.

Colette shrugged. 'It seems so. He hasn't been back to the club since. Anyway, you said something about Gavin Everett leaving me money in his will.'

'Yes,' said Abigail. 'Did you know him well?'

'Well enough,' said Colette. 'I didn't expect him to leave me anything, though. Twenty-five pounds, you said.'

'Indeed,' said Abigail. 'Before I hand it to you, do you have any identification to prove you are Eve Lachelle?'

'Why?'

'Well, we need to know the money is being paid to the rightful person. And, with respect, I was given a description of Miss Lachelle, and I must say you don't fit that description at all.'

Colette hesitated, then said, 'I've changed some things since I last saw poor Mr Everett. I had my hair done, for one thing.'

'You may have changed your hair, but I doubt if that meant also lowering your height.'

The woman thrust her hand out. 'Look, I'm Eve Lachelle, and if Mr Everett left me twenty-five pounds, then it's my money.'

'I don't believe you are Eve Lachelle, but we can soon settle this. It was Inspector Pitt at Kemp Hall police station who gave me the description of Miss Lachelle. So, if you come with me to the police station and Inspector Pitt confirms you are who you say you are . . . '

The woman scowled, hissed angrily at Abigail, 'Piss on you!', then got up and stalked out of the hotel.

Interesting, thought Abigail. She walked to the entrance and stepped out of the hotel, curious to see in which direction the woman went, although she knew she could always find her at the Quill Club. As she stepped onto the pavement, she was suddenly grabbed roughly by the arm and thrown against the wall of the hotel, and a man's guttural voice rasped at her, 'Time for payback, you nosey bitch!'

18

Abigail, stunned, stared at the man who leered in towards her, his big fist still gripping her arm tightly. His clothing was rough — a patched jacket and thick, woollen trousers — and he was wearing heavy workmen's boots.

'Listen good: forget about Eve Lachelle. Or else something very bad will happen to you.' He grinned nastily as he moved his face nearer to Abigail and muttered threateningly, 'And hurting a woman doesn't bother me.'

'That's interesting, because I feel the same about hurting a man,' said Abigail.

And, with a sharp upward jerk of her leg, she smashed her knee hard into the man's groin. He let out a high keening shriek and folded in half, then collapsed, clutching himself. Abigail knelt down beside him and said quietly, 'I am not a weak and feeble woman who's easily intimidated. And if you want me not to hurt you again, tell me who employed you to threaten me.' With that she grabbed a handful of his hair and tugged hard, making the man let out a squeal of pain.

'His name?' snapped Abigail.

'I don't know,' gasped the man.

Abigail smashed the man's face into the pavement, then pulled his head back by the hair again, making him howl.

'His name,' she repeated.

'I don't know!' he begged. 'A man pointed you out and gave me five shillings to say those words to you, to warn you off.'

'What did he look like?'

'Just an ordinary bloke. A working man.'

'Perhaps you'll have your memory jogged when the police talk to you,' said Abigail, and knelt on the man's back, holding him firmly squashed to the pavement, while still holding him by the hair. With her free hand she produced the police whistle that Daniel had given her and blew a loud blast on it.

★ ★ ★

Albert watched this unfold from his vantage point on the other side of the road to the Wilton in horror. As Abigail blew another blast on her police whistle, Albert turned and hurried off, and a short time later was rushing into the Quill Club. De Witt was checking tables and looked in surprise as his bar manager stumbled in, obviously in a state of panic.

'What on earth's the matter, Albert?'

'She beat him up.'

'What? Who?'

'The Fenton woman. I put Herb on to her to warn her off. I pointed her out to him as she was leaving the Wilton Hotel and he goes over to lean on her. Next second he's on the ground and she's banging his head on the pavement, then she blows a police whistle. How does she get one of those!'

'*She* beat *him* up?' repeated de Witt, stunned.

147

Albert nodded. 'And now the coppers will have him.'

'Will Herb say who hired him?'

'That's very likely if the police threaten him.'

'You'd better disappear,' said de Witt. He opened a drawer in his desk and pulled out some banknotes, which he handed to Albert. 'Here. Hide away somewhere, out of town. In fact, go to London.' He took a sheet of paper and wrote a few lines on it, then handed that to Albert. 'This is to Jacob Krauss at the Pelican Club in Soho. Go there for a few days. I'll send word when you can come back.'

★ ★ ★

Daniel rushed into Kemp Hall police station, having run all the way from the Ashmolean, and found Abigail sitting quite calmly in the reception area. He waved the note she'd sent him.

'You said a man attacked you,' he panted.

'Yes, but there was no need to run,' she said. 'You do fuss. If I was able to write that note, then I was obviously alright. I just wanted you here, so we could both find out who had hired the man to threaten me. Inspector Pitt is talking to him at this moment.'

'What actually happened?' demanded Daniel.

'It was as a result of my asking the women at the Quill Club about Eve Lachelle. First, a woman turned up claiming to be Eve Lachelle, when she patently wasn't. It was just a pitiful attempt to get the money I'd mentioned. Then, as I left the Wilton, this man grabbed me and told me to stop asking questions about Eve Lachelle and threatened me with violence if I continued with my investigation. I overpowered him and blew that police whistle you gave me and had the man brought here.'

'I told you to be careful! You could have been badly hurt!' said Daniel.

'But I wasn't. My attacker was.'

'But he might have been armed! He could have had a knife!'

'He didn't. And even if he had been holding a knife, he was so close to me that I still think my knee in a judicious spot would have disabled him.'

Daniel looked at her with an expression of awe. 'My God, if they ever let women into the police force and someone like you joins, they'll end up as commissioner.'

'The question it raises is,' continued Abigail, 'what happened to Eve Lachelle, and why does someone want to stop any enquiries being made about her?'

★   ★   ★

Inspector Pitt looked across the table in the interview room at Herbert Fulworth, noting again the bloody graze down one side of his face where it had been slammed into the pavement. Pitt had encountered Herb before, usually when the man had been involved in a drunken brawl, so he knew what the man was capable of. A uniformed police constable stood behind Herb,

149

ready in case the man should turn violent, but Pitt guessed there was little chance of that. The treatment he'd received at the hands of Abigail Fenton had taken away his usual bullying swagger.

'So, who hired you to threaten her?' asked Pitt.

'Just some bloke,' said Herb. 'He said it was for a lark. And then she attacked me!' He pointed at the graze on the side of his face. 'She's the one you should be arresting! That's assault, that is! She could have murdered me!'

'But we have witnesses that state that you were the one who made the first move and grabbed Miss Fenton and threw her against a wall. Now I'm wondering what to charge you with. Assault? Attempted robbery?'

'Robbery?' echoed Herb, aghast. 'I never!'

'No, you told her a man had paid you to tell her to stop asking questions about Eve Lachelle. So, I'm asking you, who was the man? And don't tell me you'd never seen him before, because it won't wash. Anyone who asks you to do that would only do so because they know who you are and what you like to do, which is be rough with women. Now this is going to be very simple: you can either tell me his name, or I'll charge you with attempted murder and have you put away for quite a few years. And I'll make sure it's hard labour. With a flogging thrown in.'

'Attempted murder?!' Herb shook his head. 'No one'll believe that.'

'Oh yes, they will,' said Pitt. 'With your record of violence. And she could have been killed. You're a strong man, Herb. So, that's your choice. A very long and rough time in jail, or you can walk out of here. What's it to be?'

Herb gulped, then said, 'His name's Albert Preston. He works as bar manager at the Quill Club.'

'How do you know him?'

'Me and him drink at the same bar: the Horse and Feathers.'

'Good,' said Pitt. 'The next thing I'm going to do is to talk to this Albert Preston and get confirmation, and if I get that, you'll be free to go.'

'He won't admit it!' burst out Herb.

'Of course he won't, but if I feel it was him, the same applies. I'll let you go.' He looked at the constable. 'You can take him back to his cell now, Constable.'

As the two men rose to their feet, Pitt added, 'A word of advice, Herb. If I were you, I'd give up this life of threatening women; you're obviously not suited to it.'

19

Daniel and Abigail got to their feet as Inspector Pitt appeared from the back of the station.

'Well?' asked Daniel.

'The man who hired him to threaten Miss Fenton was Albert Preston. He's the bar manager at the Quill Club.'

'Yes, I've met him,' said Daniel. 'But something tells me he won't have acted without authority from his boss, Mr de Witt.'

'Eve Lachelle is at the heart of this,' said Abigail.

'It would seem so,' agreed Pitt.

'One name's come up in our investigations and that's a man called Piers Stevens,' said Daniel. 'He's a member of the Quill Club and was apparently very friendly with Gavin Everett, but only after the attack on Eve Lachelle took place. Was Piers Stevens one of the men she named?'

Pitt hesitated, then said, 'That's difficult for me, because none of the men were charged, so I'm not really allowed to pass on any information about the identities of those involved.'

'But we're talking about threats being made to Abigail,' Daniel pointed out. 'Herb was just the instrument, as — I suspect — was Albert the bar manager. We need to find out where the threat emanates from.'

Again, Pitt hesitated, then nodded. 'Yes, he

was one of them. But, as I say, when we started investigating, Eve Lachelle withdrew the charges, and then just disappeared. Everyone we spoke to said she'd just upped and gone. So that was the end of it.'

'But not for Piers Stevens,' mused Daniel. 'Because, by all accounts, Gavin Everett latched onto him and started blackmailing him, and it's a bit of a coincidence that only apparently happened after the alleged attack on Eve Lachelle.'

'But why him?' asked Pitt. 'There were four men she initially named. Stevens was just one of them. What about the other three? There's been no mention of them.'

'Who were they?' asked Abigail.

Pitt shook his head. 'Sorry,' he said. 'I only talked about Stevens because you asked about him. I'd be breaching my duty if I gave you the names of the others as it turned out they had no case to answer.'

'I bet they did,' said Abigail. 'But Eve Lachelle was either frightened off or paid to keep her mouth shut.'

'I expect you're right,' agreed Pitt. 'But officially there is no case.'

'I understand,' said Daniel. 'But we will be digging, especially after what happened to Abigail. Where to now? The Quill Club?'

'Absolutely,' said Pitt.

★　★　★

Inspector Grafton stood in the Broad, his eyes on the gap in the metal railings on the other side of the road which was the entrance to the Quill Club. A discreet gentlemen's club. The lack of any sign outside the place confirmed that. That kind of discretion meant money, prestige and power, so he couldn't just go blundering in. How to go about it? Would his warrant card work here? Somehow, he doubted it. It was the same with the elite of society in London: they always knew someone who'd protect them. Until enough pressure was applied by his senior commanders, at which point that protection usually crumbled. But he didn't have his senior commanders here. He was on his own.

Suddenly he saw three figures heading towards the club: Wilson, the Fenton woman and another man. They went through the gap and down the steps.

Who was the other man? Grafton wondered. He had all the hallmarks of a copper. Plain clothes, so that meant a detective. Then he remembered where he'd seen him before. At Kemp Hall, after that cursed Superintendent Clare had ordered him off the premises, he'd seen that man in the corridor as he left.

So, the police, along with Wilson and Fenton, were interested in the Quill Club, which must mean de Witt. Why? Had they got the same information as he had, the Boer link?

He turned away, weighing up his next move. He needed someone inside the police station, someone who'd keep him informed of what they were up to. Someone who'd be impressed by his Special Branch warrant card, impressed enough to dig out information for him. The promise of a chance to get into Special Branch would work if he could find the right person. Someone ambitious and eager, and with a chip on his shoulder. Someone who resented the other police officers and felt he wasn't getting the right opportunities. It was just a question of finding them.

★ ★ ★

Vance de Witt sat at his paper-strewn desk and looked inquisitively at his visitors. Abigail had been ushered to the chair on the other side of the desk, while Daniel and Inspector Pitt stood.

'We're here because we've arrested a Mr Herbert Fulworth for launching an assault on Miss Fenton here,' Pitt said. 'Fulworth claims he was hired to carry out the attack by your bar manager, Albert Preston.'

'Nonsense!' snorted de Witt. 'Why on earth would Albert do such a thing?'

'That's what we're trying to find out,' said Pitt. 'Is Mr Preston available for us to have a word with him?'

'I'm afraid not,' said de Witt. 'He was called away unexpectedly. A family matter, I believe. He didn't furnish me with the details, just said that he needed to go away for a few days to deal with a personal issue.'

'Did he say where?'

'No,' said de Witt.

'Mr Fulworth made it clear when he attacked Miss Fenton that he was doing it to prevent her asking questions about Eve Lachelle. I remember that Eve Lachelle used to work for you as a waitress.'

'And you will also recall that she made unfair allegations against some of our members, Inspector. Which she later withdrew when they were shown to be unfounded.'

'Indeed, I remember that, Mr de Witt, but I'm puzzled why Albert Preston, your bar manager, would want Miss Fenton to stop asking questions about Miss Lachelle's current where-abouts.'

'I am puzzled, too, if that is true. Personally, I feel that to be highly unlikely. There was no need for Albert to be involved in anything to do with Eve Lachelle. I suspect this man Herbert has fed you false information.'

'Why would he do that?'

'Who knows?' De Witt shrugged. 'Criminal types often lay the blame on others, often wrongly, in order to protect themselves. When Albert returns, I will make sure he reports to you and you can ask him, but I'm fairly sure you'll get the same answer.'

'Where is Eve Lachelle?' asked Abigail.

De Witt turned his attention to Abigail, then swung back to Pitt. 'Is this lady in the employ of the Oxford police, Inspector? I'm not sure why she's here.'

'As the complainant,' said Pitt. 'She was attacked, and — as I said — according to the man who attacked her, on the orders of your bar manager.'

'An allegation which I believe to be spurious,' said de Witt. 'But I fail to see why I should answer questions from her on anything other than the alleged attack.'

'Oh, there was an attack alright,' said Pitt. 'We have witnesses, as well as the attacker who admits to it. But in that case, Mr de Witt, let me ask you the question: where is Eve Lachelle?'

'Why?' asked de Witt. 'I understood that case was closed.'

'There is another matter we wish to discuss with her,' said Pitt.

'What other matter?'

'Police business,' said Pitt. 'I'm sure you know it's an offence to obstruct the police in the course of their enquiries.'

De Witt smiled. 'I do indeed, Inspector. Well, I can only repeat what I told you before. Some months ago, Eve Lachelle failed to turn up for work. We made enquiries at her lodgings and were told she'd left that day, taking her few possessions with her. She left no forwarding address, and no one heard from her again. That's it.' He gestured at the papers on his desk. 'And now, if there's nothing else, I'd be grateful if I can continue. With Albert leaving at such short notice, I have to make arrangements to replace him temporarily, and good bar managers are hard to find.'

★ ★ ★

Daniel, Abigail and Pitt left the office and made their way through the empty club.

'Well, that wasn't much help,' commented Abigail.

157

'De Witt knows the ins and outs of the law backwards,' grunted Pitt. 'Trying to catch him out is like trying to grab hold of jelly.'

'We need to talk to Eve Lachelle's landlord,' said Abigail. 'Find out when she actually left, and what she took with her.'

'Land*lady*,' Pitt corrected her. 'She lived in rooms at a house in Market Street.'

'Can we go there?' asked Abigail. 'I'm sure she's the key to all that's happening.'

'No problem,' said Pitt. 'I met Mrs Rashford before, so I'll introduce you.'

Daniel stopped as they were about to step out into the daylight. 'You two go on. I just want to have a private word with Mr de Witt. I'll catch you up later.'

'I have a meeting with Superintendent Clare in just over an hour,' said Pitt.

'I'll see you at the Wilton and we can catch up there,' said Abigail.

'Can I say: I hope you're not going to do something stupid with Mr de Witt,' said Pitt warily.

Daniel smiled. 'No, Inspector. I promise you. Nothing stupid.'

Abigail and Pitt left the club, and Daniel made his way back to the office. He knocked at the door, then opened it and stepped in.

'Mr de Witt,' he said. 'A private word, if you don't mind?'

De Witt regarded Daniel with a cynical smile. 'Mr Wilson,' he said sourly. 'Let me, guess, you've come here to . . . what? Threaten me with physical violence if I don't tell you where

158

Albert has gone to?'

'Not at all,' said Daniel. 'Physical violence is not my forte, although I have been known to use it if pushed. No, I leave that to Miss Fenton. I'm guessing that Albert told you how she dealt with the thug who was hired to threaten her. A kick in the balls. Smashing his head against the pavement.' He smiled. 'Actually, that's quite restrained for her. When she was on an archaeological dig in Egypt, one of the local labourers caught her on her own and tried to take advantage of her. She attacked him with a shovel so savagely that he had to be hospitalised. No, when it comes to physical violence, she's the one you should be worried about. So, it is worth warning you that if you try anything like that again, next time it will be you she comes looking for, and she's liable to tear your head off and use it as a doorstop.'

De Witt had remained unsmiling during this. Now he asked, 'Is that it? You just came back to warn me off from threatening Miss Fenton? I can assure you, I have no such intention.'

'Good, but that's not the reason I came back. I returned because I'd like to know how I can contact Piers Stevens.'

'Who?' asked de Witt blandly.

'One of your members. I believe he was very close to Gavin Everett just before Everett's untimely demise.'

'All information about our members is confidential,' said de Witt tersely. 'Even as far as other members are concerned.'

'Absolutely.' Daniel nodded. 'And very understandable. I could, of course, ask Inspector Pitt to get a search warrant to look at your membership records . . . ' Daniel held up his hand as de Witt opened his mouth to speak, and finished, 'But that would be a waste of time, because by the time the warrant arrived, all your records would have disappeared. Possibly lost in an unfortunate fire.'

De Witt smiled. 'Such accidents have been known to happen.'

'No, I was thinking of pressure from another quarter to hopefully make you agree to give me that information.'

'If you're thinking of blackmail . . . ' De Witt smiled.

'No, no,' said Daniel quickly. 'I was thinking of Scotland Yard Special Branch. You've heard of them?'

Daniel could tell that de Witt had by the way the smile was wiped off his face.

'What have Special Branch got to do with the Quill Club?' he asked warily.

'Actually, not the Quill Club, but you personally,' said Daniel.

De Witt glared at Daniel.

'Explain yourself,' he snapped, and Daniel could feel the anger in the man.

'There is an inspector from Special Branch who's recently arrived in Oxford. His name's Inspector Walter Grafton. Grafton and I worked together when I was at the Yard, although it has to be said that he and I never got on. But he's tenacious. And right now, I understand he's looking into you.'

'Me?'

'Vance de Witt, manager of the Quill Club.' Daniel nodded. 'That's what my informant told me.'

'Why?'

Daniel smiled. 'Well, I could tell you what I heard about why, but I think that might be a bit one-sided. Now I could make my own enquiries to find Piers Stevens' address, I'm sure that won't be difficult, but it would save me time if you were able to furnish me with it. In my opinion, I'm not asking you to reveal anything confidential. And, in return, I'll pass on to you why I heard that Inspector Grafton is asking questions about you.'

De Witt glowered at Daniel, then he opened a drawer in his desk and took a ledger out. He opened it and turned the pages until he found the one he wanted, then took a piece of paper and a pen, and wrote an address on it, which he passed to Daniel.

'Thank you,' said Daniel.

'Your side of the bargain?' de Witt challenged.

'Apparently Inspector Grafton believes there may be a Boer connection to Everett's death. Somehow he got your name and has decided to see if you have any Boer connections.'

'That's preposterous!' snorted de Witt.

'I agree,' said Daniel. 'But Inspector Grafton has his own agenda.' He got up. 'I understand he's here independent of the Oxford police, so you won't get any information about him from Kemp Hall. But he is here on official Special

Branch business, and he's watching you.' He headed for the door, then turned and gave de Witt a small polite bow. 'Thank you for your cooperation, Mr de Witt. It's been a pleasure doing business with you.'

20

Mrs Rashford was a cheerful, friendly woman, who invited Abigail and Inspector Pitt into her homely kitchen.

'I remember you from before, Inspector,' she told them, 'and I said to myself: there's a man who won't let wrongs go unpunished. And here you are again, after all these months, still trying to get justice for that poor girl.'

'You believe that Eve Lachelle was attacked, Mrs Rashford?' asked Abigail.

'Absolutely,' said Mrs Rashford. 'I speak as I find, and in my opinion, Eve was an honest girl. I don't doubt that she lived a life very different from mine, but she never brought it into my house. She was always polite and, like I said, honest. Nothing ever disappeared if she'd been left on her own, which isn't always the way. You remember, Inspector, I told you that at the time.'

Pitt nodded. 'You did. The last time I was here was shortly after she reported being attacked.'

'That's right,' said Mrs Rashford. 'She was in a terrible state. If you remember, it was me who persuaded her to go to the police and report it. In fact, I went with her.'

'You did,' said Pitt. 'But later, she retracted.'

'She'd been got at. Pressurised. Terrible to think of those men getting away with it.'

'The trouble was, for us in the police, that

once she'd withdrawn her allegations, we couldn't do anything else other than drop the charges against them.'

'But you're here now,' said Mrs Rashford. 'So, what's changed?'

'Actually, it's not about her being attacked, but her leaving. As I understand it, one day she just left.'

Mrs Rashford looked unhappy as she said, 'Worse than that. She went out in the afternoon, and then never came back. The next morning a man turned up with a note from her saying she'd sent him to collect her things and settle up with any rent she owed. I couldn't understand it. I thought we were friendlier than that, especially after the way I looked out for her after the dreadful attack. This man wouldn't even tell me where she'd gone.'

'Did the man give a name?'

'No. Just said he was a friend of Eve's.'

'Can you describe him?'

'Yes, I can, because I was that upset over it, I remembered every part of that day. He was tall. Well built, but not overweight. He had a moustache. Not one of them big ones, but a neat one, a thin line above his upper lip.'

'Clothes?' asked Abigail.

'Smart,' said Mrs Rashford. 'A gentleman. And very polite.' She frowned. 'But there was something about him that didn't ring true. I pride myself on being a good judge of character, and there was something iffy about him. Something not right.'

'Do you keep old newspapers, Mrs Rashford?'

asked Pitt, surprising both the landlady and Abigail with the question.

'What a funny question,' said Mrs Rashford. 'Of course. Doesn't everyone? I keep 'em for lighting the fires and stove.'

'Do you still have copies of the *Oxford Messenger* for this last week?'

'I think I might,' she said. 'I keep 'em in the scullery. Why, is it important?'

'It might be,' said Pitt.

'In that case, I'll have a look.'

She left, and Abigail turned to Pitt and asked, 'Why do you need the old newspapers?'

'Because the description she gave us of the man who collected Eve Lachelle's stuff sounded remarkably like Gavin Everett, and there was a picture of Everett in the report about his death. 'Tragic museum curator', that sort of thing.'

Mrs Rashford returned with a bundle of newspapers.

'You're in luck, I hadn't used 'em yet,' she said.

Pitt took the newspapers and leafed through them, finally finding what he wanted. He showed the page with the picture of Everett to the landlady.

'Is this the man?' he asked.

Mrs Rashford took the page and studied the picture, then nodded, excited. 'Yes, that's him! The very self same man! I'm surprised I never saw it!'

'Easily missed for a busy woman like yourself.' Pitt smiled. ' 'Thank you, Mrs Rashford. You've been very helpful.'

165

★ ★ ★

Daniel sat in their room at the Wilton Hotel and listened as Abigail outlined what she and Inspector Pitt had learnt.

'So, the day after Eve Lachelle vanishes, Everett turns up at her lodgings and clears her things out. And about the same time, he becomes very friendly with this Piers Stevens, and — as far as we can tell — begins to blackmail him,' summed up Daniel. 'What's the logical conclusion?'

'That something very bad happened to Eve Lachelle which involved Stevens, and Everett was clearing up the mess. And it had to be more than just being about the attack on her, because it happened sometime after that attack, and none of the other men named seemed to be involved.'

'And, by something very bad . . . ?'

'She was killed,' said Abigail. 'By Stevens. And Everett was either there or found out about it. And finally, Stevens can't take being black-mailed, so he shoots Everett.'

'The first part, Stevens killing Eve Lachelle, and Everett being involved and blackmailing him, works for me. But as for Stevens killing Everett, we still have the other possibilities for his murder. The business of the alleged Shakespeare play, the fakery involving this Josiah Goddard, and also Special Branch's suspicions about Boer involvement.'

'Out of those, Stevens shooting Everett seems most likely,' observed Abigail.

'I agree,' said Daniel. 'So, I think our next

move is to pay a call on Mr Stevens. And fortunately, Mr de Witt gave me his address.'

'How?' asked Abigail. 'Threats?'

'Certainly not,' replied Daniel. 'We talked it over like gentlemen and he saw sense.'

'I still say you made some sort of threat,' insisted Abigail. 'De Witt didn't come across as the altruistic type.'

There was a tap at the door, and Abigail went to open it. It was Esther, looking very pleased.

'I'm sorry to trouble you,' she said, 'but I've had some good news!'

'In that case, you'd better come in,' said Abigail. 'Daniel, remember that you're a gentleman and stand up so that Esther can sit.'

'No, don't bother,' said Esther. 'I won't be staying. Honest. I just came to tell you that Mr Pinker heard from the Duchess of Charlbury. I've got an appointment to interview her in three days' time.'

'That's excellent!' said Abigail.

'Have you got any news yourselves?' asked Esther eagerly.

'Sadly, no,' said Daniel. 'We're following up a few leads, but nothing concrete as yet.' He hesitated, then said, 'But as a warning to you about being careful, Abigail was attacked today by a man who tried to stop her asking questions.'

Esther stared open-mouthed at Abigail.

'Attacked?' she said breathlessly.

'It was nothing.' Abigail shrugged. 'I dealt with it.'

'What she means is she beat the man up.'

Daniel grinned. 'And then had him arrested and questioned.'

'And I was unharmed,' stressed Abigail. 'But Daniel's quite right, we're investigating something that certain people don't want us digging into. So be on your guard.'

'Who was this man?' asked Esther.

'This isn't for publication,' Daniel cautioned her.

'No, but it will be one day. And I want to make sure I've got all the facts.'

'He was just a brainless thug,' said Abigail. 'He'd been hired by a man who works at the Quill Club.'

'The place where that man I mentioned, Mr de Witt, is the manager?' asked Esther.

'That's right,' said Abigail.

'So, do you think this Mr de Witt is involved and is part of some plot?'

'We don't know,' said Daniel. 'We're investigating.'

'And we will let you know if we find out anything that ties him to it,' Abigail promised. 'Or anything else.'

'Oh, this is so exciting!' enthused Esther. 'Murder and violence in Oxford, and I'm involved!'

'But not *too* involved, please,' said Abigail. 'Be careful.'

'I will,' Esther assured her. She gave them both a broad smile. 'And to think, you two do this all the time! That's so exciting!'

With that, she hurried to the door and left.

'I'm sorry I told her about the thug attacking

you without checking with you first,' said Daniel. 'But I thought she ought to be warned about the dangers. She strikes me as the kind of person who'll rush in blindly if she's not told to be careful.'

'I think you're right,' said Abigail. 'But I love her enthusiasm for it.' She went to the coat hook and took her coat. 'And now, let's go and find this Piers Stevens.'

⋆   ⋆   ⋆

The address Daniel had been given for Piers Stevens was a large expensive-looking house in one of the more upmarket areas of Oxford.

'What's our strategy?' asked Abigail, as they stood on the pavement studying the house. 'Do we ring the bell and ask to see him?'

'If he's involved in a possible murder, I expect if we did that, he'd simply refuse to see us,' said Daniel.

'So, what are we going to do? Just stand here and wait for him to appear?'

'I often did that with someone who was difficult to nail down when I was in the Yard,' said Daniel.

'I can't see that working here,' commented Abigail. 'This area reeks of money. Just look at the houses. Two people hanging around in the street like this, they'd suspect us of being burglars casing the joint.'

Daniel laughed. 'You are definitely picking up the argot,' he said. ' 'Casing the joint'. We'll soon have you talking like a fully fledged member of the criminal fraternity.'

The front door of the house opened, and a young man stepped out. Pitt had described Stevens to Abigail — young, short, thin fuzzy beard, spectacles — and the young man who appeared and pulled the door shut answered that description perfectly.

'We didn't have long to wait after all,' murmured Daniel.

He led the way towards the young man who was walking along, head down.

'Excuse me,' said Daniel with a polite smile. 'Mr Piers Stevens?'

The young man stopped and stared at them, and they could see panic in his eyes.

'No!' he blurted out. 'I'm not!'

He went to hurry on, but Daniel stepped in his way, and the man stopped, looking around him as if about to call for help.

'We only wish to talk to you,' said Daniel. 'My name is Daniel Wilson, and this is my partner, Miss Abigail Fenton. We've been hired by the Ashmolean Museum to look into the death of Mr Gavin Everett — '

'You've no right to talk to me!' Stevens burst out. 'Leave me alone!'

'All we want to do is talk to you about your relationship with Mr Everett, and also ask a few questions about Eve Lachelle . . . '

The effect on the short man was electric. He began to shake, and suddenly he thrust his hand into his coat pocket and pulled out a small pistol, which he held out towards them, his hand trembling.

'No!' he moaned.
'Mr Stevens — ' began Daniel.
And then the gun went off.

21

The bullet whistled past Daniel, but so close that it tore at his sleeve before hitting a brick wall.

To Daniel's horror, Stevens levelled the gun again, this time at Abigail. Swiftly, Daniel grabbed Abigail and swung her behind him, and found himself staring down the barrel of the pistol. He saw the man's finger tighten on the trigger and tensed himself for the bullet, all the time keeping his arms firmly behind him, holding Abigail in cover. Stevens' finger tightened, but the pistol only gave a dull thud and a click. It had jammed.

Steven stared at the pistol in horror and tried again, but once more it just clicked. Immediately, Daniel released his hold on Abigail and advanced towards the young man. Stevens let out a yell of anguish, threw the pistol away, and turned and ran. Daniel was about to follow him, but Abigail grabbed hold of him.

'Let him go,' she said. 'We know who he is. Inspector Pitt can deal with him.' Then she threw herself against Daniel and wrapped her arms around him. 'Don't ever do that again!' she said. 'Brave, yes, but stupid! I want you alive, not a dead hero. He could have killed you.'

'He could have killed *you*!' retorted Daniel.

He eased out of Abigail's grasp and picked up the small pistol.

'A Derringer,' he said. 'Twin-barrelled, just

172

two shots, one in each. We were lucky he chose this rather than a revolver, and we were even luckier the second barrel jammed.'

Suddenly there was a shout of 'Drop that gun!' They turned to see a police constable running towards them, truncheon drawn. Behind him ran a man and a woman.

Daniel dropped the gun on the pavement.

'It wasn't me,' he said.

'No, it wasn't!' panted the man, trying to catch his breath. 'It was another man. I saw it all! He was shorter.'

The constable looked at them, then at the couple who'd brought him, an expression of bewilderment on his face.

'He ran off,' said Abigail. 'But he dropped his gun.'

Daniel fingered the tear in his sleeve where the bullet had narrowly missed him.

'We need to see Inspector Pitt,' he told the constable. 'We're on his side.'

The constable looked at them suspiciously.

'You would say that,' he said warily. He edged towards them, then reached down and snatched up the fallen pistol. 'But I'm taking charge of this.'

★ ★ ★

Inspector Pitt studied the small pistol.

'A Derringer,' he said. 'American. We don't see many of these over here. In fact, we rarely see any guns in Oxford.'

Daniel and Abigail were sitting, along with

173

Inspector Pitt, in the office of Superintendent Clare at Kemp Hall.

'Have you put out an alert for this man, Stevens?' asked Clare.

'Yes, sir,' said Pitt. 'At the moment we've only got the description we had of him from when he fired the gun and then ran off, but I shall be going to his address and hope to get a photograph of him which we can distribute.'

Clare looked at the small pistol, an expression of concern on his face. 'We've never had a shooting in Oxford during my time here.' He looked at Daniel. 'Although I suppose it was a common occurrence for you, Mr Wilson, when you were with Scotland Yard.'

'Actually, sir, no,' said Daniel. 'Murders, yes, but they rarely involve firearms.'

'And now we have had two shootings in Oxford in the space of a week,' said Clare.

'Although it does seem that the same person was responsible for both,' observed Pitt. 'Mr Wilson asks Stevens about Everett, and Stevens pulls this gun and tries to shoot him. This points to Stevens being the person who shot Everett.'

'I don't think so,' said Daniel doubtfully.

'Why on earth not?' asked Pitt. 'A pistol. A man carrying a gun and prepared to kill with it, who fires when he's asked about Everett. It's as good as a confession.'

'Stevens was in a panic when he pulled this Derringer,' said Daniel. 'His hand was shaking, which was lucky for us, because he missed, even though we were at close range. In fact, he was in a panic the whole time, from the moment we

174

began to talk to him, and was barely able to control his movements. You told us you believed the shot that killed Everett was fired from a distance.'

'The other side of the desk,' Pitt agreed.

'The bullet hit Everett in the centre of the forehead. That shows a very steady hand and cool nerve. We both think that the killer went out, locked the door, and pushed the key back through the gap at the bottom of the door. That shows cold calm. None of that fits with what we saw of Piers Stevens.'

'Maybe he's got more edgy and nervous since he shot Everett?' suggested the superintendent.

'Maybe, sir, but it doesn't feel right to me,' said Daniel. 'The bullet that killed Everett, could it have been from a Derringer?'

'No,' answered Pitt. 'It was a .44, the same as from the revolver we found beside the body. But that doesn't mean much. If he had one gun, he could have had others.'

'Interestingly, it was the mention of Eve Lachelle that made Stevens pull out the gun,' said Abigail. 'He got agitated when we talked about Everett, but when we mentioned the name of Eve Lachelle, that was it.'

'I still think he's our best candidate for the killing of Everett,' said Pitt. 'Hopefully, we'll get the truth of it when we pick him up. Right now, while our men are out looking for him, I'm going to his home to see if they've got a photograph of him, and also to see if we can get any clues as to where he might have gone.' He turned to Clare. 'With your permission, sir, I'd like to take Mr

Wilson and Miss Fenton with me as they're deeply involved in this case.'

'By all means,' said Clare. 'And let's hope we catch this fellow before he creates more havoc.'

★ ★ ★

As Daniel and Abigail, along with Inspector Pitt and a uniformed constable, left the police station, they found Esther hovering outside.

'Abigail!' burst out Esther. 'A couple came to the newspaper office and reported that someone had been shot. They said a constable had taken a couple in charge to the station and I wondered if it was you. I should have told the editor, but I didn't tell anyone else, I just came here myself to get the story.'

'I'm sorry, miss, we're not ready to talk to the press,' said Pitt sternly.

Abigail took hold of the inspector's arm and pulled him to one side, out of earshot of Esther, although she could see that the woman was straining to hear what was being said.

'It might be better for the story that appears to be factual, rather than a made-up one that depicts Oxford as something out of the Wild West, with shootouts on the street,' she murmured quietly. 'We know Esther Maris, and she is genuine. This way you can control what she writes.'

Pitt wavered, then nodded.

'Very well, miss,' he said to Esther. 'You may accompany us to where we're going, but you must wait outside while we go in and carry out our investigation. After that, we'll provide you with the sequence of events.'

Abigail saw that Esther was about to press to be allowed into wherever it was they were going, but Abigail shot her a quick look accompanied by a firm nod to tell her it would be the wisest thing for her not to argue.

'Thank you,' said Esther. As they set off, with Pitt and the constable leading the way, with Daniel, Abigail and Esther in their wake, she asked, 'Where are we going?'

'To the home of a man called Piers Stevens,' replied Abigail. 'He's the man who did the shooting.'

'This couple said a man was shot.' She looked at Daniel. 'Luckily, I can see they were wrong.'

'Not quite,' said Daniel. 'The bullet tore a hole in my sleeve, so it'll need a repair. But nothing a needle and thread can't fix, fortunately.'

'Is that what you said when you told me to be careful?' asked Esther. 'That I might get shot if I start asking questions.'

'We hope not,' said Abigail. 'This Piers Stevens dropped his gun and fled.'

'But he might have others?' said Esther.

'He might,' Abigail admitted.

'Or other weapons!' continued Esther. And then, to their surprise, she gave a broad smile. 'This is so exciting!'

They arrived back at the house they had seen Stevens leave. Pitt mounted the steps and rang the bell while the others waited on the pavement. A nervous-looking maid opened the door.

'My name is Inspector Pitt from Oxford

police,' said Pitt. 'Are the family at home?'

'There's only Mrs Stevens,' said the maid.

'We're looking for Mr Piers Stevens,' said Pitt.

The maid gave a nervous twitch. A woman's voice from inside called, in an imperious tone, 'Who is it, Vera?'

'It's the police, ma'am,' said Vera. 'An Inspector Pitt.'

'Show him in,' called the voice. 'Bring him to the drawing room. Make sure he wipes his boots.'

'Yes, ma'am.' She looked at Pitt and said, 'Mrs Stevens says . . . '

'I heard what she said.' He turned to the constable. 'You wait here, Constable. You too, Miss Maris.'

Pitt, Daniel and Abigail entered the house and went through the motion of deliberately wiping their feet on the thick mat just inside the door, before following the maid along a passageway that smelt heavily of polish to a drawing room.

Mrs Stevens was sitting in a high-backed chair, a large woman dressed in black, the austerity of the colour offset by sparkling jewellery and a pearl necklace. She regarded them with a look of disapproval as they entered, her expression becoming more disapproving as she saw Daniel and Abigail behind the inspector.

'I assume you two are policemen, but who is this woman?' she demanded.

'This is Miss Abigail Fenton,' said Pitt. 'She is an enquiry agent employed by the Ashmolean Museum, along with her partner, Mr Daniel Wilson.'

'I do not care to have them in my house,' said Mrs Stevens firmly.

'They are here because they were the object of the attack on them by Mr Piers Stevens, who I believe to be your son.'

'He shot at us,' added Daniel. 'Before he ran off.'

'But he did not hit you,' said Mrs Stevens dismissively.

Daniel showed her the hole in his sleeve. 'Only because I moved to one side as he fired. As it was, the bullet hit my sleeve. He attempted to fire again, but the pistol jammed.'

Mrs Stevens looked at him, her expression icy, but they could see the turmoil raging inside her.

'I do not believe my son capable of such a dreadful action,' she said. 'I'm sure it was an accident.'

'I'm afraid not, Mrs Stevens,' said Pitt. 'His attempt to fire a second shot shows that.'

'Then he must have been provoked into taking such an action,' said Mrs Stevens.

'It occurred after we told him we were investigating the death of Mr Gavin Everett, curator at the Ashmolean Museum, and the disappearance of a woman called Eve Lachelle,' said Daniel. 'It was at that point he pulled out a pistol and shot at us.'

'Who is this Eve Lachelle woman?' asked Mrs Stevens.

'A waitress at the Quill Club in Oxford, of which your son is a member.'

'And why would you be asking him about this woman?' she demanded.

'Because we had been given information that he had an involvement with her,' said Abigail.

'False information!' snapped the woman.

'The fact that he reacted the way he did suggests otherwise,' said Pitt.

Mrs Stevens fell silent, then she gave a heavy sigh. 'I'm afraid that Piers has been troubled for some time.' She motioned towards a large portrait on the wall of a man in a brigadier's uniform, standing proudly before a Union Jack fluttering on a flagpole outside a castle in some rocky landscape. 'My husband had such hopes for Piers, but it was obvious that our son had no thoughts of following his father into an army career. He fell into bad company here in Oxford. I did what I could to keep him on the straight and narrow, but it became difficult after Gerald died.'

'We understand, and sympathise,' said Pitt. 'Our intention is to find him before he gets into worse trouble, or before he does anything dangerous.'

'Kills himself, you mean?' she demanded. 'In some ways, that might be the better option. Rather than bring complete disgrace on the family name.'

'We're hopeful of being able to help him before that happens,' continued Pitt. 'Can you tell us where he might have gone? Any friends of his, or relatives he might take refuge with?'

'Relatives I think would be unlikely,' she said sadly. 'I'm afraid most of our relatives have turned against Piers.'

'For what reason?' asked Pitt.

'His bad behaviour, especially when he had drunk too much,' she said. 'As to his friends, I do not know them. Piers is well aware of my attitude towards the life he leads, and I do not encourage him to bring those people into this house.'

'Does he own other weapons in addition to the small pistol he dropped?'

'Yes,' she said. 'He collected firearms. Initially, that was why Gerald hoped he might follow him into the army: his love of small arms. But it soon became apparent that collecting guns was the extent of his ambition.'

'Where does he keep his collection?'

'In his room.'

'May we see it?' asked Pitt.

Mrs Stevens hesitated, then she gave a tug at the bell pull beside her chair. Vera, the maid, appeared.

'Yes, ma'am?'

'Take them to Mr Piers' room,' she ordered.

'Yes, ma'am.'

Pitt pointed to a framed photograph on the sideboard. 'May we borrow that photograph of your son?'

'To raise a hue and cry for him?' she snapped, angry.

'We do need to find him, ma'am,' said Pitt. 'I'll see that the photograph is returned.'

'Very well,' said Mrs Stevens. 'Will you need to talk to me again after you've seen his room?' she asked.

'I don't expect so, ma'am,' said Pitt. 'Unless we find anything that raises questions.'

'I hope you don't,' said Mrs Stevens. 'I would

prefer to draw a veil over this whole sordid affair.'

22

Pitt, Daniel and Abigail followed the maid up the wide, ornate staircase and along a corridor to a closed door.

'This is Mr Piers' room,' Vera informed them.

'Thank you,' said Pitt.

As the maid withdrew, Abigail whispered to Daniel and Pitt, 'You two look at the room. I want a word with the maid.'

Abigail hurried after the maid and caught up with her just as she was about to descend the stairs.

'Excuse me,' she said. 'I'd like to talk to you about Mr Piers.'

Vera looked nervously down the stairs.

'I can't stay,' she said. 'The missus will be needing me.'

'I'll tell her we asked you to stay in the room while we looked it over to make sure we didn't interfere with anything,' said Abigail. 'Is there somewhere we can talk?'

'I'm not sure if I've got anything to say, miss,' said Vera unhappily.

'I think you might have,' said Abigail. 'And it might help Mr Piers.'

Vera hesitated, then gestured at another door. 'This is the sewing room,' she said. 'But it's hardly used any more.'

Vera led Abigail into the room, and Abigail saw that indeed it was a room made for sewing of all types, but mainly decorative: cross-stitch material was stretched on frames, ready to be patterned; a half-finished tapestry was on another frame; material of different colours hung on hangers; and threads of all sorts, some on spools, some hanging like yarn, decorated the room.

'Tell me about Mr Piers,' said Abigail. 'What sort of person is he?'

'He's not a bad person, miss. I know about the shooting, and I'm sorry about that, but he's not really bad.'

'He talked to you?'

She nodded. 'He said I was the only one he could talk to. I was the only one who didn't frighten him.'

'He's frightened of his mother?'

'And he was frightened of his father. They didn't like the fact that he's . . . sensitive.'

'You're in love with him, aren't you.'

Abigail saw tears appear in the maid's eyes.

'It was that club he went to that was the undoing of him,' she said. 'The gambling. He wasn't good at it. He thought he was, he liked to play up this image of a man about town, but he wasn't really. He lost money, and he had to keep going to his mother to pay his debts. She did, but each time she gave him the most terrible lecture, told him he wasn't a quarter of the man his father had been and that she only saved him financially to save the family name from disgrace. But each time she threatened that the next time she'd let the bailiffs take him to court.'

'But she didn't.'

'No. Because of the family name.'

'Did he ever talk about a woman called Eve Lachelle?'

'Once. After he was questioned by the police about her. He was so upset. He said it hadn't been him who'd done anything; he'd been named wrongly. He was so angry with her.'

'Did he say what had happened?'

'No. He said he couldn't talk about it, even to me.' She looked at Abigail appealingly. 'He didn't do anything really bad, did he? I know he fired the gun, but that was because he was frightened. He didn't actually hurt anyone. He won't go to prison, will he? He couldn't take it in prison. It would kill him.'

'I'm sure his mother will get a good lawyer for him, if only to protect the family name. The important thing is to find him before things get worse for him. Can you think of anywhere he might have gone? Friends? People he might turn to?'

'No, miss. When things got bad for him, he used to say I was the only one he could talk to. I was his only help.'

★　★　★

Daniel and Pitt studied the array of firearms displayed in the two glass cases hanging on the wall of Stevens' room. In the larger case were two rifles and two shotguns.

'Purdey, and Holland & Holland,' noted Pitt. 'Expensive.' He peered at the other rifle.

185

'Birmingham Small Arms,' he read.

The other case contained a variety of pistols. There were early single-shot pistols, a matchlock, a wheel lock, a flintlock and a caplock. There were also revolvers: a Colt, and a Smith & Wesson from America, along with a British Webley.

'A man who loves guns and knows how to use them,' observed Pitt.

'With a shaky hand,' said Daniel. 'I still have my doubts about Stevens being the killer.'

They set to work examining the contents of the wardrobe and dressing table, but there was little in the way of personal items.

'Strange, don't you think, the lack of letters or photographs,' mused Pitt. 'He must have had a place where he stashed things that were important to him.'

'I guess he was too afraid of his mother finding anything that she might use against him,' said Daniel.

Abigail arrived and asked, 'Find anything?'

'Nothing that will help us find him.' Pitt sighed. 'Any luck with the maid?'

'She's very sympathetic to him and I believe if she knew where he was, she'd tell us, for his safety.'

They went back downstairs, where Vera was waiting with a small parcel.

'The photograph of Mr Piers,' she said.

'Thank you,' said Pitt. 'I promise we'll take good care of it and return it as soon as it's been copied.'

Esther was waiting on the step for them as

they left the house, along with the uniformed constable.

'Well?' she demanded as soon as they appeared.

Pitt tapped the brown paper parcel. 'This is a photograph of the man we are seeking in connection with the shooting,' he said. 'I'm about to take it to the *Oxford Messenger* for them to reproduce it.'

'I can take it!' offered Esther enthusiastically. 'I'll be putting in my story about the shooting.'

Pitt looked doubtful, and once again Abigail stepped in. 'Can I suggest that Daniel and I talk to Miss Maris about what happened, and vet the story she writes before she takes it to her editor.'

'I don't want anything sensational, nor anything that might interfere with the investigation,' cautioned Pitt.

'I promise you there won't be,' said Abigail. 'And Daniel has enough experience to know what should go in a story, and what shouldn't.'

'Very well,' said Pitt. 'In the meantime, I'll get copies made of this photograph to distribute on handbills. You can come to Kemp Hall and collect it from me later.'

'Thank you!' said Esther.

As Inspector Pitt and the constable walked off, Esther turned eagerly to Abigail and Daniel. 'Where shall we go to talk?'

'Somewhere private,' said Daniel. 'Our office at the Ashmolean.'

23

Back in their office, Daniel and Abigail related the events of the shooting and the resulting search for Piers Stevens that was currently under way to Esther, while she wrote frantically in her notebook.

'There,' said Abigail when they'd finished. 'Now remember, we need to read it and approve it before you take it to your editor. We don't want anything appearing that might alert the suspects in the case of Gavin Everett's death.'

'Who are the suspects?' asked Esther. 'Apart from this Piers Stevens.'

Abigail looked questioningly at Daniel, who nodded for her to go ahead.

'We can't be specific at this moment,' said Abigail, 'but after what's just happened, obviously Inspector Pitt sees this Piers Stevens as his main suspect. Then there's the subject you overheard Inspector Grafton talking about, so the Boers offer another aspect. And there's also the one I mentioned to you before, a titled local family who might have an original Shakespeare play in their possession.'

'The ones I'm going to interview.' Esther smiled.

'But none of those last two should appear in your story,' stressed Daniel. 'Concentrate on Piers Stevens.'

'I will,' Esther promised. 'And I'll tell you

what, I'll write it here, right now. I need to get it to Mr Pinker as fast as I can to make sure it's in the first edition for tomorrow.'

Abigail again looked questioningly at Daniel, who nodded.

'That's fine,' he said. 'We have to go along the corridor and bring Mr Marriott up to date, so you can use this office.'

As they made their way along the corridor to Marriott's office, Daniel murmured, 'So you decided not to tell her about the forgeries at the Ashmolean.'

'No, that would be a betrayal of Mr Marriott's trust. We can't risk the possibility that the information might leak out, and it would seriously damage the Ashmolean's reputation.'

'But if it does turn out to be the motive behind Everett's death?' asked Daniel.

Abigail shrugged. 'In that case, we have to tell her. But we'll wait and see what happens.'

They arrived at Marriott's door, knocked, and at his call of 'Come in!', entered.

'Ah, good,' he said. 'I was just about to make my way to see you to find out if there was any news.'

'Yes, there has been,' said Daniel. 'As you know, we've tried to keep you informed of developments as the case unfolds, but without disturbing you the whole time.'

'Yes, and I appreciate that,' said Marriott. 'But do I understand from the fact you're saying this, and from the concerned expression on your faces, that something unpleasant has happened that might reflect adversely on the Ashmolean?'

'Something unpleasant has happened, but it won't impinge in any way on the Ashmolean. In fact, there's no need for the museum to feature, but a story will be coming out in tomorrow's *Oxford Messenger* about shots being fired at us.'

'Shots?' repeated Marriott in alarm.

'You remember we told you about a man called Piers Stevens, who we believed that Gavin Everett was blackmailing?'

Marriott nodded.

'We approached Mr Stevens to ask him some questions, and he pulled out a gun and fired at us. Fortunately, neither of us was hurt, but the story will be in the paper tomorrow. However, there'll be no mention of the Ashmolean,' he added hastily. 'The shooting is connected with another matter.'

'What other matter?'

'We believe that this man Stevens killed a woman, a waitress who worked at the Quill Club, and Everett was either a witness or discovered the truth about it.'

'And that was why he was blackmailing Stevens?'

'Yes, that's our belief.'

Marriott sat and let this information sink in. 'This gets worse,' he said at last.

'Yes, I'm afraid it does.'

'But you're sure you're alright? Neither of you was harmed?'

'My sleeve was damaged,' said Daniel with a rueful grin, 'but fortunately nothing else.'

'And this man, Stevens? Is he in police custody?'

'No, he managed to run away. The police have launched a search for him.'

'Do they think he was the one who killed Everett?'

'Inspector Pitt does, but I disagree,' said Daniel.

'So, what's next?' asked Marriott.

'The hue and cry over Stevens will be set in motion, and in the meantime Miss Fenton and I will pursue the other possible motives.'

'The forgeries that Everett was involved in?' said Marriott with distaste.

'That's one angle,' agreed Daniel. 'Although you can rest assured we've made sure nothing about that will appear in the press.'

'We still have the business of the titled lady with the Shakespeare play, and Inspector Grafton's idea that the Boers may be behind his killing,' added Abigail.

Marriott shook his head slowly.

'I should have seen through him,' he said sadly. 'If I had, none of this would be happening.'

'You can't blame yourself, Mr Marriott,' Abigail assured him. 'He was eminently plausible to so many people.'

'A consummate confidence trickster,' added Daniel. 'But one whose web of deceit finally caught up with him.'

★   ★   ★

Superintendent Clare studied the photograph of Piers Stevens that Inspector Pitt had handed him.

191

'A sad case,' he said. 'He looks so young and innocent. Quite naive, in fact.'

'I believe he was,' said Pitt. 'But he fell into bad company.'

'This Gavin Everett?'

'Not just him,' said Pitt. 'I feel that the Quill Club is at the centre of this.'

'It's said to be very respectable,' said Clare. 'Many of the members are very important people.'

'That may be, but I don't trust the manager there, Vance de Witt. I had my doubts about him before, over the Eve Lachelle case.'

'Which was dropped,' Clare reminded him. 'The woman withdrew her complaint.'

'Under pressure, I believe,' said Pitt. 'I'd like your permission to bring de Witt in for questioning.'

'To Kemp Hall?'

'Yes, sir.'

'Why not question him at the Quill Club?'

'Because that's his territory. He may not be intimidated by a question room in a police station, but it may go some way to unsettling him.'

'You think it will be worth the effort? Mr de Witt has some powerful acquaintances here in Oxford.'

'His bar manager was behind the attack on Miss Fenton, I'm sure of that. Everett was a member of his club. As is Piers Stevens, who tried to kill Miss Fenton and Mr Wilson. I think there's enough there to warrant him being brought in.'

Clare gave it some thought, then nodded. 'Very well, Inspector. Bring him in. But be careful. We don't want this department to run afoul of the people who run Oxford, and that includes the Watch Committee. I believe some of them are members of this club, so use tact.'

★   ★   ★

Vance de Witt sat at his desk, weighing up his options in the light of recent events. The departure of Albert, however temporary, was a big loss, one not easily replaced. Albert was not just a damn good bar manager, he was de Witt's fixer and general right-hand man.

Then there was this business of Piers Stevens shooting at people in public. News had been brought to him shortly after it happened; he had enough eyes and ears working for him in Oxford to keep him appraised of everything that went on. What on earth had driven Stevens to do such a thing? It was the act of someone insane, but was the insanity permanent or temporary?

There was a knock on his door, which opened, and Joe put his head in.

'Sorry to trouble you, Mr de Witt,' he said, 'but the police are here.'

'Not again!' groaned de Witt. 'What do they want?'

The door opened wider and a uniformed sergeant entered, followed by a constable.

'Inspector Pitt has sent us to bring you to the station,' said the sergeant.

'Well, you can tell Inspector Pitt that I'm far

too busy,' snapped de Witt. 'If he wants to see me, he can make an appointment.'

The police sergeant gave de Witt a bland look and said, 'This isn't a request. It's an order.'

'An order?' repeated de Witt, outraged. 'Who do you think you are?!'

'I'm an officer of the law carrying out my duty,' said the sergeant. 'Now, you can come with us as you are. Or, if you resist, I'll handcuff you and we'll take you in by force.' And, to reinforce his words, the sergeant produced a pair of handcuffs.

24

It was with a feeling of excitement mixed with pride that Esther entered the *Oxford Messenger* building and climbed the stairs to the first floor. This would be her first story as a proper reporter, instead of just her name on a column about 'women's issues'. She reached the editor's office and rapped with her knuckles on the door.

'Enter!' barked Pinker.

Esther strode in, doing her best to look efficient and not let her feelings be betrayed by a happy smile.

'Here you are, Mr Pinker,' she said, putting her two handwritten pages on his desk, along with the image of Piers Stevens she'd collected from Kemp Hall. 'The story about the shooting. And the picture of the suspect.'

'The shooting?' queried Pinker.

'Yes. A couple came here and told the receptionist a man had taken shots at people in the centre of Oxford, so I went to the police station at Kemp Hall to get the story.'

'Why?' demanded Pinker, glaring at her coldly.

'Because it's a story!' exclaimed Esther.

'But it's not your story,' snapped Pinker.

'It is!' protested Esther. She pushed the pages towards him. 'Here. And I've had it checked by the people who were shot at, Abigail Fenton, the archaeologist, and Daniel Wilson, the Scotland Yard detective, to make sure they're happy with it. You always say that's what to do with a story, get the approval of the people being written about.'

'You're not a crime reporter, Esther,' growled Pinker. 'You're not a reporter, full stop. You write pieces for the women's page.'

'But I thought you'd be pleased! I know Miss Fenton — '

'I'm *not* pleased!' said Pinker. 'In fact, I'm angry, and if it wasn't for the fact that your uncle owns the paper, I'd sack you here and now.'

'Sack me?'

'I'm the editor, Esther, not you. I decide who handles what. Henry Loveday is the crime reporter for the *Oxford Messenger*. Our readers will not accept a woman as a crime reporter. Or any sort of reporter, come to that, except on women's issues. Fashion. Makeup. Cooking. The home. Have you got that?'

⋆ ⋆ ⋆

Vance de Witt sat in the interview room in Kemp Hall and stared tight-lipped across the table at Inspector Pitt. If he was intimidated by being here, his manner didn't show it. Instead, it showed his barely concealed anger simmering beneath the surface.

'May I ask why I've been brought here?' de Witt demanded.

'Because we've uncovered an interesting situation, and it seems that the Quill Club is at the centre of it.'

'Oh?'

'Yes. You've no doubt heard about one of your members, Piers Stevens, shooting Mr Wilson and then running away.'

De Witt said nothing, just sat waiting, doing his best to appear calm and indifferent.

'Well, it now appears the situation was this: that Stevens killed your former waitress, Eve Lachelle, and the next morning he got Everett to go to her landlady's house to collect her things and settle up any rent that was owing. What do you think of that?'

'Very fanciful,' said de Witt dismissively.

'We have a witness statement from the landlady identifying Everett as the man who took her things.'

'She may have asked him to do that.'

'Unlikely. Because we have information that after that, Everett began to blackmail Stevens. Do you have any comment so far?'

'None,' said de Witt. 'If things did happen as you say, it's nothing to do with the Quill Club.'

'Except that when Miss Fenton started asking questions about what happened to Eve Lachelle, your bar manager hired a thug to try and warn her off. That suggests a connection.'

De Witt sat and studied Pitt silently for about a minute, then announced, 'I believe I'd like to see my lawyer.'

★　★　★

Abigail and Daniel arrived at the address that Ephraim Wardle had given them for Josiah Goddard. It was a small shop in the middle of a parade of shops, with a second-hand furniture store on one side and a shop selling mystical equipment, including Ouija boards, spell-makers and crystal balls on the other.

Abigail gestured at the display of painted plates in the window of Goddard's shop.

'See those plates. They're the same as the copies in the Ashmolean. In fact, Mr Goddard seems to have quite an industry going. There are various combinations: on some plates the figures look to the right, on others to the left, but they're all from the same pattern.'

'Making copies isn't illegal,' Daniel pointed out.

'No, but it does suggest we've found the right person.'

They entered the shop, setting a small bell above the door tinkling. At the sound, a short, wiry man in shirtsleeves appeared from a curtained entrance to the back of the shop.

'Good afternoon.' He smiled at them in greeting. 'What can I get for you?'

'I must congratulate you on the ancient Egyptian plates in your window,' said Abigail. 'And the ancient Greek ones.'

'Copies, only,' said Goddard. 'That's what I specialise in, but you won't find any others more accurate to the originals.'

'I notice they're copied from the plates at the Ashmolean,' continued Abigail.

'A connoisseur, I see!' Goddard beamed. 'You are absolutely right, madam. I frequent the Ashmolean for inspiration because they have the finest examples of ancient artefacts.'

'They do,' agreed Abigail. 'But how do you choose which of them to make copies of?'

'I go there and look, and see which ones inspire me.' Goddard smiled.

'Not because Gavin Everett has asked you to make a specific copy of something?' asked Daniel genially.

The smile was wiped off Goddard's face, and he regarded Daniel and Abigail with suspicion.

'Who?' he asked flatly.

'Gavin Everett,' said Abigail. 'An assistant curator at the Ashmolean.'

'Never heard of him,' growled Goddard.

'That's strange,' said Daniel. 'Because we were advised that you did restoration work for the Ashmolean that was commissioned by him.'

'Then you were advised wrong,' said Goddard sourly. 'Yes, I go to the Ashmolean to look at the exhibits, and I choose which ones I want to copy, and I spend time there drawing them so I get it right. It's important to get it right because people want to take something home with them as a reminder of their time in Oxford, especially the Ashmolean.'

'I'm surprised you never fell into conversation with Mr Everett while you were making your drawings at the museum,' said Abigail.

'Why should I?' demanded Goddard. 'I'm not doing anything illegal. People are always there, drawing the stuff they've got on display. Some do it for their own pleasure, some, like me, for business.' He scowled at them. 'Anyway, what's it to do with you, me being there doing my drawings?'

'My name's Daniel Wilson and this is my colleague, Abigail Fenton,' Daniel said. 'We're private enquiry agents and we've been hired by the Ashmolean to look into the circumstances surrounding Mr Everett's recent tragic and untimely death.'

Goddard remained silent while he studied them, his face showing no emotion, then he said, 'He's dead, this bloke you're talking about?'

'Yes,' said Daniel. 'I'm surprised you weren't aware of it. It was widely reported in the newspapers.'

Goddard shook his head. 'I don't read the newspapers. I don't have time. I'm busy with my work.'

'So, you've never done any restoration work for the Ashmolean?' asked Abigail.

'No,' said Goddard. 'Like I said, I go there to select things I like and make sketches, then I come back here and turn them into copies of the originals. That's it. I've never met, nor heard of, this Everett bloke.'

As they left the shop, Daniel murmured, 'He's lying.'

'The trouble is, we can't prove it,' said Abigail.

'I think we may be able to,' said Daniel. 'Providing the Ashmolean keeps accurate financial records, which I'm sure it does.'

★　★　★

Vance de Witt's lawyer was a smooth, middle-aged man called Monicker Willikins. Pitt had heard the name before, though he'd never actually met the man. Willikins was a corpulent man, but his dandified taste in made-to-measure suiting made him appear comfortable, rather than constricted by his clothes. The image of the dandy was added to by the ornate diamond pin holding his cravat in place, and his diamond and gold cufflinks. He was a man with a reputation as a legal fixer. 'One of the sharpest minds ever to grace Oxford,' a solicitor had once commented about Willikins to Pitt. 'His clients always get off.'

Trust de Witt to employ someone like Willikins, thought Pitt ruefully. He'd allowed the lawyer and his client to have a private conference in the interview room, before returning to take his previous position in the chair opposite de Witt. Willikins had settled onto a chair next to his client and smiled at the inspector in a happy, almost dream-like way.

'You've had your conference?' asked Pitt.

'We have.' Willikins beamed. 'The story that Mr de Witt was told by Mr Everett was that Miss Lachelle and Mr Stevens had had a row. As a result, Miss Lachelle told him she was leaving Oxford and refused to tell him where she was going. She then left. Everett told Mr de Witt that Stevens had begged Everett to keep the situation secret because he did not want his mother to find out that he'd had a relationship with Miss Lachelle. Mr de Witt did not know that Mr Everett had collected Miss Lachelle's possessions from her lodgings the morning after she left.

'Mr de Witt did not see Miss Lachelle again and assumed she'd made good on her threat to leave Oxford. As it was a private matter, he felt he had no right to look further into the matter.'

'Miss Lachelle was one of his employees. Didn't he feel he had the right to an explanation from her as to why she was leaving his employment?' asked Pitt.

'It often happens that a waitress decides to suddenly leave with no explanation, even in the best establishments,' said Willikins. 'It wasn't unusual.'

'Did Mr de Witt ask Albert Preston to stop Miss Fenton asking questions about Eve Lachelle?' asked Pitt.

'No. If Mr Preston did such a thing, it could only be because Mr Stevens had asked him privately to stop people asking questions about why Miss Lachelle had left so abruptly. But, until we talk to Mr Preston, we won't know for sure if that's what happened, or if — as Mr de Witt suspects — this person who assaulted Miss Fenton is simply making this up in order to protect himself.'

⋆   ⋆   ⋆

It was nearly half past five when Daniel and Abigail arrived back at the Ashmolean, and they were relieved to find Gladstone Marriott still there.

'I'm glad we caught you before you left for the day, Mr Marriott,' said Daniel.

'You have news?' asked Marriott.

'Possibly,' replied Daniel. 'We think we've traced the man who made the copies of the ancient Egyptian plates. His name's Josiah Goddard and he has a shop in north Oxford.'

'He has a shop window full of such copies,' added Abigail.

'Unfortunately, he claimed not to have known Gavin Everett, or done any restoration or copying business for the Ashmolean.'

'But you don't believe him?'

'No, we don't,' said Daniel. 'I'm assuming that you keep records of money paid out to people like restorers?'

'Yes, of course,' said Marriott. 'Although I must admit, the name of Josiah Goddard is unfamiliar to me.'

'We are assuming that Mr Everett took charge of commissioning the restoration once he began work here.'

'Only after the first six months. As I mentioned to you, Miss Fenton, I'd always found Ephraim Wardle to be excellent, and I'd assumed that Everett had continued to employ him.'

'Hopefully, that's what we'll find out from looking at the payment ledgers,' said Daniel.

'They're kept in Everett's office,' said Marriott. He got up from his chair. 'I'll show you where you can find them.'

A short while later the three of them were studying the open pages of the ledgers in Everett's office.

'There,' said Daniel, pointing at one of the entries. 'Eighteen months ago: Ephraim Wardle, restorer. The sum of two pounds fifteen shillings. And here's another for one pound eighteen shillings. And suddenly, a year ago, we have entries for Josiah Goddard, restorer, and the name of Ephraim Wardle disappears completely.'

'So now we have the proof that Goddard lied.' Abigail smiled. 'He was definitely tied up with Everett.'

'But copying itself is not a criminal offence,' Marriott pointed out.

'No, but if we can prove Goddard knew *why* Everett wanted certain pieces copied, we'll be closer to getting to the bottom of it.'

'How will you do that?' asked Marriott.

'By talking to him,' said Daniel. 'Putting some pressure on.' He looked at the clock. 'It's too late to return to his shop today; he'll be closed up. So, we'll go and see him tomorrow. It will be interesting to hear what he says when we present him with this evidence and indicate we'll be passing this information on to the Oxford police.'

25

Daniel lay in the bed and watched as Abigail went to the door of the room, opened it and picked up the early edition of the newspaper she'd ordered the night before.

God, she is beautiful, he thought. *Beautiful, dynamic, intelligent. How on earth did I get this lucky to be with someone like her?*

Abigail walked back towards the bed, flicking through the pages until she found the story she was looking for. At first, she smiled, and then her smile was replaced by a look of fury.

Oh dear, thought Daniel. *Someone is going to be in serious trouble.*

'This story about the shooting yesterday! It's outrageous! Appalling!' stormed Abigail, throwing the offending newspaper down on the table.

'Have they spelt our names wrong?' Daniel smiled.

'It's not our names that are the problem, it's Esther's. Remember she gave her copy for us to read, and check that we approved it, and I told her it was an excellent piece of reporting. And here it is in today's *Oxford Messenger*, exactly as she wrote it . . .'

'And the problem with that *is?*' queried Daniel.

'That the name attached to the article is not Esther Maris, but a certain Henry Loveday.'

'Perhaps the editor suggested she use a man's

name,' suggested Daniel. 'There is a certain prejudice against women writers in some areas of society. Mary Anne Evans had to use the male pseudonym of George Eliot, as I recall.'

Abigail shook her head. 'Esther would never agree to that. She wants to make her name known in the world of journalism. *Her* name. As soon as we've had breakfast I shall go to the newspaper offices and ask her what has happened here. Will you come with me?'

'I'm sure you don't need me for that,' said Daniel. 'I think it more important I go and confront Goddard.'

'You don't think that Piers Stevens is our killer?'

'Possibly of Eve Lachelle, but not of Everett, not in view of the cold and accurate way that Everett was shot. And it's Everett's death we've been hired to investigate.'

'You think that Goddard shot him?'

'No, but I think he might hold the key to who did. And now we've got some leverage to use on him.'

$$\star \quad \star \quad \star$$

Inspector Grafton sat on a wooden bench in the Fellows' Garden of Exeter College alongside Professor Vorster. The garden, a place of beauty and tranquillity, hidden away from the bustle of the Broad, unsettled Grafton, who was more used to the dark alleyways and criminal-infested rookeries of London. The professor had led the way through a passageway from the front quadrangle to this private place bounded on one side by Convocation House and the Divinity School, and by the Bodleian Library on the other.

'I thought this would be a good place for us to talk,' he said. 'When I got your note asking to meet me, I was intrigued by the idea that a detective inspector from Scotland Yard thinks I may have information of some use.'

The professor was a man in his sixties, white-haired, round-shouldered, bearded, dressed in a suit of tweed that looked in need of pressing — either a bachelor, or with a careless house-keeper, Grafton mused. He'd decided on his course of action: to ask the professor directly about the politics of South Africa and see how he reacted — whether the questions worried or puzzled him, or would he become shifty?

'I'm from Special Branch,' said Grafton. 'Do you know what that is?'

'No,' said Vorster. 'I don't concern myself with police investigations.'

'It's about politics,' explained Grafton. 'Particularly terrorism directed against the British state.'

The professor looked puzzled.

'Are you sure you're talking to the right person?' he asked. 'I know nothing about terrorism of any sort, except that practised in Judea two thousand years ago. My speciality is the early Christian religion.'

'Yes, but I'm more interested in the attitude of the Boer Republics in South Africa towards the British territories there.'

Vorster looked even more puzzled. 'Why would you think I can make any useful comment on that?'

'You are a Boer from South Africa?' asked Grafton.

'I left South Africa forty years ago, to come and study here in Oxford. I have not been back since. And I have no interest in the political situation in South Africa.'

'Do you have any connections with other people from South Africa living here in England?' asked Grafton.

'No,' said Vorster.

'Do you know Lord Chessington?' asked Grafton.

'No,' said Vorster. 'Who is he?'

'He is a rich businessman who lives in Oxford and owns shares in gold mines in the Transvaal.'

'Then it is unlikely our paths will have crossed, despite us living in the same city. All my interactions are with fellow academics, most of them here at Exeter College, but occasionally with other like-minded individuals from other colleges. And, before you ask, none of them, to my knowledge, is from South Africa.' He studied the inspector for a moment, then asked, 'Do I take it from your questions you are under the impression that there is some sort of Boer revolution planned in British territories in South Africa?'

'We've had such information, sir, yes,' confirmed Grafton.

'Then I would suggest your information is wrong,' said Vorster.

'And what makes you able to say that with such confidence, might I ask?'

'Do you know much about the Boer traditions, Inspector?' asked Vorster.

'No,' admitted Grafton.

'The Boer, as you know, are Dutch who migrated to southern Africa in the seventeenth century as part of a programme of colonisation by the Dutch East India Company. The rule of these colonies by the Dutch East India Company was not benign. In fact, it has been described as despotic, the company's main interest being profit at the expense of the welfare of the colonists. It was a harsh rule: the company formed the local government, made the laws, and even told the farmers what crops they were to grow. The farmers were heavily taxed.

'In most circumstances this kind of despotic rule of colonials would lead to a revolutionary movement, as happened in America when the colonists rose up to overthrow the rule of the British. But that is not the Dutch way. When faced with a brutal government, the Dutch move on. It is the tradition of the trek. Do you know about the Great Trek?'

'No,' said Grafton again, wondering where all this was leading.

'The Great Trek is the story that all Boer children are brought up on. It happened between 1835 and the early 1840s, when some 14,000 Boers, including women and children, left the British rule of the Cape Colony and walked across the great plains beyond the Orange River, and then onward through Natal and Zoutpansberg into the northern part of the Transvaal, where they settled. But this was not the first trek. The Boers had begun trekking in search of independence from repressive governments, first that of the Dutch East India Company and then of the British rule in South Africa, since the early eighteenth century. They could do this because the Boer were basically a nomadic people. They did not cultivate the soil and grow crops. They raised cattle, a movable agricultural commodity. So, when local government rules became too harsh, they moved on. They trekked. Hence the name they were given: Trekboers.'

'But they did fight back,' said Grafton. 'The Boer War of 1880.'

'That was not a war,' said Vorster. 'It was a series of skirmishes. And it came about because of British greed. Wherever the Boer settled on a tract of land, the British would arrive and claim it for their government. They did this with the Transvaal in 1877. The thing about the Boers is that they may be always moving on, but they are not weak. On the contrary, their lifestyle has made them a hard people. And they resent it when grave injustices are heaped on them, especially unfair and often illegal taxes. This was what happened in 1880. A Boer living in the Transvaal refused to pay a tax that everyone agreed was illegally inflated. British government officials seized his wagon and tried to auction it off to pay the tax, but his fellow Boers turned up en masse, disrupted the auction and reclaimed the wagon. The government sent troops after them to try and take the wagon back, but the Boers resisted, and in December the Transvaal formally declared its independence from Britain.

'The thing the British had omitted to take into consideration was that the Boers, although having no regular army, as cattle farmers they'd spent most of their working lives in the saddle, and they were also skilled hunters with rifles. The British soldiers weren't trained to fight this way but to line up in ranks and fire volleys. British army garrisons all over the Transvaal became besieged.

'In all, this so-called 'war' lasted about ten weeks. At the end, in March 1881, the British government accepted defeat and signed a peace treaty giving the Transvaal self-government, but with an acceptance of the Queen as the Republic's nominal ruler.

'And that was it, Inspector. The British lost after bringing this war upon themselves. The Boers of the Transvaal had no desire to take over any further territories from Britain, as far as they were concerned the matter had been settled. And that is why your suggestion that the Boers are in some way planning an insurrection in South Africa to take over the British territories is ludicrous.'

★　★　★

Abigail marched into the reception area of the *Oxford Messenger* and demanded to see Esther Maris. The man at the reception desk was about to ask the purpose of her visit, but one

211

look at the obvious fury in Abigail's eyes and the steely set of her mouth, and he chose to avoid any sort of confrontation with this obviously formidable woman and sent a messenger through the doors with a note. A short while later Esther appeared, but a very different Esther from her usual bubbly, excitable persona. The young woman looked haggard, and Abigail could see from the red rims of her eyes that she'd been crying.

'Follow me,' Abigail ordered. 'It is my turn to buy us coffee.'

Abigail led the way to a coffee house nearby, where she ordered drinks for them both, then turned to Esther while they waited for them to be brought over and flourished the edition of the *Messenger* at the unhappy young woman.

'Who is this Henry Loveday?' she demanded.

'He's the *Messenger*'s crime reporter,' said Esther miserably.

'But this is your story,' said Abigail. 'It's word for word as you wrote it and gave it to me to read.'

'Yes, but Mr Pinker says the readers of the *Oxford Messenger* won't put up with a crime report by a woman. So, he took the piece away from me and gave it to Henry Loveday.'

'And what did this Henry Loveday actually do with it? Because it seems to me he hasn't altered any of your words.'

'He changed my name to his,' said Esther. She groaned. 'I thought this would be the start of a proper career for me as a journalist. As a crime reporter. But it's all gone now. I suppose I was fooling myself. It was just a silly dream.'

'No,' Abigail told her firmly. 'It's an ambition, and an ambition can be achieved.'

'But how? Mr Pinker threatened me with the sack for daring to write the story in the first place. He's told me to stick to writing about women's interests: furnishings, clothes, cookery.' She shook her head miserably. 'And if that's all the *Messenger* will let me do, there's no chance of my being able to write what I want for any of the bigger newspapers. The nationals.'

'Do you really want to do this?' asked Abigail.

'I do,' said Esther. 'More than anything.'

'Then let me have a word with Mr Pinker.'

'No!' exclaimed Esther, alarmed. 'That's the worst thing you can do for me! He'll sack me for certain!'

'I don't think so,' said Abigail. 'After all, I'm a world-famous archaeologist. You said so yourself in the article you wrote about me, so it must be true. And I don't think Mr Pinker will want to upset me by doing anything so bad as sacking you.'

★   ★   ★

Daniel stood outside Goddard's shop and looked at the handwritten sign stuck to the glass of the door: *Gone away. All enquiries at Madame Angel's next door.*

Daniel looked at Madame Angel's, the shop window filled with the same motley jumble of tarot cards, crystals balls, Ouija boards and other-worldly paraphernalia, and wished the sign

213

had directed him to the second-hand furniture shop on the other side.

He strode to Madame Angel's and pushed open the door. A large woman with a blaze of red and orange tints in her hair was sitting behind a counter, peering into a crystal ball.

'Good morning,' said Daniel. 'I wonder if — '

'No! Wait! Don't tell me!' said the woman, and she came from behind the counter and moved close to Daniel, looking intently at him.

This was a mistake, Daniel groaned inwardly. *I should have tried the furniture shop anyway.*

'Give me your hand,' ordered the woman.

'What?' said Daniel, bewildered, but before he could stop her the woman had grabbed his left hand and held it in both of hers.

'I see why you are here,' she intoned intently. 'You come to ask where Josiah Goddard has gone.'

Daniel stared at her, stunned, his mouth dropping open in amazement.

Madame Angel let go of his hand, and suddenly burst into laughter.

'Oh dear!' she chuckled. 'If you could see your face!' And she laughed again.

Daniel tried to regain his composure.

'Yes, but . . . ' he began.

'Nothing supernatural about it, dear.' The woman smiled at him. 'I saw you and a woman arrive here yesterday to call on Joe at his shop. And after you'd gone, he comes in here and says he's got to go away for a while, and for me to collect any post that comes for him, and he'll pick it up when he returns. And there's no

214

getting away from it, you look like a copper. You got that air about you. So, it didn't take much to add two and two and come up with the answer that Joe's done a runner because you're after him, and you want to know where he's gone. How am I doing? Think I'd make a good detective?'

'You'd make an excellent detective,' said Daniel admiringly.

'So, what's he done?' asked Madame Angel.

'We're not sure,' said Daniel. 'But we've got some questions to ask him. Do you know where he is?'

Madame Angel shook her head.

'My detecting powers don't stretch that far,' she said. She gestured at the wares on display. 'Course, I could try using a crystal ball, but it'll cost you, and I can't guarantee a result.'

'Do you know where Joe — Mr Goddard — lives?'

'I do, as it happens.' She stood beaming at him.

'Let me guess, I have to cross your palm with silver,' said Daniel.

'It's traditional,' said Madame Angel.

Daniel pulled a shilling from his pocket and handed it to her. She looked at it doubtfully, then shrugged. 'Well, it could be worse, I suppose. It could have been a sixpence.'

'Or I could have gone to make enquiries about him at Kemp Hall and saved myself any money at all,' said Daniel.

The woman shook her head as she pocketed the coin. 'No, you don't want to do that, dear, not unless you want the curse of darkness to follow you.'

'You do that as well, do you?' said Daniel. 'Put spells on people?'

'Seventh daughter of a seventh daughter,' said Madame Angel. 'You'd be surprised at the powers I can conjure up.'

'Let's just have his address,' said Daniel. 'And if I need any witchery to help me further, I'll be back.'

26

Abigail strode along the corridor to the door marked 'Editor'. She rapped upon it smartly and had opened it and stepped in before Pinker had the chance to call, 'Come in!' He looked enquiringly at her, wondering who this stranger was and how she'd managed to get to his office without prior arrangement.

'Mr Pinker, I'm Abigail Fenton.'

'Ah, Miss Fenton!' Pinker beamed, stepping forward and shaking her hand. 'It is a great pleasure to meet you! Your reputation as an archaeologist, of course, preceded your arrival in our wonderful city. I was delighted to read the piece that our Esther Maris wrote about you in the women's column. Did you see it?'

'I did, and I was very impressed by Miss Maris's work.'

'I'm delighted to hear you say that. We have high hopes for her.'

'In that case, why did you take the story about the shooting in Oxford away from her and give it to someone else? I have read Miss Maris's account, and also the account that appeared in your newspaper under the byline of one Henry Loveday, and I can see no difference in the wording. It seems to me that Mr Loveday took Miss Maris's copy and simply put his own name where hers should have been.'

Pinker gulped. 'Er . . . well, that's because

there is a procedure to these things. Mr Loveday is the acknowledged crime reporter for this newspaper . . . '

'By simply copying what other people write and adding his own name to their work? I believe that is called plagiarism and is a criminal offence.'

'No, no, madam! It is procedure! As I explained to Miss Maris, our readers expect stories about unsavoury things such as crimes to be written by a man.'

'What nonsense!' exploded Abigail. 'Have you ever read *Frankenstein*? The story of the creation of a murderous monster?'

'Of course,' said Pinker.

'And who wrote it?'

'Mary Shelley . . . '

'A woman! And I'm sure you're familiar with the works of the Brontë sisters, particularly *Wuthering Heights* which features a very brutal central character capable of terrible criminality.'

'Yes, but . . . '

'There are no 'buts' about this, Mr Pinker. Mr Wilson and I agreed to give the details of the shooting to Miss Maris because we have met her and trust her. We could have taken the story to one of the national newspapers, such as the *Daily Telegraph* or *The Times*, because Mr Wilson has a good rapport with the crime reporters on those papers due to his excellent reputation.'

'Yes, I am aware of his reputation — ' began Pinker.

Abigail held up a hand to silence him.

'Regardless of your 'procedure', the next time something happens on any case that we are involved in that takes place here in Oxford, we shall insist that the story is covered by Miss Maris, or we shall circumvent the *Oxford Messenger* and take our exclusive side of the story to one of the nationals.'

'But — ' began Pinker.

'I say again, there are no 'buts',' said Abigail firmly. 'The choice is yours. We believe we may be able to bring a very big case here in this city to a conclusion very shortly. We will give our account of it to Miss Maris if it is understood that the story that appears in your papers does so with her name attached, and as sole contributor to it. Otherwise we will take our story to the nationals and leave your Mr Loveday to pick up the crumbs from them.'

★ ★ ★

Inspector Grafton weighed up his options as he left Exeter College and headed back to his room at the Swan Inn. He was convinced that if Everett's death had been the result of a Boer conspiracy then Professor Vorster wasn't involved. His years of experience as a detective had given him 'the nose', the ability to sniff out guilt, and Vorster didn't have that taint. Grafton was sure Vorster was exactly what he appeared to be, an academic whose interests began and ended with his own particular strand of study. However, he'd been interested by what the professor had said about the Boers and their attitude towards politics and power. If he was correct — and Grafton felt he spoke with authenticity — then the politics of power could be ruled out. Which left the other alternative: riches. And in the case of South Africa that meant gold, and the one person he'd been told of in Oxford who fitted that bill was Lord Chessington.

It was time to take a close look at his lordship.

★   ★   ★

It was with a feeling of frustration that Daniel arrived back at their office at the Ashmolean. Abigail was sitting at the desk, looking — he thought — smug and pleased with herself.

'I gather from your expression that you had a successful chat with Esther,' he said. 'You made her feel better?'

Abigail smiled. 'Better than that. I had a successful chat with the editor of the *Oxford Messenger*, pointing out to him the error of his ways in taking the byline away from Esther and giving it to someone who had no involvement in the story.'

Daniel chuckled. 'I wish I'd been there. You giving a newspaper editor a ticking off would have made my day. I'd also have told him he was lucky you didn't beat him up.'

'I do not beat people up,' retorted Abigail primly.

'Yes, you do,' said Daniel. 'I've seen you beat up two men. In fact, I was wondering if you'd ever thought of taking up prizefighting as an extra career.'

'I assume from your expression when you came in that your trip to Goddard's shop was unsuccessful.'

Daniel sighed. 'Sadly, you're right. He's done a runner, and according to Madame Angel of the occult shop next door, there's no way of knowing for how long, or where he's gone. I did get his address from her, but his landlord said the same: Mr Goddard left abruptly after settling up his rent to date, leaving no forwarding address.'

'We seem to be causing a mass exodus from Oxford just by asking questions,' observed Abigail. 'Albert, the bar manager at the Quill Club. Piers Stevens. And now Josiah Goddard.'

'If Goddard is innocent as he claimed to be, why did he flee?' asked Daniel.

'Because he knows we'd have found out that he lied about not knowing Everett,' said Abigail.

'Obviously.' Daniel nodded. 'He knew we'd check up on that and return. But he still could have insisted that making the copies for Everett was all he did.'

'Unless he ran because he killed Everett,' suggested Abigail.

'What's his motive?'

'Thieves falling out. He felt he was being cheated by Everett over the amount he was getting for making the copies.'

'It still doesn't make sense to kill him. Goddard was making money from it. If he kills Everett, that source of income dries up.'

'Perhaps he threatened Everett with a gun, not

meaning to kill him, and the gun went off accidentally.'

'It's possible,' said Daniel, but his face showed his doubt.

'The question is, do we tell Inspector Pitt about Goddard?' asked Abigail.

'I don't know,' admitted Daniel. 'He's hard stretched as it is. He's got a hue and cry going for Piers Stevens, as well as trying to find Albert the bar manager. Not to mention any other cases he'll be working on, and from my experience when I was a detective, there'll be plenty of those. Plus, if we tell him about Goddard, we'll have to tell him about the fake artefacts here at the Ashmolean, and you were reluctant to let that information out, out of respect for Gladstone Marriott and the reputation of the museum.'

'Yes, true.' Abigail nodded. 'I agree, for the moment we'll keep it to ourselves while we try and track down Goddard. But if it turns out that he is the person who killed Everett . . . '

'In that case, we'll have to tell the inspector everything,' Daniel finished.

'So, what's our next move?' asked Abigail.

'I thought I'd tail Inspector Grafton,' said Daniel.

'You think that might lead anywhere?'

'Well, we've drawn a blank with our other options. Inspector Pitt is searching for Piers Stevens, we don't know where Josiah Goddard has vanished to, and until Esther actually does her interviews with the two women . . . ' He searched his memory for the names.

'The Duchess of Charlbury and Baroness Whichford,' Abigail reminded him.

'Yes. There's not a lot we can do until Esther reports back on which of those two is likely to be the mystery lady with the alleged Shakespeare play for sale. So, I thought I'd check out what Grafton has been up to. In case there is anything in the Boer connection he talked about.'

'You think that's a possibility?'

'To be honest, no. But I learnt from bitter experience during my years on the force not to dismiss things, however remote. You never know where things might lead. What about you?'

'I don't know,' said Abigail. 'I might go and see Esther again, chase her up about getting those interviews. And make sure her spirits are still positive.'

27

First Daniel checked that Inspector Grafton was still in his room at the Swan Inn by running his eye over the board where the room keys were kept and noting that the key to Grafton's room was not there. That done, he went back out into the street and moved to a position down the street from the hotel entrance and in the cover of a doorway. He had to wait over an hour before his quarry appeared from the hotel. Grafton didn't even bother to look around to check if he was being followed.

Daniel followed the Special Branch inspector along a few streets until they arrived in the very same expensive area where Piers Stevens lived, and where he'd shot at Daniel.

Was Grafton heading for Stevens' house? Daniel wondered. If so, why? As far as Daniel was aware, Stevens had no Boer connections, and the Boers seemed to be the main thrust of Grafton's investigation.

But instead of making for Stevens' house, Grafton headed for an imposing residence in its own grounds set apart from the other houses. Instead of going to the front door, the inspector moved into the shadows from a few trees whose branches hung over one of the walls surrounding the house.

So, he's watching the house, mused Daniel. *Why? Whose house is it? Is he waiting for a contact of his to come out?*

Daniel waited and watched from a corner. The inspector stood in the shadows, also waiting.

That's what we policemen spend so much of our time doing, reflected Daniel: *just waiting and watching and trying to be inconspicuous.*

The time passed, and Daniel wondered how long he'd have to be there, like the inspector, waiting and watching, but after about half an hour a woman appeared from a side entrance.

A servant, decided Daniel. A lady of the house would come out through the front door. The woman was middle-aged and carrying a large and empty basket. Doing errands, decided Daniel. Most likely shopping.

As Daniel watched, Grafton detached himself from his surveillance point and stepped into the path of the woman, causing her to halt. At the same time, Grafton reached into his pocket.

What's going on? wondered Daniel.

★ ★ ★

'One moment, if you please, madam,' said Grafton tersely. He produced his warrant card and showed it to her, saying 'Police. Scotland Yard.'

The woman stared at him.

'Scotland Yard!' she burst out, horrified.

'Ssh!' he said sharply. 'This is a delicate operation. I saw you come out of Lord Chessington's house. I assume you work there?'

'Yes, sir. I'm his housekeeper. Mrs Brent.'

'What I'm about to ask you concerns Lord

225

Chessington, but is not to be repeated to anyone, and that includes his lordship. If you do, you will be in breach of government secrets. Do I make myself clear?'

The poor woman began to tremble. 'I've not done anything, sir. I've always been law-abiding. I'm a poor widow woman who's just doing a job to earn a crust.'

'Yes,' said Grafton dismissively. 'You won't be in any trouble as long as you answer my questions honestly. Does Lord Chessington have anything to do with Boers?'

Mrs Brent looked at him, bewildered.

'Boars?' she repeated. 'Pigs?'

Grafton stared at her, equally bewildered, until the penny dropped.

'Not pigs,' he grunted, annoyed. 'Boers as in people from South Africa. We were at war with them, if you remember.'

Mrs Brent shook her head. 'Not me, sir. I've never been at war with anybody. My last husband was in the war with the French, but that was years ago.'

Patiently, Grafton said, 'Lord Chessington has business interests in South Africa, doesn't he.'

'I believe he has, sir, but he's never talked about them to me. I'm only the housekeeper.'

'Who does he talk about them to?'

'No one really, sir. I only know about them because I heard him mention something about his shares going down when he was reading the business papers.'

'Who was he talking to?'

'His butler, William. William's been with him

226

years. His lordship was upset about it. The shares, I mean. He said something about pulling out of . . . ' She frowned as she struggled to remember the right word. 'It sounded like Tenvale, or something. Tunvale?'

'The Transvaal?' prompted Grafton.

She nodded. 'Yes, that was it. But the next day he was much happier, his shares had gone up again.'

'Did he ever meet any South Africans?'

'I suppose he must have when he was in South Africa.'

'I mean since he's been back in England,' said Grafton impatiently.

'Oh, sir, he's been back in England for years.'

'And have any South Africans ever visited him at his house?'

'Not to my knowledge, sir. If they did, they didn't come while I was there.' She looked anxiously along the street and asked, 'Is that all, sir? Only I've got to get the things for his lordship's supper, and the butcher sells out of the best cuts very quickly.'

'Just one last question: where does Lord Chessington keep the documents to do with his business dealings? Does he have an office in Oxford?'

'No, sir, he doesn't need one. He does all his business from his home. He has his office at the back of the house, next to the conservatory.'

'Is it kept locked?'

'Oh yes, sir. He's the only one allowed in. None of us servants ever go in, except Millie the cleaning maid, and she can only go in when his lordship's there in the room.'

'Thank you, Mrs Brent. You've been very helpful. You may go now and get to the butcher's. But remember what I said, you're not to tell anyone about this conversation. Is that clear?'

★   ★   ★

Daniel watched the woman scurry away. He was tempted to go after her, ask her what Grafton had wanted with her, but the inspector had obviously terrified the poor woman and he didn't want to make her distress worse. Also, it was quite likely that Grafton had asked her to tell him if anyone questioned her about their meeting, threatening her with jail if she didn't. That was certainly Grafton's way: intimidation of those he thought he could bully. And Daniel didn't want Grafton alerted to the fact that he was following him.

He wondered whose house it was that Grafton had been watching, and out of which the woman had come. He strolled back to the house and stood admiring it. It was a large house, built in the Georgian style, with a well-stocked, colourful garden at the side. A series of short steps led up from the pavement to the black wood front door adorned with brass furnishings in the form of a knocker, letter box and door handle, with a brass bell pull set at one side in the brick doorpost. A fence of ornate metal railings ran the length of the property, and a high brick wall protected the back of the house from intruders.

As Daniel stood there, he saw a postman approaching, a bulging sack hanging from his shoulder.

'Excuse me,' he said. 'I was just admiring that magnificent house there and wondered to whom it belonged.'

'That house?' said the postman. 'Why, that's Lord Chessington's. One of the richest men in Oxford.' He scowled. 'It's only the rich what can afford a place as plush as that.'

With that, he moved on.

Lord Chessington, thought Daniel. The name that Esther had mentioned to them when she reported Grafton's conversation with the editor of the *Oxford Messenger*. So, Lord Chessington was Grafton's quarry.

28

Ever since she'd discovered that one fake exhibit among the ancient Egyptian artefacts in the glass display case, Abigail had taken every opportunity to carry on examining the other items on display, when she wasn't involved in directly investigating the death of Gavin Everett. Her immediate examination of the other artefacts had exposed three other fakes, one Egyptian and two ancient Greek. All four of the fakes had been decorated plates. Without examining every item in the museum in minute detail, she had to admit to herself that she couldn't be sure there were no others. She'd discounted the Native American costumes on display; the work in them was so intricate it would have cost more than the originals were worth to make copies of them. Similarly with most of the sculptures, although it was possible that wax impressions of some of the small metal pieces could have been made and copies cast in the moulds. But, again, Abigail felt that was unlikely; the cost of a smelting process and the artistry and skill needed to make a perfect copy would be expensive. As far as she could tell, Everett's scheme had been to make copies as cheaply as possible.

She paused before a display case in the Greek Room and reflected that this particular item was absolutely not a copy. It was the Parian Chronicle, also known as the Parian Marble.

Discovered on the island of Paros and bought by an agent of the Earl of Arundel in the seventeenth century, and later presented to Oxford University, the marble tablet chronicled events in ancient Greece from 1582BC to 299BC. Here were entries for events that were legendary — the Trojan War, the Voyage of the Argonauts — often considered to be myths but inscribed in detail here as historical facts. As always, when gazing upon a direct and tangible link with the ancient world, Abigail was filled with a sense of awe and wonder.

'The Parian Marble,' said a voice close by her, reading the identifying label. It was Esther. 'It's not very easy to read the inscription on it, is it,' she added.

'It needs work to do it, but it can be done. In fact, it was done by John Selden, who deciphered it quite brilliantly soon after it came to London.' She gave a smile of delight. 'Wonderful, isn't it!'

'Yes, I suppose so,' said Esther, but without the same enthusiasm. Then her tone brightened in expectation as she said, 'I got your note asking me to call. Has anything happened?'

'No, just that I thought it better if we met here rather than me come to the *Messenger* office,' said Abigail. 'Especially in view of the conversation I had with your Mr Pinker.'

'Yes, that was strange,' said Esther. 'Whatever you said must have done something to him, because he was nice to me.'

'That's good,' said Abigail.

'But it was strange,' said Esther, puzzled. 'He's not usually kind to me. I get the impression he thinks I'm an encumbrance.'

'Take the opportunity while it's there,' Abigail advised her. 'While he's being kind and considerate, now's the time to press for one of your news stories to get into the paper, and under your own name.'

'I'm still not sure if he'll agree,' said Esther doubtfully.

'Oh, I think he might,' said Abigail. She looked around to check that there was no one else within earshot, then lowered her voice to say, 'Although the thing I wanted to ask was how the interviews with the Duchess of Charlbury and Baroness Whichford are going.'

'Actually, I'm seeing the duchess today.' Esther beamed. 'So, I was going to come to see you anyway to ask what sort of things you think I should question her about.'

'The same sort of things you asked me,' said Abigail.

'Yes, but this is different,' said Esther. 'We're trying to find out if she's the one selling the Shakespeare play. So, should I mention something about it?'

'I don't think that's a good idea,' said Abigail. 'At least, not directly. If she is the one selling it, it'll make her suspicious.'

'But if she starts acting suspiciously that will mean she's the one,' said Esther.

'Not necessarily,' said Abigail. 'There's lots of reasons why people act suspiciously. Perhaps you can mention how long her husband's family have been in the area, and the famous people they must have known in the past.'

'Like Shakespeare!'

'Yes, but it would be too obvious to say his name. Perhaps mention other famous playwrights of the time.'

'I don't know any others,' said Esther.

'Christopher Marlowe,' said Abigail.

'Oh yes, I've heard of him,' said Esther. '*Doctor Faustus*.'

'*Doctor Faustus?*' said Daniel, suddenly joining them. 'This sounds like a very literary conversation.'

Abigail shot a look of censure at Esther. 'We were talking too loudly,' she said. 'We'll make sure we hold these conversations in the office in future.'

'All I heard was talk about Christopher Marlowe and *Doctor Faustus*,' said Daniel.

'Yes, but someone else might have heard the earlier part of our conversation,' said Abigail, concerned.

'There was no one else but you two here in this room when I arrived,' Daniel reassured her. 'But if there's anything we three need to discuss . . .'

'Not really,' said Esther. She smiled. 'I'm just off to do my interview with the Duchess of Charlbury.'

'Of which there's no more to be said until you return,' said Abigail firmly.

'Of course.' Esther beamed. 'I'll see you later.'

After she'd gone, Abigail let out a rueful groan. 'I'm such an idiot. I should have insisted that we didn't talk about anything until we'd got to the office.'

'That's no guarantee of anything,' Daniel pointed out as he led the way towards the stairs. 'Remember, Esther picked up much of her information by listening at doors.'

Neither spoke until they were back in the office and the door was firmly shut.

'I think Inspector Grafton is planning another burglary,' said Daniel. 'This time at Lord Chessington's house.'

'The man that Esther mentioned to us?'

'That's him. Grafton was definitely checking the house out and questioning one of his servants.'

'So, what should we do?'

'We do nothing,' said Daniel. 'I intend to follow him this evening and if he does break into the house, I'll catch him when he comes out and ask him what he's up to.'

'I doubt if he'll tell you.'

'I think he might. He won't like the idea that I'll have caught him in the act and I think he'll try and buy my silence. My price will be information.'

★ ★ ★

As the hansom cab drove down the long drive towards the huge mansion that was Charlbury Court, set in the vast estate of Charlbury Park, Esther was seized by a sudden moment of panic.

How does one address a duchess? 'Your Duchess'? 'My Lady'? Frantically, she racked her brain, and then remembered a book on etiquette she'd read some time ago. The first time you talk

234

to a senior member of the aristocracy you address them by their title, then thereafter as 'Your Grace'. So, it would be 'Duchess' to begin with, then 'Your Grace'.

Doing these interviews had seemed such a good idea at the time, but now the reality was here, Esther couldn't stop herself feeling nervous. Not about finding information for Abigail and Daniel, but about getting things wrong and upsetting Mr Pinker. Despite what Abigail said, Mr Pinker was already angry with her. If she upset the duchess it could mean the end of her prospective career as a journalist, certainly as far as the *Oxford Messenger* was concerned.

The hansom deposited Esther at the main entrance to the mansion, and as she stepped down from the cab Esther had qualms: should she have gone to the rear, the tradesmen's entrance? What was the protocol here?

A liveried footman came down the steps towards her.

'Good day,' said Esther. 'My name's Esther Maris from the *Oxford Messenger* and I'm here to meet the Duchess of Charlbury.'

'Yes,' said the footman. 'The duchess has just returned from her ride. If you'll wait here, I'll go to the stables and inform Her Grace you've arrived.'

He left her. Esther instructed the driver of the hansom to park his vehicle to the side of the house. 'I'll come and find you as soon as I've finished,' she added.

The cab driver jerked the reins, and the horse

trotted to the side of the large mansion.

Esther stood at the foot of the steps and waited. After about ten minutes, the footman reappeared. Behind him rode a stern-faced woman in riding gear, riding side-saddle on a dark brown horse. A young man in breeches and a waistcoat trotted beside the horse.

The woman pulled the horse to a halt beside Esther and slid down from the saddle.

'You may return him to the stable,' she ordered.

'Yes, Your Grace,' said the groom. He took the horse's reins and led him away.

The woman stood and studied Esther, and Esther was sure the look she gave her was one of disapproval. But not blatant disapproval, this woman was too reserved for that. She was in her forties, slim, dark-haired, and her expression suggested she was used to getting her own way.

'So, you're the person from the *Oxford Messenger*,' she said, unsmiling.

'Yes, Your Grace,' said Esther, and she bobbed in a curtsey. Even as she did it, she cursed herself: *Damn, I should have called her 'Duchess' at first.*

If the duchess was offended by the omission, she didn't show it. But then, her face showed nothing, except possibly distaste.

'Follow me,' she instructed. 'We'll go to the conservatory.'

So, I'm not to see inside the actual house, thought Esther as she followed the duchess along the house's frontage, then round a corner to where a large conservatory stretched along one wall. A footman was waiting by the door of the conservatory and he opened the door for them as they approached.

'Lemon with ice,' ordered the duchess curtly as they entered the conservatory.

The footman bowed and withdrew.

The duchess gestured for Esther to sit on a hard-backed wooden chair, then settled herself on a cushioned armchair close to it.

Just to let me know my place, thought Esther.

'Your editor wrote to my husband asking for this interview,' said the duchess. 'If it had been left to me, I'd have said no. I dislike the vogue for poking around in people's lives just because they are rich. It smacks to me of parasitism. But my husband insisted.'

'I'm very grateful to His Grace,' said Esther.

'What do you want to know?' demanded the duchess.

'First, let me assure you that I will let you examine what I write for your approval,' said Esther.

'My husband will read it,' said the duchess. 'I have no interest.' Then her attitude changed slightly as she said, 'Your editor's letter said this was to be a series. I assume you have other ladies of title to interview?'

'Yes, Your Grace,' said Esther.

'Who?'

'Baroness Whichford.'

'And others?'

'Not at this moment. My editor wants to see how the readers react to these first two interviews.'

'And have you already interviewed the baroness?'

'No, Your Grace. Yours is the first.'

This seemed to please the duchess, because Esther noticed a fleeting smile of satisfaction cross her face.

'As it should be,' said the duchess. 'My husband's family is the oldest in the county.'

'Yes. I believe the title comes from the fifteenth century.'

'My husband's ancestor received the title from Henry VII in appreciation of his military support which helped Henry gain the throne. It is said that without Charlbury, there would have been no Tudor monarchs.'

The footman reappeared, with two glasses filled with iced lemon water, which he placed on a small table between the two women. Esther took a notebook and pencil from her bag.

'With your permission, Your Grace, would it be alright if I kept notes? I want to make sure that what I write is accurate.'

'If you must, if your memory is at fault,' said the duchess dismissively. She sipped at her lemon as Esther opened her notebook, then asked, 'What exactly do you want to know?'

'About your life here at Charlbury Court,' said Esther. 'What your interests are.'

'I ride and I hunt,' said the duchess. 'If you expect me to wax lyrical about needlework or poetry, which I believe most titled ladies are expected to devour, you will be disappointed. I ride as well as my husband and pride myself on shooting better. But then, my father was Earl

Wenham, one of the best shots in England, and he trained me and my brother in firearms.' She smiled. 'I was better with both a pistol and a rifle than my brother, which delighted my father, but upset my brother's pride deeply.' She took another sip at her iced lemon, then said, 'I understand your uncle owns the *Oxford Messenger*.'

'Yes, that's right.'

'I assume that's why you were taken on. Money has its own power.'

There was no mistaking the sneer in the duchess's voice, but Esther forced herself to keep the smile on her face.

'I'm sure that had something to do with it at first, but I'm trying to prove my worth,' she said.

'Your name: Maris. Where does that come from? It's not English, is it?'

'I believe my family were originally from France.'

'Yes,' said the duchess, with a definite sneer of superiority this time. 'I believe a lot of Jews came over from France.'

29

Daniel was outside the Swan Inn as darkness began to fall. As before, he'd checked that Grafton's key was absent from its hook at the reception desk before he took up his watch point almost opposite the hotel entrance. Tonight, he was given cover by the large number of students who'd congregated in the area, indulging in childish games such as leapfrog and tag, many of them already seeming to be the worse for drink. *Another problem for the local constables*, reflected Daniel. Most of the students would be from wealthy, and certainly influential, homes and their families would object if their precious sons were arrested for unruly misbehaviour — 'high spirits', their families would call it — which meant that the constables would stay away and let them carry on with their anarchic actions.

Give me a decent criminal any day of the week rather than these overgrown and pampered children, thought Daniel.

Grafton appeared at half past ten. He didn't appear disturbed by the students who blocked the pavements; in fact, he just barged his way between them, sending some of them stumbling into the road. Daniel set off after him. He had considered waiting near to Lord Chessington's house, but — although he was sure that Grafton intended to burgle that house this evening — he didn't want to take the chance of being wrong and discovering later that Grafton had another target in mind.

His initial suspicion was right: Grafton led him to Chessington's house. Daniel found a hiding place beneath a tree where he could observe Grafton, as the Special Branch detective inspector made for the wall that surrounded the property. Grafton took a look around to make sure he wasn't being watched and failed to spot Daniel in his hiding place. The rest of the street was deserted. Grafton hauled himself to the top of the wall, then disappeared over it.

So, he's committed himself, mused Daniel. It was now just a matter of waiting for the inspector to reappear and then confronting him. Daniel smiled to himself as he pictured the look of consternation, then embarrassment, on Grafton's face when he stepped out from his watch place and greeted the inspector.

He wondered if he'd have a long wait. The general rule of burglary was not to stay in a property for too long as it increased the risk of discovery. But Grafton was not a burglar, just a Special Branch detective who employed the technique. If he was caught, Daniel was sure he'd bluster his way to freedom on presentation of his Special Branch warrant card.

Daniel had been in his hiding place for about fifteen minutes when he was startled to hear the sound of a gunshot from within the house. What on earth had happened? Had Grafton shot someone?

As he watched, the door of the house opened,

and the figure of Grafton staggered out, half fell, then pushed himself back upright again and began to stumble down the steps to the pavement, before falling and tumbling to the ground.

Daniel left his hiding place and ran towards the fallen detective, reaching Grafton just as the figure of a man appeared in the doorway, silhouetted in the light from inside the house. Daniel knelt down and checked Grafton's breathing, and was shocked to find none.

'There's his accomplice!' shouted the man in the doorway, and Daniel looked up to see the gun being swung up and aimed at him as the man yelled, 'Stay where you are!' This was followed by a cry of, 'Don't just stand there, get him!'

Daniel became aware that two men had rushed out of the doorway and were hurrying down the steps towards him. He got to his feet and began to say, 'I am . . . ', but one of the men swung a punch that smashed into the side of his head, sending him staggering, his head ringing. As he tried to right himself, he saw a poker in the other man's hand swinging towards him, and the next second it connected hard with his skull, and as his head exploded with pain, he felt himself falling, falling . . .

★   ★   ★

Slowly, Daniel came round. Through eyelids that flickered he saw that he was in a darkened room and he was lying down on something hard. His

242

head throbbed. He breathed in and picked up the smell of urine and damp. He pushed himself up, but as he did so the pain in his head exploded again and he fell back with a groan.

'Don't try and get up,' said a voice.

The voice was familiar, but not familiar enough to place at once.

'You got a really bad crack on the head. The doctor thinks you might even have a fracture of the skull.'

Inspector Pitt.

'Where am I?'

'Take a guess.'

Carefully, Daniel turned his head and looked around. It was a police cell, light filtering through the glass porthole in the metal door. Daniel was lying on a hard wooden bunk chained to the wall, with just a blanket beneath him. The inspector was sitting on the bunk at the other side of the cell, looking at him, and even in the dim light, Daniel could see the look of concern on Pitt's face.

Daniel put his hand gingerly to his head, and his fingers touched a thick bandage that completely encased his skull from his eyebrows upwards.

'What were you doing?' asked Pitt, and Daniel was aware of the tone of exasperation in his voice.

'I was following Grafton.' The image of the scene came into his mind: Grafton staggering down the stone steps and falling onto the pavement, and the man appearing in the doorway. He saw again the gun in the man's hand.

'He shot him,' he said. 'The man in the house shot Grafton.'

'Yes, he told us.'

'He told you?' repeated Daniel, puzzled.

'His name's Lord Chessington and he said he found a burglar in his house, going through his private papers. The man looked dangerous and seemed about to attack him, so Chessington took the pistol he always keeps for his protection and fired at the man, intending to wound him, he says. Apparently, Grafton made a run for it, at which point Chessington summoned two of his servants to help him.'

'Grafton came out of the house and then fell,' said Daniel. 'I went to help him, but I'm fairly sure he was dead. There was no sign of him breathing.'

'He was dead,' Pitt confirmed. 'According to Chessington, he saw you bending over him and assumed you were the burglar's accomplice, so he set his men on you.'

Slowly, Daniel pushed himself up to a sitting position. His head still throbbed, but the slowness of the action prevented the sharp and excruciating pain he'd suffered before.

'If you're involved, you must have told him who I was, that I was no burglar,' said Daniel. He waved his hand at the walls. 'So why am I in a police cell?'

'If I had my way, you'd be in a hospital, under observation,' said Pitt. 'But the decision to keep you under lock and key was made by powers far above us here in Oxford.'

'London?' asked Daniel.

Pitt nodded. 'We telegraphed the War Office once we realised that it was Grafton who'd been killed. We told them that you'd also been attacked. They telegraphed back almost immediately with orders that you were to be kept here, in a cell, and not be allowed to talk to anyone. They're sending someone down to question you. They should be here sometime tomorrow morning.'

'Does Abigail know?'

'No,' said Pitt. 'The orders were that no one's to know anything.'

Daniel looked at Pitt, a look of appeal on his face.

'Please, tell her something, just to let her know I'm alive,' he implored. 'You don't have to tell her the details, just that I'm safe, and I'll be in touch as soon as I can.'

Pitt hesitated, obviously torn between his orders and the heartfelt appeal from Daniel. Then he said, 'Alright. I'll go and see her at the Wilton.'

★   ★   ★

It was two o'clock in the morning as Inspector Pitt walked into the reception of the Wilton Hotel. The night receptionist on duty looked at him inquisitively.

'Yes, sir?' he asked. 'Can I help you?'

Pitt produced his warrant card and showed it.

'Police,' he said. 'I'm here to see one of your guests.'

'Which one?' asked the receptionist.

'For the moment, that's police business,' said Pitt. 'But your guest is expecting me.'

He made for the stairs to the first floor. It was a lie, Abigail Fenton wasn't expecting him, but he didn't want to get into a lengthy explanation with a receptionist.

He wondered how to approach this situation, how much to tell her. Officially, he shouldn't even be telling her that Daniel Wilson was in police custody. And there was a ban on imparting any information about the shooting of Inspector Grafton, or Lord Chessington's role. But he knew, from his brief acquaintance with her, that a simple statement that Daniel was physically alright wouldn't satisfy her. But how much to tell her without putting his own job at risk?

He arrived at the door of room 14 and knocked as quietly as he could, not wanting to disturb the neighbours and bring them into the corridor to see what was going on at this hour of the morning.

There was the sound of movement from inside the room, then the door opened and Abigail, wearing a dressing gown over her nightclothes, looked out, and immediately the look of relief that Pitt guessed was intended for Daniel vanished and was replaced by one of fear. Her hand went to her mouth and she gasped. 'Daniel?'

'He's alive,' said Pitt.

She stumbled back from the doorway as if she'd been struck, then she recovered herself and opened the door wider.

'Please, come in,' she said.

Pitt hesitated.

'I'm not sure if it's allowed,' he said. 'A man coming into a single woman's room at night . . .'

'Oh, for God's sake!' she burst out angrily. 'Something dreadful's happened to Daniel, and you're worried about decorum? If the hotel doesn't like it, they can turn me out. Anyway, you're a police officer, here doing your duty. Now come in!'

Awkwardly, Pitt entered the room, and Abigail shut the door and gestured to one of the armchairs.

'I know I'm going to need to sit down for this, and I'm guessing you'll need to as well,' she said.

Pitt sat down, while Abigail took the other chair.

'You say he's alive,' she said. 'But how badly is he hurt? Was he shot?'

'No, but another man with him was.'

'Inspector Grafton?'

Pitt frowned. 'You knew what Daniel was up to?'

'Of course! We're partners. We tell each other what we're doing. I've just been waiting here for him to return, unable to sleep because of the worry. I ask again, how badly is he hurt?'

'He was hit over the head with a metal poker. It's possible his skull may be fractured, but he's conscious and seems to be alright, except for a terrible headache. It was he who asked me to come and tell you about it.'

'Which hospital is he in?'

'He isn't,' said Pitt. 'He's in a cell at Kemp

Hall police station.'

Abigail stared at him. 'What? Why?'

'Miss Fenton — Abigail — I'm not supposed to be telling you anything at all!' said Pitt awkwardly. 'I'm defying orders from London, for which I could lose my job. But because Daniel asked me to let you know he was alive, and safe, and because I know and like him, I've come here to tell you that, so you wouldn't worry about him.'

'Of course I'm worried about him!' burst out Abigail angrily. Then she composed herself. 'You're right. I apologise, Inspector. You're putting yourself at risk by coming to tell me this, and I appreciate that. Please, tell me what you can.'

'You know he was following Grafton?'

'I do,' said Abigail. 'He believed that Grafton was going to burgle the home of Lord Chessington.' She looked at Pitt with a firm stare. 'As I know that Daniel doesn't carry a gun, I assume that either this Lord Chessington, or one of his people, shot Inspector Grafton.'

'You're very astute,' said Pitt. 'But officially I can't tell you.'

'If Daniel was hit over the head with a metal poker, Lord Chessington and his people must have seen Daniel watching the house after the shooting and erroneously assumed that Daniel was Grafton's accomplice.'

Pitt gave her a look of helplessness and said, 'But I haven't told you any of this.'

'Not a word,' said Abigail. 'Can I see him?'

'No,' said Pitt.

'Why not?'

'The same orders from London that instruct me not to say anything. He's being held for questioning.'

'Who in London has sent these orders? Special Branch?'

'I'm not allowed to say,' said Pitt. He hesitated, then said, 'You can ask me that again.'

'Special Branch?' Abigail asked again.

This time, Pitt silently shook his head, then rolled his eyes upwards.

'So, higher than Special Branch,' said Abigail.

'I've said nothing,' said Pitt.

'No, you haven't,' said Abigail. 'Tomorrow morning I'll call at Kemp Hall to report my partner as missing. It would be unusual if I didn't take such an action.'

'I understand.' Pitt nodded. 'No one will be able to give you any information about him. All I'll be able to do is take a note of your enquiry and promise to look into it.'

This time it was Abigail's turn to say, 'I understand.' She stood up and held out her hand. 'Thank you for making this visit, Inspector. And I apologise for giving you a hard time. But Daniel is very important to me.'

'Yes, I think I know that,' said Pitt, shaking her hand. 'I'll see you at Kemp Hall in the morning, where I will unfortunately have to send you away.'

'And I will go without a fuss,' Abigail assured him. 'What time will you be there? I assume, as you've been on duty until the small hours . . . '

'Ten o'clock,' said Pitt.

'I'll see you at ten,' said Abigail.

30

It was half past ten the next morning when Pitt arrived at Daniel's cell with a mug of tea.

'Here,' he said.

'Thanks,' said Daniel.

'How's your head?'

'It still hurts if I move it.'

'Once we get you out of here, we'll get a proper doctor to examine you.'

Daniel touched the bandage around his head. 'The one who did this wasn't a proper doctor?'

'A locum,' said Pitt. 'He was the best we could get at one o'clock in the morning. But he seemed to know what he was doing. And your interrogators have just arrived from London. Two of them.'

'Special Branch?'

'Somehow I think not. I get the impression they're a step up. Their ranks, for example. As well as their names. Commander Smith and Captain Jones.'

Daniel gave a wry smile. 'Not very imaginative. Mind, they could be their real names. And the ranks suggest either War Office or Secret Intelligence. Either way, it's the same thing. Are they in uniform?'

'No. Plain clothes. Dark suits. It looks like they go to the same tailor. And Miss Fenton has just been here. And, before you ask, yes, I did go to see her and told her where you were, and that you were alive, if not well.'

'You didn't tell her about the rest of it? The shooting of Grafton?'

'I didn't need to. She worked it out while I sat there silently listening to her tell me exactly what happened.'

'Yes, she's very clever. Is she still here, waiting in reception?'

'No, she agreed to leave.'

'How did you manage to persuade her to do that?'

'We had an agreement,' said Pitt. 'I told her my job was at stake if she caused a fuss.'

'She must think a lot of you,' said Daniel. 'That doesn't usually stop her.' He sipped at the tea. 'When do Commander Smith and Captain Jones see me?'

'As soon as you've finished your tea,' said Pitt. 'A word of warning: they don't look friendly.'

★ ★ ★

Esther stared at Abigail, her eyes and mouth wide open in shock.

'Inspector Grafton was shot?!' she said.

'Yes,' said Abigail.

They were sitting in the office at the Ashmolean. Esther had come in to report on her interview the previous afternoon with the Duchess of Charlbury, but instead had been informed by Abigail of the events of the previous night.

'And killed?!' exclaimed Esther.

'Yes,' said Abigail again, adding, 'But you can't

251

use this story. And that's not just you. No one at any newspaper is allowed to write about it.'

'Why?'

'Because it involves something secret to do with the government.'

'And Mr Wilson . . . ?'

'Is still being held at Kemp Hall police station.'

'They surely don't think he killed Inspector Grafton!'

'Inspector Pitt says some very important officials are coming down from London to question him about what happened.'

'What *did* happen?'

'Until I talk to Daniel, I won't know myself.'

'They won't let you talk to him?'

'No.'

'But isn't that against the law? I thought all people locked up could receive a visit from a friend or relative.'

'The people who have given these instructions about secrecy are the people who make the laws.'

'But — '

Abigail held up her hand. 'It's no use speculating, Esther. All I know for certain is that Inspector Grafton was shot and killed last night, and Daniel was assaulted and taken to the police station where he was locked up and has been ever since.'

'Was he hurt?'

'I understand he received a blow to the head.'

'Who shot Inspector Grafton?'

'Again, I'm not sure,' said Abigail. 'I have my

opinion, but I'm not prepared to speculate until we know for sure.'

'When will that be?'

'When Daniel is released.'

'When will that be?' she repeated.

'I don't know. In fact, there is a danger he may not be released. That all depends on these people from London.'

'Who are they?'

'I wasn't allowed to know. The main thing is, and I stress again, this is *not* a story for publication. Now, how did you get on with the duchess?'

'She was horrible!' said Esther. 'I hope it's her! She was sneery about everything. She's a dreadful woman.'

'Did she talk about the Shakespeare play?'

'No,' admitted Esther unhappily. 'I tried to lead the conversation around to writers and poets the duke's family might have known, but she's got no interest in anything literary. The only things she's interested in are hunting and shooting.'

'Was there any sign of the duke?'

'No. It seems he goes away for weeks at a time. Not that she seems bothered.' She gave a secretive smile. 'There was a handsome young stable groom she seemed fond of.'

'How could you tell?' asked Abigail, intrigued.

'It was nothing either of them said or did, it was just a feeling I got between them,' admitted Esther. 'But it may have been because I didn't like her and wanted to find some nasty secret about her.' She hesitated, then asked tentatively,

'What's our next move?'

'For you, I suggest you see if you can arrange your interview with Baroness Whichford. For me' — she sighed — 'I'm going to wait until Daniel's released, and then we'll see. We were going to start searching for a man called Josiah Goddard.'

'Josiah Goddard?' repeated Esther. 'The artist?'

'That might be a bit overstating it,' said Abigail, surprised at Esther recognising the name. 'He says he's a restorer.'

'Yes, that's him,' said Esther.

'You know him?' asked Abigail, intrigued.

'I know *of* him,' explained Esther. 'I did an article on his sister, Jenny, who does wonderful cross-stitch, and she told me she came from an artistic family and that her brother was an artist. She said his name was Josiah Goddard.'

'Where would we find this Jenny Goddard?' asked Abigail.

'Jenny Woodman,' said Esther. 'She's married to a farmer. They live just outside Oxford near a village called Stanton St John.'

★ ★ ★

Pitt escorted Daniel along a corridor to an interview room. He opened the door and gestured Daniel in. Two grim-faced men in identical dark suits sat side by side at a table. An open notebook was in front of the younger of the two. The older man, who Daniel guessed must be Commander Smith, gestured at the empty chair opposite them on the other side of the table.

'Sit,' he said.

Daniel sat. Pitt moved to stand at the wall.

'Thank you, Inspector. There's no need for you to stay,' said Smith. Pitt frowned.

'This is our police station,' he said. 'We are responsible for the people in our charge.'

'And your superintendent has seen our credentials,' said Smith curtly. 'If we need you, we'll call.'

Pitt hesitated, then nodded and left. The two men fixed their gaze on Daniel. The younger man, who Daniel guessed to be Captain Jones, took a pencil from his pocket and poised it over the open notebook in front of him.

'Your name is Daniel Wilson?' said Smith.

'It is,' confirmed Daniel.

'Until two years ago you were a detective inspector with the Metropolitan Police at Scotland Yard.'

'I was,' said Daniel.

'Why did you leave?'

'Is this relevant?' asked Daniel.

'Yes,' said Smith curtly, and looked at Daniel and waited.

'Possibly it was prompted by Inspector Abberline retiring to become a private enquiry agent. It made me think I could do the same.'

'Not because you have a problem with authority?'

I wonder who you've been talking to, thought Daniel. Aloud, he said, 'No.'

'But you do have a problem with authority,'

insisted Smith. 'Your superiors reported you for insubordination.'

'A few of my superiors may have done, but Inspector Abberline never did, as far as I know,' Daniel countered.

'Do you agree that you were insubordinate to some of your superiors?' Smith pressed.

'In their opinion,' said Daniel. 'I do not agree I was being insubordinate. Sometimes I questioned a decision if I felt it was the wrong one. But I always carried out orders.'

'In many cases with reluctance and doing your best to continue on your own path,' said Smith.

'Is there a point to this line of questioning?' asked Daniel. 'I thought we were here to discuss what happened to Inspector Grafton.'

Smith and Jones exchanged the briefest of looks, then Smith said, 'We are just trying to establish how strong your anti-establishment feelings are.'

'I have no anti-establishment feelings,' said Daniel.

'Your record indicates the opposite.'

'Any such comments on my record were written by some people who didn't like me and the fact that sometimes I questioned a decision.'

At this, Jones made a note in his notebook.

'How well did you know Lord Chessington?' asked Smith.

'Not at all,' replied Daniel. 'I'd never met nor seen the man before last night. And even last night I only saw him in silhouette and I had no idea who he was.'

'What were you doing with Inspector Grafton going to Lord Chessington's house last night?'

'I didn't go with Inspector Grafton to his house.'

'Then why were you there?'

'I followed the inspector.'

'Why?'

'Because I was curious to find out what he was up to. I'm sure you're aware that I've been hired by the Ashmolean Museum to look into the death of Mr Gavin Everett. Apparently, Inspector Grafton was here on the same mission. To that end, he had burgled my hotel room, and also Mr Everett's lodgings, in his search for information. I was curious to see who he would burgle next.'

'Had you heard the name Lord Chessington before last night?' asked Jones, speaking for the first time.

Daniel paused. This was the crunch. If he said no, he was sure they would then question Abigail, and he didn't want her falling into their clutches. But if he said yes, then he'd have to do it without naming Esther Maris and putting her at risk.

'Well?' pressed Smith.

'Yes,' said Daniel. 'I'd heard the name just a few days before.'

'How?' asked Smith. 'In what context?'

'I went to the offices of the *Oxford Messenger* to try and see if I could find out any information on Everett, and I happened to see Inspector Grafton going into the editor's office. So, I eavesdropped.'

'Not a very gentlemanly thing to do,' said Jones.

'It's one of the things detectives do to gather information,' said Daniel. 'I understand that Special Branch are very good at it. As are the Secret Service.'

This brought a scowl from Smith, who snapped, 'What did you hear?'

Daniel cast his mind back to Esther reporting the conversation between Grafton and Mr Pinker that she'd overheard. 'Inspector Grafton asked Mr Pinker, that's the editor of the *Messenger*, about possible Boer sympathisers in the Oxford area. Mr Pinker said he knew of no such people. When Inspector Grafton pressed him for the names of local people with connections to South Africa, including the Boer colonies of the Transvaal and the Orange Free State, Mr Pinker told him that Lord Chessington had business interests in the Transvaal and was a major partner in some gold mines there with some Transvaal businessmen.'

Smith and Jones waited for more. When none was forthcoming, Smith demanded, 'And?'

'And, nothing.' Daniel shrugged. 'That was the extent of their conversation. Then Grafton left the editor's office.'

'Did Grafton see you?'

'No,' said Daniel. 'When I heard the door opening, I took evasive action.' He looked at them both and added, 'You can check with Mr Pinker at the *Oxford Messenger* about what was said.'

'Did you see Inspector Grafton shot?' asked Jones.

'No,' said Daniel. 'I was waiting outside the house for him to reappear.'

'Why?'

'I'd decided to ask him what he was up to. I was of the opinion that we could both benefit if we shared information.'

'Had you suggested that to the inspector before?'

Daniel gave a wry smile. 'The inspector had made it perfectly clear that he had no interest in working with me. He'd also tried to have me stopped from investigating Everett's death. My hope was that when he discovered that I was aware of his activities, he might decide it would be beneficial for us to pool our resources.'

'Go back to his being shot,' said Smith. 'You said you didn't see it.'

'No,' said Daniel. 'I heard a gunshot from inside the house. Then the door opened, and Inspector Grafton came out. He seemed to be in distress. He stumbled, and then fell down the stone steps at the front of the house and landed on the pavement. I ran to him to see if I could help him.'

'Was he conscious?'

'No. I checked his breathing and realised that he was dead. He'd just made it out of the house before dying.'

'So, he didn't say anything?'

'No,' said Daniel. 'Not a word.'

'And then?'

'Then this man appeared in the doorway. He was holding a gun. He called these two other men from inside the house and shouted, 'There's his accomplice!', pointing at me. I rose to my feet and started to explain who I was, but before I was able to say anything, the two men attacked me and knocked me unconscious. The next thing I remember is waking up here in a police cell.'

Smith and Jones studied Daniel in silence for a few moments, then Smith asked, 'Have your investigations into Mr Everett's death suggested any motive for it?'

'So, we are ruling out suicide?' said Daniel with an amused smile. Neither of the men smiled back at him. 'One or two possibilities have arisen,' Daniel continued. 'One is that Everett was involved in the faking of ancient artefacts and selling the originals to private collectors. This may have resulted in anger from the other criminals he was involved with doing this. Another is that he was blackmailing a certain man over an alleged rape.'

'Who is this man?'

'His name's Piers Stevens. He's currently being hunted on a charge of attempted murder after he took a shot at me when I confronted him. Inspector Pitt has the details.'

'At any time during your investigations, did the suggestion arise that South Africans could be involved in his death? Particularly Boers?'

'Only from Inspector Grafton.'

'But nothing you have discovered, apart from that?'

'No,' said Daniel.

'What was your opinion of Mr Everett?'

'I never met him,' replied Daniel. 'But, from what I've discovered about him, I'd say he was a crook. A forger, a blackmailer, a confidence trickster. By all accounts charming, but completely corrupt and absolutely not to be trusted.'

The two men fell silent as Jones once again wrote something in his notebook.

'Is that it?' asked Daniel. 'Are we finished? If I'm not to be charged with anything, can I go?'

'One last thing,' said Smith. 'At no time during this exchange have you made any mention of Miss Abigail Fenton. Why?'

Immediately, Daniel was alert, concerned about where this was leading.

'You never asked me any questions in which she figured,' he said.

'We understand she is your partner in this investigation. And she also partnered you in previous investigations.'

'Yes,' said Daniel. 'Where it needed someone with historical expertise. She has a first class degree in history from Girton College in Cambridge and is a well-known and highly respected archaeologist with an international reputation.'

'What has been her role in this investigation?'

'She uncovered the fact that Everett was having copies made of certain ancient artefacts, so he could sell the originals.'

'Did she have any contact with Inspector Grafton?' asked Jones.

'No,' said Daniel. 'Absolutely none.'

31

Abigail sat at the desk in the office at the Ashmolean, moving pieces of paper around, then moving them again to a different place, just to keep herself busy. Where was Daniel? How was he? Inspector Pitt had asked her not to go to the Kemp Hall police station, telling her that he'd be in touch to let her know what was going on if Daniel himself didn't appear at the museum. She looked at the clock. Three o'clock and there'd been no sign of either Daniel or Inspector Pitt. After what Esther had told her about Josiah Goddard's sister, she'd been bursting to find out more about the farm where Jenny Woodman and her husband lived, how far it was from the city, and how best to approach the Woodmans without causing Josiah Goddard to flee, if he was — as she was sure — hiding out there, but she hadn't left the office for fear of Daniel arriving and her not being there to meet him.

She'd felt that going to Kemp Hall to inform Inspector Pitt about Jenny Woodman was valid, but she knew she'd only really be going because she was worried about Daniel. She knew she needed to tell Daniel about the Woodmans first. But where was he? Why hadn't he been released? The horrible thought struck her that these people from Special Branch, or the War Office, or wherever they were from, might be taking Daniel back to London for further questioning.

What would she do then? What could she do?

'I'm glad you're still here,' said a voice from the doorway.

Daniel!

Abigail pushed herself out of the chair and flew at him, wrapping her arms around him in a tight hug and kissing him hard on the mouth. He kissed her back and smiled.

'You missed me then?' he said.

'When did they let you go?' she asked.

'About an hour ago.'

'An hour ago!' she exploded, furious. 'I have been sitting here, worrying myself to death over you — '

'That was the Secret War Office people, or whoever they were,' said Daniel. 'Inspector Pitt then brought in another doctor to examine my head before he let me go.'

'And?'

'No fracture. But he's told me to be careful. So be gentle with me. No hitting me around the head.'

'I've never hit you around the head,' said Abigail indignantly.

'No, but I thought I'd mention it just in case you were thinking of doing it.'

She hugged him tightly again. 'Oh, my love. You could have been killed!'

'Twice,' he reminded her. 'There was also Piers Stevens and his gun. And you might have been killed when that thug set on you. I never thought of Oxford as being such a dangerous place. Have you told Gladstone Marriott what's happened?'

263

'No, because Inspector Pitt said he wasn't allowed to tell me anything.'

'He told me you'd worked out what had happened. Grafton being shot. Me being attacked, and then arrested.'

'Yes, but I didn't know officially.'

'So you've kept it to yourself.'

Abigail hesitated, then admitted, 'Not completely.'

'Oh?'

'Esther was here.'

'Esther!' burst out Daniel. 'You told a reporter!'

'I did not,' insisted Abigail. 'I told her I'd heard something, all unconfirmed, but I swore her to secrecy.'

'And you think she'll keep to it?'

'Yes, I do. And, more importantly, she gave us a lead on Josiah Goddard. It seems he's got a sister called Jenny Woodman and she's married to a farmer, and their farm is just outside Oxford. It's just a guess, but I think he might have gone there.'

'Yes, you could be right,' said Daniel. 'We need to take this to Inspector Pitt. We'll need help in bringing Goddard in if he's there, especially if his brother-in-law comes to his aid.'

A thought struck Abigail, and she asked, 'Was it Lord Chessington who killed Inspector Grafton?'

'Yes,' said Daniel.

'Has he been arrested?'

'No,' said Daniel. 'According to Inspector Pitt, his lordship found Grafton in his study, apparently burglarising it. Chessington had heard noises in the room and brought a gun with him. He has a fear of burglars. According to Chessington, the burglar — Grafton — was acting in an aggressive manner and reached into his pocket, and Chessington thought he was going to produce a weapon. At that point, Chessington says, he shot at Grafton to wound him. It was a single-shot pistol, hence he only fired once. He said Grafton pushed past him and ran for the front door. The police have agreed that Chessington acted in self-defence, so he won't be charged.'

'It might have been a different situation if he'd just been an ordinary householder,' commented Abigail.

'True,' agreed Daniel. 'But then, being a lord has major advantages.'

'You can get away with shooting burglars, for one,' said Abigail.

'You can get away with a lot more than that, as I learnt during my time at Scotland Yard,' said Daniel ruefully. 'Now, we ought to go and see Marriott and bring him up to date, before we go and tell Inspector Pitt about Goddard's possible hideaway.'

★   ★   ★

They found Gladstone Marriott in his office, studying a letter with a perplexed expression on his face. The puzzled expression remained as they entered.

'I'm glad you're here,' he said. 'I was just

about to bring this to you.' He held out a sealed envelope to Daniel. It was addressed to 'Daniel Wilson Esquire'.

'It was in a note I received from Lord Chessington literally a moment ago, delivered by messenger, asking me to pass it on to you.' He looked again at the letter in his hand. 'His note to me says, 'Please pass the enclosed to Mr Wilson. I wish to make amends for his dreadful suffering last night.'' He looked at Daniel, still puzzled. 'What dreadful suffering?'

Daniel explained, relating the story of the previous night. As he did so, Marriott's expression became more and more horrified.

'Lord Chessington shot and killed Inspector Grafton?!' he said, shocked.

'Yes, but that's not to be passed on,' said Daniel.

'I wasn't able to come and tell you earlier, Mr Marriott, because the police had ordered me not to tell anyone,' said Abigail.

Marriott stared at them both, as if he couldn't comprehend what he was hearing.

'And you were kept in the police station all night and interrogated by these people from London?' he said to Daniel.

'Yes,' said Daniel. 'It was only after they were satisfied I had nothing to do with Grafton's death that they let me go. And that was just an hour ago.'

'And Lord Chessington?' asked Marriott.

'He's not to be charged with anything,' said Daniel. 'It's seen as he acted in self-defence.'

Marriott shook his head in bewilderment.

'I never thought such a thing would ever happen in Oxford,' he said. 'I'm so sorry for the suffering you endured.'

'I'm afraid that sometimes goes with the job,' said Daniel. 'Sadly, Inspector Grafton had the worst of it.'

'So, do you think his idea that Everett's death was the work of the Boers . . . ?'

Daniel shook his head. 'I don't think so. Everything we've uncovered points to it being connected to the waitress from the Quill Club who went missing, possibly murdered; or to the fraudulent ancient Egyptian plates Everett switched for the real ones, or the business of the possible Shakespeare play.'

Marriott let out a groan.

'I really didn't think it would turn out to be as bad as this,' he said.

'Let's see what Lord Chessington is writing to me about,' said Daniel as he opened the envelope and took out a single sheet of paper. He read the few brief lines, then handed the letter to Abigail to read, and she in turn passed it on to Marriott for his perusal.

'He's invited you both to afternoon tea,' said Marriott. 'Today.'

'It's a bit late for tea,' said Abigail, looking at the clock.

'Any time is the right time for tea,' said Marriott. 'Especially in his lordship's world.'

'It will be interesting to hear what he has to say,' said Daniel. 'Especially on why he really shot Grafton.'

'You don't think the story of him thinking he

was a burglar rings true?' asked Abigail.

'It still seems a bit of an extreme action to take,' mused Daniel.

'You said that Lord Chessington claimed he only intended to wound him,' Abigail reminded him.

'True, but I would expect his lordship to be a better shot. An arm or a leg is for wounding. Grafton was shot in the chest.' He put the note back in the envelope and tucked it into his pocket.

'It's interesting that he's invited both of you,' observed Marriott. 'Considering only Mr Wilson was involved in the events of last night.'

'It suggests Lord Chessington has been making enquiries,' mused Daniel.

'Not to me,' said Marriott.

There was a tap at the door and the figure of Hugh Thomas appeared. He stopped when he saw Daniel and Abigail.

'My apologies,' he said. 'I came to see Mr Marriott and I didn't realise he was occupied. I'll come back later.'

'No, don't go on our account, Mr Thomas,' said Daniel. 'In fact, you're the very person we need at the moment.'

'I am?' said Thomas, puzzled.

'Along with Mr Marriott. Did either of you ever meet a man called Josiah Goddard? He took over the restoration work for the Ashmolean after Ephraim Wardle.'

Marriott frowned. 'No, I can't say that I did. And the name's unfamiliar. Restoration work, you say?'

268

'Yes.'

'Josiah Goddard,' said Thomas. 'Yes. I did meet him.' They looked at him and he enlarged. 'I came into Mr Everett's office for something, and a gentleman was in here with him. 'Mr Thomas, this is Josiah Goddard,' said Everett. 'He's going to be doing some restoration work for us, so if you see him studying any of the exhibits and making drawings of them, that's with my permission.' I remember being surprised that Ephraim Wardle was being replaced, because he'd always done an excellent job, but I thought that Mr Everett must've known what he was doing.'

'Did you see Goddard again at the Ashmolean after that?' asked Daniel.

'Indeed, sir. Just as Mr Everett said, he was in here a few times making sketches.' He frowned, thoughtfully, then added, 'In fact, he was here the day Mr Everett died.'

Daniel and Abigail exchanged looks of startled surprise.

'Here? In the museum?' asked Abigail.

'No, in the street outside the main entrance. It was just after we'd officially closed. As I left, I saw Mr Goddard outside by the main entrance, as if he was waiting for someone.'

'What time was this?'

'Half past five, the time I always leave.'

'Did you tell Inspector Pitt this?' asked Daniel.

'No, sir,' said Thomas. 'There didn't seem any need. He was just a person outside in the street. There were quite a few people outside in the street that day. It's leaving time, after all.'

32

As Daniel and Abigail walked back to their office, Daniel said, 'This latest information from Mr Thomas definitely points the finger of suspicion at Goddard.'

'Shall we go and tell Inspector Pitt what we've learnt and get the farm raided?'

'Later,' said Daniel. 'If he's there, that's where he'll stay for a while because he knows he's safe. First, we have this invitation to tea from Lord Chessington to attend to. Personally, I feel there are still some questions hanging over his lordship's role in this matter.'

★ ★ ★

The last time I was here, I saw a man die, and I was beaten unconscious, thought Daniel as he and Abigail mounted the steps to Lord Chessington's front door. Their tug at the bell pull was answered by a man in a butler's uniform opening the door.

'Good afternoon,' said Daniel. 'Daniel Wilson and Abigail Fenton for Lord Chessington.'

'Yes, sir. His lordship is expecting you. If you'll follow me.'

He led the way along a passageway, and a man appeared from one of the rooms. He was in his fifties, stout and balding, and formally dressed in striped trousers and a morning jacket over a starched white shirt, enlivened by a red and blue cravat. He smiled as he saw them.

'Ah, my guests!' he said, holding out his hand and shaking theirs. 'I thought I heard voices.' He turned to the butler. 'William, tell Mrs Brent we'll take tea in the conservatory.'

'Yes, m'lord.'

William departed, and Daniel and Abigail followed Lord Chessington along the passage and then through a door into a large conservatory where different varieties of roses were growing in colourful profusion. Chessington took a deep breath as he gestured them to comfortable armchairs.

'I love the scent of roses,' he said. 'So heady!'

As they all seated themselves, Chessington said apologetically, 'Originally I had only intended to invite Mr Wilson in an attempt to make amends for the dreadful suffering he experienced at the hands of my people, but when I learnt that he was here in partnership with you, Miss Fenton, I couldn't resist the temerity to invite you as well. I have long been an admirer of your archaeological work, especially your explorations at Giza.'

'My work at Giza was simply following in the footsteps of others: de Maillet, Greaves, Pococke and Norden, and especially Nathaniel Davison, who was the first to enter the chambers above the King's chamber in Khufu's pyramid.'

'Yes, but you were *there*!' enthused Chessington. 'Inside those pyramids! Uncovering antiquities that had lain undiscovered for thousands of years!'

He sat back, shaking his head in open admiration. 'How I envy you, Miss Fenton! To have actually touched the final resting places of the gods.'

'In their view, and that of their people, they were gods, but our excavations showed their very human aspect.'

'In what way?'

'Well, for example, at Meidum, in the chapels of Nefermaat's mastaba, the figures of the people represented were cut deeply into the stone, and these deep cuts filled with coloured paste. Previously, the colouring had been done on the surface, but it's as if Sneferu was aware that time would make these images vanish. By etching them into the stone he made sure the images lasted. As a god, he wouldn't have needed to take this step because he would have felt assured that they would be there for all eternity. As a *human* king, he needed to make sure the images would last.'

'Fascinating, and truly wonderful!' said Chessington. 'And to hear these names spoken by someone who has been where these kings and their families actually were: Sneferu! Nefermaat! Khufu!'

Suddenly he looked apologetically at Daniel.

'Mr Wilson, my apologies. I was lost in listening to Miss Fenton and had almost forgotten my reason for inviting you. I cannot express enough how sorry I am for what happened to you.'

There was a discreet cough from the open door of the conservatory, then the woman Daniel had seen talking to Grafton the previous day entered bearing a tray with tea pots, cups and saucers. Behind her came the butler, William, carrying a second tray, this one with plates and displays of biscuits and cakes.

'Shall we serve, sir?' asked William.

'Do!' said Chessington. To Daniel and Abigail, he added, 'Just tell them how you'd like it. Milk or no milk. Sugar or no sugar. And do help yourself to some fancies.'

After they'd been served, and the servants had left, Chessington continued with, 'I had a visit from Superintendent Clare explaining the sequence of events. He said that the man I mistook for a burglar was actually a detective inspector from Special Branch at Scotland Yard in London.'

'Yes, sir. That's my understanding,' said Daniel.

'But what on earth was he doing in my house?'

'That's what I hoped to find out, your lordship. That's why I'd followed him.'

'And you saw him break in?'

'I didn't actually see him break in. I saw him disappear round the back of your house, and assumed he was planning to gain entry. My intention was to confront him when he came out and ask what he was looking for, in case it gave us an insight into our enquiry into Gavin Everett's death. I don't know if Superintendent Clare mentioned it, but the Ashmolean has hired us to look into why Everett died.'

'That's what I don't understand; why would this Inspector Grafton think I'd have anything to do with Everett's suicide?'

'That's something I was intending to ask him, but now I guess we'll never know.'

'You knew this inspector?'

'I did. I knew him when I was a detective with Scotland Yard, and I'd met him here in Oxford since Miss Fenton and I arrived. He warned me not to continue investigating Everett's death, which is why my curiosity was aroused.'

'And the police have no idea what he was up to in my house?'

'Not to my knowledge.'

'Superintendent Clare says the man was from Special Branch. Does that mean they are looking into me, for some reason?'

'I have no idea, sir,' said Daniel. 'Superintendent Clare might be able to throw more light on it than me.'

'I asked him. He said he had no idea.' He looked troubled. 'I can't think of any reason why they should be looking into me. My business affairs are open for anyone to see. I have no involvement in politics, and my understanding is that Special Branch was set up to investigate political troublemakers, treasonable people, assassins, that kind of thing.'

'Yes, sir. That's my understanding as well.'

'And Grafton never said anything to throw any light on why he was interested in me? Interested enough to burgle me?'

'No,' said Daniel. 'In fact, he refused to give me any information as to why he was here in Oxford.'

Chessington frowned, puzzled, and muttered,

'Most mysterious.' Then his face brightened, and he said, 'But enough of this morbidity! I don't know if Gladstone Marriott mentioned it to you, but I am somewhat of a collector of historical pieces. Alas, not the wonders that you have seen, Miss Fenton, but one or two pieces of which I am very proud have come my way through auction houses, and I'd be most grateful if you'd allow me to show them to you.'

'It would be my pleasure,' said Abigail.

'I hope this won't bore you, Mr Wilson, two devotees of history indulging this way.'

'Not at all,' said Daniel. 'Through Miss Fenton, I've learnt to appreciate history and historical artefacts.'

'Splendid!' Chessington stood up. 'Then follow me!'

He led the way into the adjoining drawing room where some ancient artefacts were on display. Most, Abigail noted, were small sculptures from the Roman period, along with a few items such as combs and pottery.

'Many of these came from archaeological surveys at Roman sites here in Britain,' he told them proudly. He pointed. 'That is from Bath, that from St Albans, and that one from Hadrian's Wall.'

Suddenly something caught Abigail's attention through a half-open door into an adjoining room.

'And it looks as if you have other treasures in here, My Lord,' she said, interested.

At a speed surprising for a man of his age and bulk, Chessington moved swiftly and pulled the door shut, just as Abigail was about to enter, and turned the key in the lock.

'My sincerest apologies,' he said humbly to Abigail. 'But that's my private room, my study, where I keep very important business papers. Even my servants aren't allowed inside. I was in there just before you arrived and obviously forgot to lock the door after me. Once again, my apologies.'

'We quite understand,' said Abigail. 'I would be the same with my own private papers.'

★   ★   ★

'What private papers?' asked Daniel half an hour later as they walked down the steps from the house, having made their farewells to Lord Chessington.

'I don't have any,' replied Abigail. 'I just wanted to allay Lord Chessington's fears that I might have seen something in that room that he wouldn't want me to see.'

'And did you?'

'Yes.' Abigail nodded. 'I caught sight of the original plate from the Ashmolean, the one that Goddard copied, just before he shut the door.'

'You're sure?' asked Daniel.

'Absolutely,' said Abigail firmly. 'Remember, ancient Egyptian artefacts are my speciality.'

'So, it looks as if Lord Chessington was one of the customers for Everett and his stolen artefacts,' said Daniel.

'It does indeed,' said Abigail.

'And now we may have a different and more

sinister reason why Chessington killed Inspector Grafton,' said Daniel. He gave a determined look at Abigail and said, 'I think it's time we let Inspector Pitt know about the forgeries and Josiah Goddard, and this connection with his lordship.'

33

When they got to Kemp Hall they were told that Inspector Pitt had gone for the day.

'But he left a message that if either of you called asking for him, and if it was urgent, we were to give you his home address for you to call on him there,' the duty sergeant informed them.

Daniel and Abigail exchanged looks, then both said simultaneously, 'Yes, it is urgent.'

As they left the police station, Abigail asked, 'Is it really urgent enough to disturb him at home?'

'Inspector Pitt seemed to think so, otherwise he wouldn't have left the message,' said Daniel. 'And policemen are used to having their home lives disturbed.'

The address they were given was of a neat, well-kept terraced house in a short cul-de-sac. Their knock at the front door was answered by a girl of about nine, who looked at them enquiringly.

'Good afternoon,' said Daniel. 'Is Inspector Pitt at home?'

'It's actually good evening, because it's after six o'clock,' the girl corrected him. 'Who wants him?'

'Mr Daniel Wilson and Miss Abigail Fenton.'

'If you wait here, I'll see if he's available.'

With that, she shut the door.

'Well, that put me in my place,' said Daniel ruefully.

'I like her,' said Abigail approvingly. 'A girl after my own heart.'

The door opened, and this time Inspector Pitt looked out at them. He grinned. 'I hear you just met my daughter, Edie, who said she corrected you about the time of day.'

'Indeed, she did,' said Daniel.

'And quite rightly,' said Abigail. 'She should be encouraged.'

'Edie needs no encouragement,' said Pitt. He looked momentarily concerned as he said, 'The fact you're calling suggests something's happened.'

'More like information received,' said Daniel.

'In that case, you'd better come in.'

'You sure we won't be disturbing you?' asked Daniel.

'A policeman's job is to always be disturbed,' said Pitt. 'You should know that better than anyone, Mr Wilson.'

'Daniel,' said Daniel.

'In that case, as I'm off duty and it's after hours, I'm Bradley.'

He led them into the narrow hallway and called, 'Martha!'

A woman appeared from the back of the house, wiping her hands on a towel. Behind her came three children: their daughter, Edie, along with two boys, both younger.

'Daniel and Abigail, I'd like you to meet my wife, Martha. Martha, this is Daniel Wilson and Abigail Fenton, who I've told you about.'

'It's a pleasure to meet you,' said Martha.

'And a pleasure for us,' said Abigail, shaking her hand. 'We apologise for disrupting your household.'

Martha smiled. 'I'm used to it.'

'And this is Edie, who you've already met, and her brothers, Tom, and Richard the youngest.'

'It's a pleasure to meet you,' said Abigail, and she and Daniel formally shook the children's hands.

'We need to talk business, so I'm going to take them into the parlour,' Pitt said to his wife. 'And some tea's in order I think, Martha, if that's alright.' He winked at her. 'With a slice of your special fruit cake, if you please, especially after what Mr Wilson's been through.'

'Thank you, but actually we've just had afternoon tea,' said Daniel. 'We were invited to Lord Chessington's and we've just come from there.'

Pitt looked at them, stunned. 'Lord Chessington!'

'I don't think I can serve you anything like you'd have been given at his lordship's,' said Martha unhappily.

'Nonsense!' said Abigail. 'His lordship's was all thin biscuits, not enough to slake the appetite of a grasshopper. If you don't mind, Mrs Pitt, I'd love to take a slice of your fruit cake. And Daniel was just trying to be polite. I know he'd love some, too.'

'Yes, I would.' Daniel smiled. 'If it's no trouble.'

'No trouble at all!' said Martha, happy again.

Pitt led them into the parlour, and Daniel was pleased to note that, unlike the parlour of his own parents and most of his relatives which was kept for only the most solemn of occasions, notably after funerals, and so dark and oppressive in its furniture and decor, this room was light and cheerful, and obviously used by the family regularly.

Pitt gestured them to chairs, then asked, 'So, what's this about you going to tea at Lord Chessington's?'

'He invited us,' said Daniel. 'He said he wanted to make amends for the way I'd been treated. But I suspect his real motive was he wanted to meet Abigail. He's apparently a collector of note, especially of pieces from ancient Egypt and Greece, and as that's Abigail's speciality . . . '

'Did he talk to you about shooting Grafton?'

'He did, and it was very much as you described it. He found a burglar in his study and believed he was in danger, so he shot him.' Daniel frowned thoughtfully. 'The thing that still doesn't ring true for me is his claim that he only intended to wound him. Lord Chessington comes across as a man used to handling firearms, so if he just intended to wound this burglar, why shoot him in the chest where he's more likely to kill him?'

'The heat of the moment?' suggested Pitt.

'Possibly,' said Daniel. 'But I wondered if he wanted to make sure this burglar didn't reveal what was in the study.'

'And what was in the study?' asked Pitt.

Daniel turned to Abigail.

'I think it's for you to explain to the inspector about the fakes, as you discovered them,' he said.

'The fakes?' asked Pitt.

'What we're about to tell you is not for public knowledge,' said Abigail. 'Not yet. Unless it turns out to be the real motive for the murder of Gavin Everett.'

'Go on,' said Pitt.

Abigail was about to enlarge, when the door opened, and Martha appeared bearing a tray with teapot, cups, milk, sugar and plates with three slices of cake.

'Here you are,' she said brightly.

'Thank you, Martha!' said Pitt, getting up to take the tray from her and putting it on a small table.

'Is there anything else?' she asked.

'No, this will be perfect.' Abigail smiled. 'Thank you, Mrs Pitt.'

'Then I'll leave you to your business,' said Martha, and she left, closing the door behind her.

Pitt set about pouring tea and distributing the cake, while Abigail told him what she'd discovered at the Ashmolean.

'Gavin Everett was running a racket,' she said. 'He was getting certain ancient artefacts copied — mainly decorated plates, from what I can see — and selling the originals to private collectors. And today, at Lord Chessington's, I saw one of those stolen plates in his study. But he shut the door very quickly as soon as he saw me looking in.'

'So, what we're wondering is, how many other pieces stolen from the Ashmolean does he have in that room?' added Daniel. 'And did he shoot Grafton — believing him to be a burglar — to prevent him talking about seeing the stolen items?'

'How sure are you of this?' asked Pitt. 'The fact that Everett had these items copied?'

'I got suspicious about one of the plates on display,' said Abigail. 'I examined it and found that it was definitely a copy, and not a very good one. I then found another three items that were copies.'

'And you didn't tell me this before because . . . ?' asked Pitt.

'We decided to keep it secret because the reputation of the Ashmolean was at stake,' said Abigail.

'And they are the ones paying our wages,' added Daniel.

'But you told Gladstone Marriott about these fakes?'

'Yes.'

'Why have you decided to tell me now?' asked Pitt. 'Because of seeing the original at Lord Chessington's?'

'No,' said Daniel. 'That was a bonus, telling us that Chessington was one of Everett's secret clients. We're telling you because we tracked down the man who did the copies for Everett, and there's a possibility that he may be able to throw some light on why Everett was killed, if the motive for his death is due to these fakes.'

'Who is this man?'

'His name's Josiah Goddard and he has a shop in the north of Oxford. But, after we went to see him, he did a runner. Vanished.'

'Suggesting he's guilty of something,' said Pitt.

'Exactly,' said Daniel. 'And we think we know where he might be hiding. His sister, a Mrs Jenny Woodman, is married to a farmer, and we think he might be hiding out at their farm. We wondered if you could arrange a raid on the farm.'

'Where is this farm?'

'It's near a small village outside Oxford called Stanton St John.'

Pitt gave a rueful grimace.

'That's outside our boundary, I'm afraid,' he said.

'But all of the county of Oxford comes under the city's police,' said Daniel.

'Yes, but it's about manpower,' said Pitt. 'We're quite a small force, so the Police Board prefer that crimes committed outside the city are handled by the local constabulary.' Then he smiled. 'Stanton St John, did you say?'

'Yes,' said Abigail.

'Fortunately, I know the sergeant who operates there. Sergeant Jasper Mills. A good man. I'll give you a note to introduce you. You tell him what you want, and that you're working with me, and I'm sure he'll be helpful. Plus, it's always better to have the local man on the job. Jasper will know these Woodman people, which means he'll know the best way to handle them.'

He got up and went to a small bureau, from

which he took writing paper, an envelope, and a pen and ink.

'Thank you,' said Abigail, as Pitt sat down and began to compose his letter.

'Luckily, there's not the same rivalry between us in the city and the Stanton St John station as there is with some others in the county. I'm sure you'll find Jasper Mills welcoming to you.'

As Daniel watched the inspector write, he asked, 'How are you getting on with your search for Piers Stevens?'

Pitt shook his head.

'We've drawn a blank so far,' he said, ruefully. 'There's no sign of him.'

'I think I may have an idea where he's hiding,' said Daniel thoughtfully.

Both Pitt and Abigail looked at him in surprise.

'Where?' asked Pitt.

'At his house,' said Daniel.

Pitt stared at him.

'Impossible!' he said. 'His mother was very clear about her attitude towards him. She wouldn't allow it.'

'But the maid, Vera, is different. Abigail said she thinks the maid's in love with Stevens.'

'She is,' said Abigail. She looked at Daniel, impressed. 'I think you're right! Stevens is a young man used to having everything done for him. He's not the kind who could survive easily on the streets, and even less so in a wood, or somewhere rural. He has no access to money. He can't trust any of his acquaintances from the Quill Club.'

'Exactly,' said Daniel. 'The only place he would seek refuge is the only place he knows, his home. He'd throw himself on the mercy of the maid, beg her to hide him, and not tell his mother.'

'But where could he hide in there?' asked Pitt.

'A cellar. An outhouse,' said Daniel. 'Somewhere the maid could deliver him food. In my opinion, I think it would be worth you making a return visit to the house, ostensibly to update Mrs Stevens on the lack of success in the search for her son. And while you're there, question the maid. Tell her you know she's hiding him and you only want to help him. Promise that you'll take him without violence and that you'll make sure he has a fair trial, a proper hearing.'

'And if she doesn't believe me?'

'Search the house, especially the areas that are rarely used. As I said, the cellar or an outhouse. After all, you haven't had any luck finding him so far, so you've got nothing to lose.'

*　　*　　*

As Daniel and Abigail walked away from Pitt's house, making their way back to their hotel, Abigail said, 'You are very clever, Daniel Wilson. I didn't think of Stevens hiding at his house.'

'You would have,' said Daniel. 'You were the one who worked out that the maid was in love with him, so where else could he go?'

'However, there's one thing you're not very knowledgeable about,' said Abigail.

'What's that?'

'The importance of cake being served,' said Abigail.

'It's cake,' protested Daniel. 'It's not special!'

'That's where you're wrong,' said Abigail. 'It's more than cake. It's about proud hospitality. I learnt that from my sister, Bella. These things are very important to some people. And with nice people like Inspector Pitt and his wife, respect has to be shown.'

'I'll remember that in future,' said Daniel. 'The next time I'm offered cake I'll weigh up whether they are the sort of person I need to show respect or affection to, in which case I say yes, or if I loathe and despise them, in which case I refuse.'

'Good,' chuckled Abigail. 'You're learning social skills.'

34

In his office at the War Office, Commander Atkinson sat stiffly upright and faced Commander Smith and Captain Jones. On his desk in front of him lay their report following their recent visit to Oxford.

'So, you don't think the Boers were involved in Everett's death?' he said.

'No, sir,' said Smith. 'From what we've heard from Wilson, I tend to agree with him that Everett was a crook. It's my belief he spun the tale about the Boers to get money. It was a confidence trick, pure and simple.'

'So, who did kill Everett?'

'Possibly one of his victims, but there will be no official police investigation into his death. Officially, the Oxford police are describing it as suicide.'

'But this man Wilson and this Fenton woman are still poking around.'

'Officially, to see if they can find out why Everett killed himself.'

'But unofficially?'

'They are trying to find out who killed him. The evidence of the gunshot, the lack of powder burns around the wound — all point to him having been murdered.'

'But that won't come out in public?'

'No, sir. And, even if it did, it wouldn't affect us. As I say, I'm confident the Boers weren't involved in any way.'

'What about this Lord Chessington? The man who killed Grafton?'

'As we say in our report, sir, he believed that Grafton was a burglar, and shot him to defend himself and his property.'

'Did you talk to him while you were in Oxford?'

'No, sir. We felt the least that was known about our presence in the city the better. The police seemed fairly satisfied with the explanation. This Lord Chessington seems to be a man of good character.'

'And wealthy,' commented Atkinson.

'Yes, sir. And with important contacts in Parliament.'

Atkinson looked thoughtful, then he produced a telegram from beneath the papers on his desk, which he passed to Smith and Jones.

'I sent a telegram to a diplomatic contact in South Africa asking for any information about Chessington.'

The two men read the reply.

Chessington has business interests in the Transvaal over goldfields. Ten years ago, he killed a man called Benjamin Wildman in the Transvaal, after which he left and returned to England. No legal action was ever taken against him. No warrant over the death exists.

'Who was this Benjamin Wildman?' asked Smith.

'I've sent another telegram asking for more information,' said Atkinson. 'As yet, I've had no reply. But this suggests that Chessington is — or was — a dangerous man, capable of killing. Could he have been the person who shot Everett? They both have a South African connection. Perhaps Everett discovered about Chessington killing Wildman in South Africa and tried blackmailing him. Everett was obviously a crook and quite capable of it, by all accounts.'

'It's possible, sir,' said Smith. 'But without further investigation, it's just conjecture. Do you want us to return to Oxford and interview Lord Chessington?'

'No,' said Atkinson. 'Our task was to find out if there was a Boer connection that might put this nation at risk. You've done that and found there is none. Anything else is of no interest to us. Now we have to ensure that this whole business is closed so that there is no chance of what happened to Grafton becoming public knowledge.'

★　★　★

Esther looked out of the window towards Whichford Hall as the hansom cab journeyed down the long drive. As had been the case when she'd arrived at Charlbury Court, she felt slightly overawed at the vastness of the mansion she was approaching, and the huge area of the lands surrounding the house. In her hand, she clutched the letter she'd received at the *Messenger* offices from Baron Whichford, which had been addressed to *her*, not to Mr Pinker, inviting her to come to the hall to meet the baroness.

She wondered how they would be towards her. Would they be cold and sneering in a superior way, as the duchess had been?

As she stepped down from the hansom, a man came down the steps to meet her. But this wasn't a footman, as had been the case at Charlbury; everything about him said 'gentleman', from the cut of his clothes, his riding boots, his whole bearing. He smiled at her as he drew near and held out his hand.

'You must be Esther Maris,' he said. 'I'm Baron Whichford.'

Flustered at the baron himself coming to greet her, Esther took his hand and at the same time dropped into a curtsey.

'My Lord,' she said.

He chuckled. 'There's no need for that. Richard, please. You are our guest, after all. And may I call you Esther?'

'Indeed, My Lord . . . Richard. That's very kind of you,' said Esther, straightening up.

'I trust your journey out here was pleasant? Some parts of the roads are in need of repair and the journey can be quite bone-shaking.'

'The journey was fine, thank you.'

He gestured towards the huge house. 'I'll take you in and introduce you to Deborah — that's the baroness, my wife — in a moment. But before I do, I hope you don't mind if I mention one or two things.'

'Not at all, Richard,' said Esther. 'I'd be

grateful for any pointers you can give me when meeting the baroness.'

'The thing is, she didn't want to do this, at first, but I thought it would be good for her. Help to get out of herself, lift her spirits. You see, a short time ago, a cousin whom she was very close to died in a tragic accident.'

'Oh dear,' said Esther. 'I am sorry.'

'As a result, Deborah has rather gone in on herself. So, I'd be grateful if you could keep the topics you ask her about . . . you know . . . on happy things.'

'I promise,' said Esther earnestly. 'I'll do my best to keep our conversation light. Do you have any suggestions for topics which might interest her?'

'Well . . . clothes. And the decor of the house. She's been the key person in turning this rather imposing and large house into a home.'

'Your children?' suggested Esther.

The baron gave her an unhappy look.

'I'd rather you didn't, if you don't mind. Sadly, we have been unfortunate in that respect too. My wife has been with child twice, but — alas — both times something . . . went wrong.'

'I understand,' said Esther. 'And please accept my sympathies. I'll avoid any talk about children.'

'By all means you can talk to her about the children of the workers on our estate. She's been very active in that area, doing a lot of charitable work for the less fortunate.' Then he frowned as he thought it over, and added awkwardly, 'On second thoughts, it might be better to stick to clothes and decor. And her sewing. She does wonderful cross-stitch. And, of course, the paintings in the hall. She's very much the art connoisseur.' He gave her an apologetic smile. 'I hope you don't mind my saying all this to you, but my wife's well-being is the most important thing to me.'

'Of course, Richard. I absolutely understand, and I promise I'll make sure I do nothing to upset Her Grace.'

As the baron led the way towards the hall, Esther reflected how different her reception was at Whichford to that she'd received at Charlbury, the kindness and friendliness of the baron, and she fervently hoped that the baroness wouldn't turn out to be the guilty one.

★　★　★

The rural village of Stanton St John was too small to merit an actual police station. Instead, the police house where Sergeant Jasper Mills lived with his family served that purpose. Daniel and Abigail had caught a hansom to the village and hoped they would find the sergeant at home before he set out on his rounds. They were in luck. When they knocked at the front door, Mrs Mills directed them to the rear of the house where her husband was hard at work fixing one of the wheels of his small two-wheel cart.

Sergeant Mills studied the letter of introduction from Inspector Pitt that Daniel handed to him, then studied Daniel and Abigail.

'Daniel Wilson,' he said. 'Would that be the same Daniel Wilson that was with Abberline?'

Daniel nodded. 'Indeed.'

Mills put out his hand. 'May I be permitted to shake your hand, Mr Wilson.'

'It's my pleasure, Sergeant Mills,' said Daniel.

Mills then turned his attention to Abigail. 'Bradley says in his letter that you're an investigator too, Miss Fenton.'

'Yes,' said Abigail. 'That is correct.'

The sergeant obviously had difficulty computing this concept, because his face became a frown, and he asked, 'Are women coming into the force now? Is this a London thing?'

'We're private investigators,' explained Daniel. 'But I can assure you that Miss Fenton is as qualified as I am to investigate the kind of situations we look into.'

'What would those be?' asked Mills.

'So far we've investigated murders. Now, we're investigating an allegation of fraud.'

'Oh? Who against?'

'A man named Josiah Goddard. He's the brother of Jenny Woodman. We understand that she and her husband have a farm here in Stanton St John, and we think he might have taken refuge with them.'

Mills nodded.

'Joe Goddard,' he said. 'Yes, he grew up here. Always a bit troublesome. You think he's hiding out at Toby Woodman's place?'

'It's a possibility. If he is, he needs to be taken to Oxford for questioning, but Inspector Pitt and the Oxford police have no jurisdiction here, and

Miss Fenton and I, as private investigators, have no authority to arrest him, which is why Inspector Pitt suggested we came to see you.'

'Yes, well, as you can see, I've got a bit of a problem with transport,' said Mills, indicating the broken axle of his cart. 'But we'll soon sort that out. I was about to go and see Jeb Pick, our village blacksmith, who also happens to be a deputy constable. He's a good man and I'm sure we can use his wagon. If you'll wait here while I put my uniform jacket on, just so we make this official.'

The sergeant disappeared into the house, and Daniel and Abigail walked back to the front of the house to wait for him.

'I note we haven't been offered cake,' observed Daniel.

'This is a different situation,' said Abigail. 'We know Inspector Pitt and were invited to his house. Also, we arrived in the late afternoon. Here, we're on an official errand and we have no relationship with the sergeant and his family. Also, it is too early for cake.'

'So, there are rules for when cake is served?' said Daniel.

'Of course,' said Abigail. 'At least, so I'm informed by Bella.'

'It's been a while since we've seen your sister,' commented Daniel. 'In fact, the last time was at her wedding to Dr Keen, and that was some months ago. Do you think we ought to pay them a visit?'

'I'm not sure if Bella approves of us.' Abigail sighed. 'She considers you have made a fallen woman of me, living in sin as we do, in her eyes.'

'Perhaps we should visit them, even if only to show her that we are not at all sinful, but very happy together.'

'I have thought of it,' said Abigail. 'Perhaps I'll write to her and suggest it, and we'll see what she says.'

Mills reappeared from the house, now properly attired in his sergeant's uniform.

'I've told my wife we're off on official business,' he told them. 'It's not far to Jeb's forge.'

They set off along the road, passing other houses and an inn, the Flying Cow.

'You say Joe Goddard used to live in the village and that he was troublesome,' said Daniel. 'What sort of trouble are we talking about?'

'Just silly stuff, mostly, when he was a kid. But there was a bit of thieving.'

'Did he ever go to prison?'

Mills shook his head. 'His sister, Jenny, always appealed for him, said it would be the death of him — and of her — if he went inside. She swore she'd get him to mend his ways. Not that he did, but he never did anything big enough to warrant sending him for trial. No one ever got injured by him, although I think that was because he was a bit of a coward and was frightened that if he tried robbery he'd get hurt. And everyone had too much of a soft spot for Jenny to want to cause her grief. She brought him up from when he was tiny after their parents died. In the end, he went off to the city, which was a relief to most of us here in Stanton St John.'

'Does he come back much?' asked Daniel.

'No,' said Mills. 'It's like now he's in the big city he's shaken this village off. He's come back a couple of times, but not for long. I suspect it was to borrow money off his sister.'

'How does he get on with his brother-in-law, Toby Woodman?'

'Toby can't stand him. But he stays quiet about him because he knows how much Jenny cares for her brother, and Toby loves his wife and wouldn't want her upset.' He gestured at a wooden hut from which they could hear the banging of metal on metal, and from whose chimney dark smoke belched.

'Here we are, Jeb's forge,' he said.

They walked along a short path and into the wooden hut, whose interior walls were blackened, and encountered a fierce heat from the glowing coals in the forge. A giant of a man wearing a stained undervest was hammering a piece of metal into shape on an anvil, and he stopped as they entered and nodded in greeting.

'Jeb, these people have been sent by Inspector Pitt from Oxford,' said Mills. 'He wants us to go with them to Toby Woodman's and see if Joe Goddard's there, and if he is, we're to arrest him and take him to Kemp Hall. The trouble is, my cart's broken its axle, so I was going to come to see you anyway to ask for your help with it, but now I need you in your role as constable to see if we can find Joe. Are you available for that?'

'Ar.' Pick nodded.

He took his off his leather apron and walked

to a hook where his constable's tunic was hanging. As he pulled it on, Mills added, 'We'll need to take your wagon.'

'Ar,' said Pick again.

He buttoned his tunic, then went to a cupboard, from which he took his police helmet and a long, stout truncheon, which he hung from his belt. That done, he left the forge and made his way round the back. Daniel and Abigail followed Mills, who followed Pick. There was a horse grazing in a small meadow next to the forge, and Pick whistled it over, then led it towards a four-wheeled wagon and hitched it up.

'Does the truncheon mean he's expecting trouble?' asked Abigail.

'No, but he's had dealings with Joe before, when Joe lived in the village.'

'What sort of dealings?'

'Just enough to know not to trust him.'

★   ★   ★

Esther sat in the drawing room studying Baroness Whichford, who sat near her on a chaise longue, and thought she'd never seen anyone so nervous. The baroness had been kind in her welcome, very different from the cold, superior sneers of the Duchess of Charlbury. The baroness had taken both Esther's hands warmly in greeting before guiding her to the chair she now sat in, and had smiled, but Esther could sense that the smile — although it appeared genuine — hid an inner turmoil. She was unhappy, deeply unhappy, and the way her hands twisted a piece of chintz she had picked up showed she was battling against agitation.

'Thank you so much for seeing me, Baroness,' said Esther. She looked admiringly around the room, taking in the portraits that adorned the walls. 'You have such a beautiful house, and in such a wonderful setting.'

'Yes, we have been very fortunate,' said the baroness. 'But at the same time being the current inhabitants of Whichford Hall is a huge responsibility. Mainly for my husband, of course. The years of history here make demands on him.'

'And on you, I would suggest,' said Esther. 'The lady of the manor has her own responsibilities. The estate workers and their families.'

'My husband looks after them, along with his general overseeing of the estate.'

'But you give him support. You know what they say: behind every great man is a woman.'

'My husband is indeed a great man. Certainly, the greatest I've ever known.'

'You've been married for a long time?'

'Twenty years,' said the baroness. 'The happiest twenty years of my life.' She gave a wistful smile as she added, 'For me, my husband was my salvation.'

'In what way, My Lady?' asked Esther.

The baroness hesitated, then said, 'In the way it is for any woman when a good man enters her life.'

'Of course,' said Esther. She gave a rueful smile. 'For some of us, we are still waiting for that moment.' The baroness gave a kind but weak smile in response. Esther pointed at one of the portraits. 'That's by Gainsborough, isn't it?'

'Yes,' said the baroness, turning to look at it. 'One of Richard's ancestors, but I can't remember which number baron he is. I'm sure my husband will know.'

'This house must have seen many famous people in its time,' said Esther. 'Like Thomas Gainsborough. Artists. Musicians. Writers?'

'I'm sure,' said the baroness.

'Do you know who might be the most famous who was here?' asked Esther.

35

Inspector Pitt pulled at the brass handle of the bell beside the front door of Stevens' house. The door was opened almost immediately by the maid, Vera, who looked nervously out at the inspector and the constable with him.

'Good morning. Is Mrs Stevens at home?' asked Pitt.

'Yes, sir. I'll tell her you're here.'

The maid disappeared into the house, returning a few minutes later.

'The missus says for you to come in. But only you, sir. She'd prefer it if the constable came inside but waited by the door.'

'Of course.' Pitt turned to the constable and said, 'Did you hear that, Constable?'

'Yes, sir.'

Pitt left the constable waiting inside the front door while he followed the maid into the same drawing room he'd met Mrs Stevens on the previous occasion.

'Well, Inspector. Have you found my son yet?' Mrs Stevens demanded.

'I'm afraid not, ma'am. Which is why I've returned. There is a possibility that there may be some clues in his room as to where he may have gone, or who he may have sought refuge with, and with your permission I'd like to search it.'

'I thought you searched it before,' she snapped.

'I did, but I may have overlooked something. A note left in a drawer, or something.'

'Very well,' she said. 'But I don't want your men tramping all over my house.'

'I can assure you, ma'am, it will be just me. And, in order to make sure that nothing is disturbed, or if it is it's replaced properly, I wonder if I could trouble you for your maid to accompany me while I'm in your son's room.'

Mrs Stevens hesitated, then nodded.

'Very well. Just in case anything needs putting back the way it was.' She turned to the maid, who was waiting nervously, and said, 'You may accompany the inspector, Vera.'

'Thank you, ma'am,' said Pitt.

He gestured for the maid to lead the way and followed her out of the drawing room and up the stairs to Piers Stevens' room. Once inside, he turned to her and said gently, 'I'll be frank, miss. I haven't come to search Mr Piers' room, I've come to search the house, because it's my belief that he's hiding here.'

She stared at him, her face going white, and she began to tremble.

'No,' she said. 'He's not.'

'Yes, he is,' said Pitt, firmly but gently. 'Now, I can call in a large squad of policemen who will comb every part of this house, from the attic to the cellar, and every outhouse. But that will upset Mrs Stevens very much, and there is the risk that when we find him, he will make a run for it and could be seriously injured as he attempts to escape. Or, you can tell me where he is, and I'll go and have a gentle word with him and persuade him it's in his best interests to come along with me quietly, without all the hoo-ha of a full-scale search. I promise you he'll be treated fairly and gently, and he'll be safe. I give you my word on that.'

He fixed his eyes on the maid, who averted her head from his gaze.

'He's not here,' she said weakly.

Pitt said nothing while he studied her, then he said, 'In that case I'll go to Mrs Stevens and tell her what I suspect, and institute a full search. If she asks me why I think that, I'll have to tell her because I believe you've given him sanctuary here and kept him supplied with food while he's been in hiding. When we find him, which I know we will, and my suspicion is shown to be correct, I'll leave it to you to consider what Mrs Stevens' attitude to you will be.' He saw tears fill the maid's eyes, and berated himself for bullying her, but he knew it was the only way to get her to admit his quarry was hiding in the house. 'However, if you tell me where he is, and I take him quietly, I'll tell Mrs Stevens later that it was a clue I found in his room that led me to find him elsewhere, and there will be no suspicion that you were involved. Either way, I'll take him in. But doing it with a full search puts him at risk, and also your position here when Mrs Stevens discovers he was in the house all the time.'

Vera's head dropped, and she began to cry. Gently, Pitt led her to a chair and sat her down while she sobbed.

'He needs help,' he said. 'He can't spend his

life being hunted. It will be the death of him. You know that.'

'It wasn't his fault,' she moaned.

'I know,' said Pitt. 'And I'll help him all I can. Now, where is he?'

'In the cellar,' she whispered.

'How many cellars are there?' asked Pitt.

'Just the one. There used to be a wine cellar, but that was knocked through into the other one.'

'And the entrance?'

'Outside the back door,' she said, her voice barely more than a whisper. 'It's a low door set into the wall. The steps go down.'

'Thank you,' said Pitt.

He turned and headed for the door, and behind him her voice begged, 'You promise you won't hurt him.'

'I promise,' said Pitt.

★ ★ ★

The wagon, with Jeb Pick at the reins and Sergeant Mills beside him, and Daniel and Abigail sitting in the back, trundled through the village, then about three miles over a rough unmade road before pulling to a halt in front of a two-storey farmhouse with two small outbuildings next to it, and two large barns across a courtyard from the house.

As they dismounted from the wagon a woman appeared from the house.

'Good morning, Jenny. Is your brother, Joe, about?' enquired Mills.

Jenny Woodman immediately looked worried and cast a nervous look back towards the house.

'Joe? No. Why should he be?'

'These people here are from Oxford and they've got orders for Joe to be taken to Kemp Hall to answer some questions.'

'What sort of questions?' demanded Jenny. 'About what? Joe hasn't done anything wrong!'

'Then he won't worry about answering the questions,' said Mills.

'Well, he's not here,' she said defiantly.

A man wearing rough clothes appeared from a barn and approached them.

'What's going on?' he demanded. 'I heard raised voices.' He looked at Mills and Pick and asked, 'What are you here for, Jasper? And you, Jeb Pick, both in your uniforms?'

'We've come to talk to Joe, if he's here,' said Mills.

'I've told them he isn't!' shouted Jenny. 'Why can't you leave us alone?'

'Now, now, Jenny, there's no need for that shouting,' said Mills gently.

'Unless she's doing it to alert someone in the house,' Daniel murmured to Mills.

Mills nodded. 'And there he is,' he said, gesturing at a figure who'd appeared from the back of the house and was running towards a barn. 'He's going for a horse.' He turned to Pick and said, 'Constable.'

'Ar,' said Pick.

He leapt down from the driving seat of the wagon and, to Daniel's and Abigail's surprise for a large man, ran at an astoundingly fast pace in

305

pursuit of the escaping Joe Goddard.

'No!' howled Jenny Woodman.

While Daniel and the sergeant ran after the speeding blacksmith, Abigail went to comfort the distraught farmer's wife.

'They won't hurt him,' she told her.

'He's getting away,' said Daniel, as he realised that Goddard had quickened his flight and was definitely putting distance between himself and the blacksmith. Goddard had decided to abandon running to the barn and was instead making for open countryside, sure that the wagon wouldn't be able to follow him at speed.

Suddenly, Pick stopped and reached down, and Daniel saw he'd picked up a small stone. Pick stood, as if weighing the stone in his hand, and suddenly he threw it.

The stone hit Goddard on the back of the head, sending him tumbling to the ground, where he lay.

Jenny Woodman let out a scream. 'You've killed him!'

But Goddard wasn't dead, just dazed, because they saw him trying to struggle to his knees. But before he could push himself up, Pick was on him, pushing him back to the ground. Daniel and Mills hurried and joined the blacksmith, and Mills dropped to his knees and clapped a pair of handcuffs on the fallen Goddard's wrists, hauling him to his feet.

'That was an incredible throw!' said Daniel in admiration to the blacksmith.

'Ar,' said Pick.

At a nod from Mills, he took hold of Goddard

and marched him towards the wagon.

'Jeb's the star of our cricket team,' said Mills as he and Daniel followed them. 'As a fielder he's second to none. He can throw a ball and demolish a wicket from the boundary.' He then stopped and lowered his voice and added, so that only Daniel could hear him, 'This is also payback for Jeb for the way Joe made his life a misery when they were kids growing up here. You see how big Jeb is. Well, he was always big, and a bit slow, both in his movements and his thinking. He was alright, don't get me wrong, nothing wrong with him, but he took a bit longer that most to understand some things, and Joe used to tease him. Well, more than teased him. He was cruel. He used to call him Jeb Thick. And he'd take Jeb's stuff and hide it and get him into trouble with Jeb's dad, and Jeb's dad was a hard man. Very hard. There was no softness about Reuben Pick. He had the forge before Jeb. Jeb was his dad's apprentice and he took it over when his dad died. And now he's got Joe Goddard in handcuffs.'

'Everything comes round in the end and catches up with you,' said Daniel. 'I was told the Indians call it karma.'

'I expect they're right,' said Mills. 'They usually are.'

Jenny Woodman was standing sobbing, but she broke off as her brother neared her and made to go to him.

'It's alright, sis,' said Goddard airily. 'They've got nothing on me. It's all a mistake. You'll see.'

'I promise you, I'll see he comes to no harm,'

Abigail assured the unhappy woman.

Toby Woodman stood and watched the scene, his face showing his anger. 'I told you it was trouble, him coming here!' he stormed at his wife. 'It always is with him!' Then, as Jenny Woodman subsided into more sobs of misery, he went to her and pulled her close to him in a comforting hug. 'I'm sorry, lass,' he said.

* * *

Pitt stood in the rear yard, looking at the low door and wondering if Stevens was still hiding in the cellar, or if he'd sneaked out. But the yard was enclosed by a high brick wall, with no rear access. If he had sneaked out, he would have had to pass the constable at the front door.

Pitt tried the handle of the door, and as it opened, he heard a scuttling sound from below. The sound was too heavy for rats.

He stepped into the darkness and sat down on the top step of the short flight that led downwards.

'Mr Stevens,' he said quietly. 'This is Inspector Pitt from the Oxford police. I know you're here and I've given my word to someone who cares for you very much that I won't harm you. I made that promise and I intend to keep it.

'If you come with me now, there is no need for your mother to know that you were hiding in the house, and that the maid has been looking after you. As I say, Vera cares for you, and I believe you care for her. I don't think you'd want her to be dismissed from this house, without a reference, which is what will happen to her if your mother discovers she's been harbouring you here.

'So those are the two options. One, you come with me quietly and your mother will never know you were here, and I promise you will be looked after and not mistreated in any way. The other: I send in a squad of policemen who will take you out forcibly, and the resultant fuss and noise will mean that Vera's role in hiding you will be revealed to your mother. The choice is yours.'

There was silence, and for a moment Pitt wondered whether he'd been wrong, and Stevens had managed to get away and he'd just been talking to himself. But then there came a shuffling sound, and a nervous voice asked, 'You promise Vera won't be named?'

'I promise,' said Pitt.

'And my mother won't know I was here?'

'I promise,' repeated Pitt.

'And you won't hurt me?'

'I promise,' said Pitt for a third time.

There were more shuffling sounds, then from the darkness a short, forlorn, dishevelled figure emerged from the darkness with his hands held up in surrender.

★ ★ ★

As Inspector Pitt led Piers Stevens quietly along the passageway to the front door, he heard Mrs Stevens call out imperiously from the drawing room, 'Is that you, Inspector?' Pitt glanced at Stevens, who looked panicky.

'Yes, ma'am,' he called back. 'I was just coming to see you to say goodbye.'

He ushered Stevens to the front door, where he handed him over to the constable.

'Keep an eye on him,' he whispered. 'But don't hurt him.'

With that, Pitt hurried back to the drawing room. Just before he entered, he saw Vera standing on the stairs, looking anxiously down at him. He nodded and gave her a thumbs up sign, then stepped into the drawing room.

'You've been an inordinately long time, Inspector,' Mrs Stevens reprimanded him.

'Yes, and my apologies for that, ma'am. But I may have found some information that will help us find your son. As soon as I've located him, I'll report back to you.'

'Please don't,' said Mrs Stevens. 'I don't wish to be involved any further in this sordid affair. If you find him, then deal with him as you see fit. I have no wish to receive any further information about him. As far as I'm concerned, he is dead to this family, so I don't anticipate seeing you again.'

'I understand, ma'am,' said Pitt. 'And please accept my condolences.'

'Your expressions of concern in this matter are irrelevant to me,' said Mrs Stevens stiffly. 'I wish you goodbye.'

Pitt bowed, and left. Stevens was waiting by the front door next to the constable. Pitt noticed he was still trembling. The inspector took him by the arm and guided him out of the house to the street. As he closed the door behind them, his last sight was of the forlorn and desolate Vera, still standing on the stairs.

36

The handcuffed Josiah Goddard had remained silent during the journey to Oxford, after one defiant statement of 'I'm innocent!' just before the wagon set off. Sergeant Mills drove, having left Jeb Pick behind to mend the broken axle of his cart. 'Jeb can do it quicker than I can, and make a better job of it,' he told Daniel and Abigail. Daniel and Abigail also remained mostly silent during the journey, not wanting to say anything that might give ammunition to Goddard when it came to Inspector Pitt interviewing him. Mills was happy to do the talking as he drove, pointing out places of interest they passed, the sergeant obviously very proud of the Oxfordshire countryside and keen to show it off to these visitors from London.

They pulled into the courtyard at the rear of Kemp Hall, and Daniel helped Goddard down from the back of the wagon while the sergeant tethered the horse. That done, Daniel, Abigail, Mills and Goddard made for the entrance to the police station, with Goddard uttering a last defiant, 'I've done nothing wrong!'

As they entered the station, they were surprised to see Inspector Pitt waiting for them.

'You were expecting us?' asked Abigail.

'No, I'd just brought in a prisoner myself and handed him over to the turnkey when I saw the wagon pull into the yard.'

'You found Piers Stevens?' queried Daniel.

'I did. He was exactly where you said he'd be, in the cellar of his house.' He turned to Mills, who was holding Goddard by the collar of his coat. 'It's good to see you again, Jasper.'

'And you, Bradley. And as you can see, I've brought you something. Meet Josiah Goddard, who I believe you're looking for.'

'I am indeed,' said Pitt.

'I've done nothing wrong!' said Goddard defiantly.

'What do you want done with him?' asked Mills.

'We'll hand him over to the turnkey for safe passage to a cell, and then you and I can go to my office and do the paperwork. Let's have a brew together and catch up. It's been a while since I've seen you.'

'Sounds good to me,' said Mills.

Pitt turned to Daniel and Abigail. 'Give me half an hour and then we'll talk to Stevens.'

'You haven't done that yet?' asked Daniel.

'I was waiting for you to return.' He grinned. 'You have a knack of getting people to talk, Daniel. I want to see it in action.'

'That suits us,' said Daniel. 'We'll get a coffee and see you back here in half an hour.'

Daniel and Abigail left the station and made their way to a nearby coffee house.

'Cake?' Abigail asked Daniel as the waitress took their order for coffee.

'No, thank you,' said Daniel. 'The whole protocol of when and when not to have cake is starting to disturb me. I shall go without.'

'It will be interesting to see what Stevens says,' said Abigail.

'He'll protest his innocence,' said Daniel.

'He might not,' said Abigail. 'He didn't strike me as a particularly resilient character.' She sipped at her coffee reflectively, then added, 'But then, he doesn't have to be to plead his innocence.' She looked thoughtfully at Daniel, then said, 'Inspector Pitt is right, you know. You do have the knack of getting people to talk. When I try and question people they seem to clam up or get evasive.'

'I think some of them feel intimidated by you,' said Daniel.

'I'm not intimidating!' protested Abigail.

'Yes, you are.' Daniel smiled. 'When I first met you, I was intimidated by you.'

'And now?' demanded Abigail.

'Now, I just love you. I still think you're formidable and you'd make a terrifying opponent, but I've seen the softness underneath, the good heart and compassion. For me, that's the real you. Along with the fact you're the most clever person I've met.'

'Nonsense!'

'No, it's true. You're clever and tenacious. When you feel you're right, you stick to it like a terrier.'

'So do you.'

'Yes, but not so obviously.'

'Is that what I am: obvious?' she demanded.

'In a way,' said Daniel. 'Although I prefer to use the word 'honest'. Straight.'

'That's two words.'

314

'And pedantic,' said Daniel.

They finished their coffee and returned to the police station, where Pitt was waiting for them.

'Sorry to keep you waiting,' apologised the inspector. 'It would have been rude to just send Jasper off without offering him a cup of tea and catching up.'

'Absolutely understood,' said Abigail. 'You never know when you might need his help again.'

'It's not just that. Jasper's had to deal with a lot of troubles over the past few years. One of his young sons drowned, then his father killed himself, but with all that to cope with he's kept to his work and done a really good job out in that area. He's very reliable, but sadly reliable people often aren't appreciated by the powers that be; the go-getters seem to get the promotions and any awards that are going. So it's nice to let Jasper know he's appreciated.' Then he gave a grin at Abigail and said, 'And, of course, I never know when I might need his help again. Shall we go and talk to Piers Stevens?'

* * *

Abigail had elected to sit by a side wall of the interview room and observe, while Daniel and Inspector Pitt conducted the questioning. The men sat side by side at a table. Piers Stevens was brought in by a constable, who placed him on the empty chair on the other side of the table, then went to stand guard by the door, ready to spring into action if the prisoner showed any sign of fight.

315

There'll be no need for that, reflected Abigail. She didn't think she'd seen so miserable a person as Piers Stevens. The way he sat, cowed, made her think of a depressed hamster, hunched over, his hair matted, his clothes stained, and his body giving off a pungent smell from the lack of bathing.

'We know that you killed Eve Lachelle and that Everett was blackmailing you because of it,' said Daniel.

Stevens said nothing, just sat, trembling.

'We found Everett's diary,' added Daniel gently.

At this, Stevens let out a howl of anguish and lowered his head to the table. Abigail and Pitt both shot sharp looks at Daniel, but he shook his head, his attention on Stevens.

'It was an accident,' moaned Stevens, sitting back upright. 'Does he say that? He must say that!'

'Tell us about the accident,' said Daniel.

Stevens fell silent, sagging on the chair, then he swallowed and said, 'It was her fault. She shouldn't have named me. That was wrong. It wasn't me! I never attacked her! I came in when the others were finishing with her, but I never touched her.'

'Where was this?' asked Pitt.

'The storeroom at the back of the club.' He shook his head. 'She shouldn't have named me. That was unfair!'

'But she'd retracted her statement.'

'It made no difference! She'd *named* me!'

'And so you confronted her about it,' said Daniel.

Stevens nodded. 'It was a few days later. I was at the club and she was there. I was still so angry, and when she went into the back room where all the crates are stored, I followed her and told her off.'

'Had you had much to drink?' asked Daniel.

Stevens hesitated, then nodded again. 'I couldn't have faced her like that if I'd been sober. I got angry with her and . . . and I hit her. Just a slap across the face because I was so angry, but she fell and hit her head on the corner of one of the beer crates. That was it. It was an accident!'

'But you panicked,' said Daniel.

'Yes. And then Gavin Everett came in. He'd been standing by the door and he said he'd seen what happened. I begged him to come with me to the police, tell them it was an accident, but he said they'd never believe me. He said we had to get rid of her body, tell everyone she'd gone away. He said he'd arrange everything.'

'And you let him?'

'I was scared! In a panic! She was dead, and I'd killed her, and even though it was an accident, Everett said they'd hang me because the rape charges she'd made against me and the others gave me a motive for killing her. To silence her. I didn't know what to do. I was confused.'

'How did you get rid of the body?' asked Pitt.

'Doesn't Everett say in his diary?'

Pitt looked at Daniel, who shook his head. 'No,' he said.

'Then I'm not saying,' said Stevens. 'Without her body you haven't got any evidence.'

'We've just heard you confess,' said Daniel. 'Three of us. That's evidence enough.' When he saw the anguish in Stevens, twisting the young man's face, he said in the same gentle tone, 'We've been told you're a good man with a good heart.'

'Who said that?' he said, scornfully.

'Your mother's maid, Vera,' said Daniel.

At this, all the defiance seemed to go out of Stevens and he sagged in the chair again.

'She was the only one who was ever kind to me,' he mumbled.

'She saw the goodness in you,' continued Daniel. 'And I believe her.'

Stevens looked at Daniel, surprised. 'You do?'

'I do. And that's why I ask you, as a good and honest man, to tell us where we can find Eve Lachelle's body so that we can return it to her family for proper burial. They have that right.'

'She didn't have any family,' said Stevens.

'Everyone has family somewhere,' said Daniel. 'And surely, as a human being, she has the right to a proper burial, with a headstone to mark the fact that she lived. If you do have the good heart that Vera says you have, and that I also believe you have, then tell us where Eve Lachelle's body is so that she can be properly laid to rest. You owe her that.'

Stevens sat, silent, his head bowed, then finally said, 'She's out on some waste ground at Summertown.'

'Do you know where?'

Stevens nodded, his head still bowed, unable to face them.

'Did you go with Everett when he buried her?' asked Pitt.

Stevens nodded again. 'Everett and another man. I don't know his name. I'd never seen him before, or since.' Suddenly he raised his head and they saw the tears spilling out of his eyes and running down his cheeks. 'I didn't want to go with them, but Everett made me. It was . . . horrible. They . . . they wrapped her in a blanket and tied it up with rope. She was put on the back of a cart. The other man drove it, and Everett and I sat in the back. When we got there, they carried her and dumped her in a pond.'

'A pond?' queried Pitt.

'It was marshy ground. There were a few ponds.'

'But you know which one they put her in?'

Stevens nodded and hung his head again.

'I remember everything about it. The path. The trees. There were rabbits. They put her in a small, deep pond by some trees.'

'We'll need you to show us,' said Pitt.

Stevens looked at them appealingly.

'Do I have to?' he begged.

'We won't find her without you showing us which pond,' said Pitt gently.

'You're doing this for Eve,' said Daniel. 'To say sorry to her. And then she'll forgive you.'

Stevens suddenly broke down, crumpling on the chair so that his head lay on the table as he cried, his body heaving with his sobbing.

Pitt looked at Daniel and Abigail.

'I'll make the arrangements for a party to go out there and recover her,' he told them. 'In the

319

meantime, we'll return Mr Stevens to his cell while we talk to our next guest.' He turned to the constable. 'Take him back to his cell but be gentle with him.'

'Yes, sir.' The constable nodded. He went to the sobbing Stevens and tapped him gently on the shoulder. 'Come on, sir. I'll help you back to your cell.'

As Stevens pushed himself to his feet, his posture a picture of misery, Pitt told him, 'Thank you, Mr Stevens. I've just got a few things to sort out, and then we'll travel to Summertown. And if everything is as you say, we'll see that you get fair representation.'

The constable led Stevens out of the room, and Abigail turned to Daniel and said accusingly, 'You lied to him. You said we'd found Everett's diary.'

'I didn't say it said anything about him killing Eve Lachelle,' said Daniel.

'But it was still a lie.'

'It was an exaggeration,' said Daniel. 'Like your story you told those women of working for a solicitor to give Eve Lachelle her inheritance.'

'And it got us what we wanted: a confession,' said Pitt. 'And, more importantly, the place where the body was buried.' He stood up. 'Now, let's see what Josiah Goddard has to say for himself. And, after this last one, I suggest you take the lead again, Daniel. But this time with Miss Fenton sharing the questioning. After all, you are the history expert.'

★ ★ ★

Goddard was brought from his cell to the interview room, still handcuffed.

'Are these necessary?' he demanded, angrily.

Pitt looked at the constable who'd accompanied Goddard.

'He started to get difficult, sir,' explained the constable. 'Verbal abuse. So I thought it best to restrain him as a precaution in case he tried to escape.'

'Quite right.' Pitt nodded. 'But I think you can take them off now.'

The constable unlocked the handcuffs, and Goddard sat down in the same chair that Piers Stevens had occupied only moments before, but the difference in attitude of the two men was very marked. Whereas Stevens had been beaten down and distraught, Goddard was aggressively defiant.

Abigail had now moved to join Daniel and Inspector Pitt at the table across from Goddard. It was Daniel who opened the questioning.

'You were seen hanging about outside the Ashmolean just before Everett was shot,' he said.

'Well, that was nothing to do with me,' said Goddard. 'I didn't shoot him.'

'But you went to see him.'

Goddard hesitated, then nodded. 'He owed me money,' he said.

'For the copies you made for him,' said Abigail.

'Yes.'

'We've seen the financial ledger. He paid you as you delivered each one.'

Goddard hesitated, then mumbled, 'Yes, but

not enough. I didn't realise what he was using them for at first.'

'Putting them on display at the museum in place of the originals?' asked Abigail.

'He told me he wanted them as replacements in case the originals needed to be taken out for cleaning. But I saw that some of my copies were on permanent display. So, what had happened to the originals? I knew then that he was selling them to private collectors.'

'So you challenged him?'

'I did. I told him I knew what he was up to and I wanted my share. He said I was already getting enough from selling the other copies I made. I said that was a separate business, and I wasn't making as much from them as he was from selling the originals.'

'What did he say?'

'He challenged me to prove he was selling the originals. I said I didn't need to, all I had to do was tell Mr Marriott some of the stuff on display had been done by me, and I could prove it, and he'd have difficult questions to answer.' He gave a sly grin. 'That made him change his tune. He said he'd think about it.'

'And?' prompted Daniel, as Goddard fell silent.

'Well, after a week or so when I hadn't heard anything, I went back to see him. He said he was still thinking about it. I told him the time for thinking was over. I wanted a share of what he'd made. He said he was still waiting for the people to pay him the money, but he'd settle with me once he'd got it. I wanted to know how much.

He said he'd give me ten per cent of what he'd got. I said it wasn't enough, I wanted half. After all, I was the one who'd done the work. In the end, we settled on a quarter for my share. The trouble was, I didn't know what he'd sold the pieces for, and I didn't trust him. So, I set about trying to find out who might have bought them.'

'And did you find out?'

Goddard shook his head. 'No. I don't move in those kind of rich circles. But I just knew Everett was trying to cheat me. When I still hadn't got the money I was owed, I went back to see him, but I decided to wait until everyone had gone. I didn't want anyone coming in and overhearing what we were talking about.'

'And that was the day he was shot,' said Daniel.

'Yes, but it wasn't me! He was alive when I left his office!' Then he suddenly remembered something. 'I can prove it. There was a woman who was waiting at the bottom of the stairs when I came down. The only person she could have been waiting for was Everett because he was the only person in the building. Find her. She'll tell you he was still alive when I left.'

'Who was this woman?'

'I don't know. I'd never seen her before.'

'Describe her.'

'I can't. She had a hood over her head, so I couldn't see her face. But I could tell she was a proper lady by the clothes she wore. She had on a long cloak, and her shoes must have cost a pretty penny. I notice things like that because I'm an artist.'

'The copies you made,' said Abigail. 'You must have done drawings of the originals.'

'Not just drawings,' said Goddard. 'Proper reproductions, with all the right colours where they should be.'

'And you did these in a sketchbook, I presume,' said Abigail.

'Of course,' said Goddard. 'Just like any artist would.'

'We'll need those sketchbooks.'

'Why?' demanded Goddard. 'They're mine, and they're precious.'

'They may also be what stops you going to jail,' said Abigail. 'Providing you make a note against those sketches to show which ones Everett asked you to make copies of.'

'You're going to try and recover the originals?' said Goddard.

'We'll do our best,' said Abigail.

Goddard shook his head. 'Like I've already said, I don't know who Everett sold the originals to, so I can't see how you can.'

'That's up to us,' Abigail told him. 'But what I can promise you is that if you don't give us your sketchbooks, with the notes of which ones Everett asked you specifically to copy, we'll see that you go to prison for a very long time.'

'On what charge?' demanded Goddard. He turned to Inspector Pitt, who'd stayed silent during all this. 'Copying ain't illegal!'

'Conspiracy to defraud is,' said Daniel. 'As is conspiracy to commit theft. And, as a former Scotland Yard detective, I can assure you that the courts go very hard on any conspiracy charge.

Hard labour is assured, and there's the serious possibility of transportation.'

Goddard swallowed hard and looked at them, agitated. 'And if I give you my sketchbooks?'

'That will help convince us you weren't an accomplice to any crime, but an unknowing dupe who'd been conned by Everett.'

'And I'll get off?'

'That depends on Inspector Pitt,' said Abigail. She looked at Pitt. 'What do you think, Inspector?'

'If these sketchbooks are handed over and they help in solving a crime, I'm sure that might go a long way to convince us that you were, as Miss Fenton has just said, an unwilling dupe in this case, and therefore innocent.' He looked directly at their prisoner. 'Well, Mr Goddard?'

'If you come with me to my shop, I'll give 'em to you,' said Goddard. Then he added sharply, 'But I want 'em back after!'

'Good,' said Pitt. 'However, at this moment we have another journey to make. When we've done that, we'll take you to your shop.'

'You mean I've got to stay locked up here!' said Goddard, aghast.

'Only for a while,' said Pitt. 'It will give you a chance to think about your situation if you hadn't decided to help us. If that had been the case, you'd have been occupying a cell for much longer, and in a far harsher environment than a police station.'

37

Daniel and Abigail rode in the interior of the police van, along with two uniformed constables. Inspector Pitt sat at the front with Piers Stevens, who was sandwiched between him and the driver.

A long-based hearse from a local funeral director's followed the police van.

'Isn't it strange for Everett to have taken Stevens with them when they disposed of Eve Lachelle's body?' asked Abigail, puzzled. 'Surely he would have wanted the dumping place kept secret from Stevens in case he revealed it.'

'No,' said Daniel. 'It was part of Everett's strategy to keep Stevens under his control. You saw the effect the whole business has had on Stevens: it's made him a wreck. Making him witness the body being dumped like that would have made him feel absolutely dreadful. Terrible guilt. And, by going with them, it implicated him in the whole business. No, Everett knew what he was doing alright. He knew how weak Stevens was and this was all part of him tightening the screws.'

The van lurched slightly, then began to shudder and jerk as it rolled forward. Daniel took a look out of one of the small, barred windows.

'We've left the road. We're going along a rough track that runs at the back of a church, passing a graveyard, by the look of it.'

The journey got bumpier, and Daniel, Abigail and the two constables took firm hold of the bars in the rear compartment to stop themselves from being thrown from their seats. Finally, the vehicle stopped. There was a knock on the roof, then Pitt's voice called, 'We're here. All down.'

One of the constables let Daniel and Abigail out first, then the two policemen began to gather the equipment up they'd brought with them in the van: two spades and a grappling hook on a rope.

Stevens and Pitt had already dismounted, the young man looking tiny and shrunken beside the tall figure of the inspector. Daniel and Abigail stayed back and watched as Stevens led the way across the uneven ground, stumbling now and then. Pitt and Stevens were making for a small clump of trees, and finally they stopped. Pitt raised his arm and called for the others to join them.

Daniel and Abigail let the constables and the four funeral directors go first, then followed in their wake. The ground beneath their feet was soft and squelchy, and there were various places where the water from the ponds on either side of the narrow path had turned the path to mud. The funeral directors carried a long wooden box between them, using a handle at each corner.

'Careful you don't slip,' cautioned Daniel.

'When I was in Egypt — ' began Abigail.

'Yes, alright. You've done this kind of thing before.' Daniel sighed.

Pitt and Stevens were standing beside a pond

filled with reeds and grasses.

'Here,' said Stevens, pointing.

Pitt gestured for the two constables to drop the grappling hook into the pond, then withdrew, tugging at Stevens' sleeve to move him away from the pond.

As the constables pulled at the rope, Daniel took a large handkerchief from his pocket and passed it to Abigail.

'Here,' he said. 'You'll need this.'

She took it but regarded it with puzzlement.

'Why?' she asked.

'When they start to reveal the body.'

She offered the handkerchief back to him.

'You forget, I'm not unfamiliar with seeing dead bodies. And I don't get tearful over people I don't know.'

'Yes, but those have either been recently dead, or thousands of years old. This body has been here for three months or so. In that time, the creatures in the pond will have been at work, the flesh will have decayed and started to decompose, and the stench will be awful.' He produced another handkerchief from his pocket. 'I'll be covering my nose and mouth with this. If you look, you'll see that Inspector Pitt and the constables are doing the same.'

Abigail looked and saw that the constables had, indeed, tied cloths around the lower part of their faces, as had the funeral directors, while Pitt had his handkerchief ready in his hand.

'Thank you,' said Abigail. 'I shall know to come prepared in future.'

Their first drag of the pond was unsuccessful,

the grappling hook appearing from the pond with just grasses caught up in it. The constables moved their position a few yards to one side and dropped the hook in again, and once more it came up empty.

Pitt looked enquiringly at Stevens, who began to tremble.

'She was here!' he burst out. 'She was! This is the place!'

The grappling hook was thrown in a third time, and again came up with just a tangle of grasses.

'Throw it nearer the middle,' Pitt told them.

They did, and this time as they began to pull on the rope, it snagged on something. The two constables hauled at the rope, but they were having difficulty. Inspector Pitt stepped forward and joined them, grabbing the rope, but even with three of them heaving at it, whatever they had caught hold of refused to appear. Daniel left Abigail and joined them, taking a section of the rope in his hands, and now the four men looked like a tug of war team. Pitt called out commands to coordinate their efforts, and very slowly the rope came upwards out from the pond water, until finally a piece of cloth broke the surface. As it did so they saw that a broken branch had become tangled with a bundle, causing the hook to snag below the surface.

The four men continued pulling at the rope, and soon the large bundle of cloth was being dragged from the water in the claws of the grappling hook and pulled to lay on the grassy ground clear of the water.

Daniel rejoined Abigail, and Pitt resumed his place beside the miserable figure of Stevens, at the same time gesturing for the funeral directors to come forward.

The four men lifted the wooden box and carried it to where the bundle lay, putting it down beside it. Two of them began to lift the bundle, and as they did so the cloth, which had rotted, parted, and something that was not wholly human, yet not completely a skeleton, fell out onto the grass. As it hit the ground it began to move, and for a moment Abigail was stunned — how could a dead body move? Then she saw the different creatures come crawling and flapping out of the body. Suddenly the appalling stench hit her, and she was glad of the handkerchief Daniel had given her.

The whole thing — the sight of the decomposing body tumbling out of its rotted blanket, the creatures, the smell — was too much for Piers Stevens, who fell to his knees and vomited, and kept vomiting.

38

The remains of the body of Eve Lachelle had been taken by the funeral directors to the hospital mortuary to be examined by the resident pathologist. Piers Stevens had been returned to a cell at Kemp Hall to be held on remand pending the outcome of the medical examination. Josiah Goddard had been released after taking Inspector Pitt, Daniel and Abigail to his shop and handing over his sketchbooks.

Abigail's first desperate desire after the exhumation had been to soak herself in a bath at the Wilton Hotel to try and rid herself of the stench of decayed corpse that she felt still enshrouded her, but she had forgone that in order to get her hands on Goddard's notebooks. Now, bathed, she and Daniel were back in their room at the hotel.

Abigail had the sketchbooks open on the dressing table and was leafing through them, but her mind was running over the final part of Goddard's statement about the mysterious lady he claimed to have seen waiting outside the Ashmolean on the evening Everett was shot.

'It seems as if we're back to this mysterious titled lady with the Shakespeare play,' she said. 'Which means either the Duchess of Charlbury or Baroness Whichford. Except now, one of them might well be our murderess. From what Esther told me about interviewing them both, I'd put my money on the duchess. Esther said the baroness was a fragile woman, very nervous. I can't see her holding a pistol and firing such a good, firm shot to kill Everett. According to Esther, the duchess, on the other hand, is an excellent shot and sounds like she's got nerves of steel.'

'No,' said Daniel, who was lying on the bed, deep in thought. 'It doesn't make sense.'

Abigail looked at him inquisitively.

'Think about it,' enlarged Daniel, getting up from the bed and joining her at the dressing table. 'She's agreed to meet Everett and bring him the play. She arrives as scheduled. Except she shoots him. Why would she do that?'

'Because something changes,' suggested Abigail. 'Something she doesn't expect to happen.'

'But she's brought a gun with her. Why?'

'She planned to shoot him.'

'Again, that makes no sense. If she's going to kill him, why do it at the Ashmolean? It's too risky. Far better to make arrangements to see him somewhere private and secret, and then shoot him there.'

'So, what do you suggest?' asked Abigail.

'Someone else arrived. They'd found out about the prospective sale and followed her in order to stop it.'

'Her husband?'

'It has to be.'

'So our killer is either the Duke of Charlbury or Baron Whichford.'

'Yes,' said Daniel. 'The problem is, at that level of society, we can't arrest one of them without

332

being absolutely sure it's him. Superintendent Clare and Inspector Pitt wouldn't entertain it.'

'So how do we identify which one is the killer?'

'By working out how one of them would have known his wife was planning to sell the family heirloom. Which means, which one had the play in his family's possession?'

'That's impossible to find out,' said Abigail. 'If they're asked direcdy, the guilty one will simply deny it.'

'But Everett found out that one of them had the play,' said Daniel. 'According to Marriott, he was told about it by some man acting as an intermediary for the wife. But I have my doubts about that. Everett lied about nearly everything. I'm pretty sure the story about an intermediary was a cover. I think he found about the play some other way, and then took advantage of it.' Suddenly his face brightened and he smiled. 'Everett was an eavesdropper. I think he heard someone brag about his family owning such a play. And where might he have heard this talk? At a place where gentlemen meet to play cards, talk, and socialise.'

'The Quill Club?' asked Abigail.

'Exactly,' said Daniel. 'I wonder if either the Duke of Charlbury or Baron Whichford is a member?'

'I don't know,' said Abigail doubtfully. 'Even if one of them is a member, it doesn't mean he's the one who shot Everett. It's all circumstantial, and if just one strand of your thinking turns out to be wrong, your whole theory collapses. At the moment it's all just speculation. You're guessing. You don't *know*.'

'I do,' insisted Daniel. 'It's my detective's nose. It's led me to this point, and it's rarely wrong.'

'Rarely isn't good enough,' said Abigail. 'Without proof you have nothing.' She weighed up that thought, then said, 'We need to talk to Inspector Pitt.'

★ ★ ★

When Daniel and Abigail arrived at Kemp Hall, they discovered that Inspector Pitt was busy with a visitor.

'But I'm sure you can go in,' the duty sergeant told them. 'It's Dr Lennox from the hospital, come to report about the body that was brought in.'

'Dr Lennox,' said Daniel as he and Abigail walked along the corridor towards Pitt's office. 'He was the doctor who examined me after the War Office people, or whoever they were, let me go.'

'He's worked fast,' said Abigail.

'Too fast,' said Daniel doubtfully. 'He can't have done a proper examination in this short time.'

They entered the office and found Doctor Lennox leaning on the inspector's desk as the two men looked at a sketch of a human head. The doctor smiled as he saw them and stretched out his hand in greeting.

'Good to see you again, Mr Wilson. I hope

334

your head has recovered.'

'Indeed, it has, Doctor. Thank you for your ministrations.' He indicated Abigail. 'This is my partner, Abigail Fenton.'

'Good to meet you, Miss Fenton,' said Lennox, shaking her hand.

'Dr Lennox was explaining about the cause of death of Eve Lachelle,' said Pitt.

'Yes. As I explained to the inspector, I haven't had time to do a proper examination, but Inspector Pitt specifically asked me one question to which he said he'd appreciate a speedy answer, so I concentrated on that. The full examination of the cadaver will follow over the next couple of days.'

'I wanted to know if Stevens' defence was plausible,' said Pitt. 'You remember he said he hit her and she fell and struck her head on a beer crate.'

'And the answer is, yes, that's a very possible explanation,' said Lennox. 'She died from a fracture of the skull as the result of a blow from a pointed object made of wood. The sharp corner of a wooden beer crate would fit. There were splinters of wood embedded in the fracture. Unfortunately for the woman, she had an exceptionally thin skull, so if she fell and hit her head against the corner of a wooden beer crate, that would be a probable cause in my opinion.' He looked at Daniel and smiled. 'Unlike your head, Mr Wilson. Even without doing an autopsy on you, my examination of you showed that you are fortunate in having a thick bone structure to your skull.' He looked at his watch. 'Well, I'd better get back and continue with examining the rest of the body. I'll be able to let you have my full report in a couple of days.'

'Thank you, Doctor,' said Pitt. 'I appreciate you coming in and letting me know this.'

After Lennox had gone, Daniel said, 'You're thinking the charge could be involuntary manslaughter.'

Pitt nodded. 'Which is a far less serious charge than either murder or even voluntary manslaughter.'

'You want him to avoid prison,' said Abigail. 'Even though he killed the woman.'

'There'll be a prison term, but he won't face the hangman,' said Pitt. 'But that decision won't be up to me. All I can do is pass the evidence to Superintendent Clare, and he'll decide what the charge will be.' He looked at Abigail. 'I trust you've recovered from the ordeal of the exhumation?'

'I still have the smell in my nostrils,' said Abigail.

'Yes, it takes some getting used to,' said Pitt sympathetically. 'What can I do for you? Have Goddard's sketchbooks produced a result?'

'Not yet,' said Abigail. 'We need to talk to you about our prime suspects for the murder of Gavin Everett.'

'This mysterious lady that Goddard talked about,' said Pitt.

'No, her husband,' said Abigail.

'Her husband?' echoed Pitt, surprised. 'And does he have a name?'

'He's a choice of two,' said Daniel. 'Either the

Duke of Charlbury or Baron Whichford.'

Pitt looked at Daniel, stunned. Then he said, 'This is getting above my pay grade. I think we need to go and see Superintendent Clare.'

★ ★ ★

'So you think that either the Duke of Charlbury or Baron Whichford murdered Everett,' said Clare thoughtfully.

Daniel, Abigail and Inspector Pitt were in the superintendent's office, and Daniel had just set out his theory behind the shooting of Gavin Everett.

'I do,' said Daniel.

'But you have no proof.'

'The evidence so far is circumstantial, but it does point to the killer being one of those two.' Daniel enumerated his train of thoughts. 'The person who killed Everett was a good shot with a steady hand. According to Gladstone Marriott, Everett was due to meet a lady, or the lady's representative, at six o'clock in his office at the Ashmolean to arrange to buy a Shakespeare play from her, which her husband's family had owned since the sixteenth century. Her husband's ancestor had bought the play from Shakespeare himself. The only two families that fit that possibility are those of the Duke of Charlbury and Baron Whichford.

'Just before Everett was shot, a lady was seen by Josiah Goddard, the man who was Everett's confederate in the fraudulent artefacts racket, waiting to go into the Ashmolean. He described her as appearing distinguished in her dress, although he never saw her face. This points to her being either the Duchess of Charlbury or Baroness Whichford.'

'Very circumstantial,' said Clare. 'She could have been any lady, going into the Ashmolean for any number of reasons.'

'True,' admitted Daniel. 'But I feel it was one of them.'

'Feeling is not proof,' said Clare.

'But we can get proof,' said Daniel.

'Daniel's got a theory that Everett learnt about the existence of the play from a conversation he overheard at the Quill Club,' said Abigail.

'Yes,' said Daniel. 'And if we see Mr de Witt and insist he tells us which of those two, the duke or the baron, is a member . . . '

'No,' said Clare.

The firmness of his tone surprised them.

'But we are very close to solving the murder,' insisted Daniel.

'No,' said Clare again. He opened a drawer in his desk and took out a letter, which he passed across his desk to them. 'There is no murder.'

The letter was from the War Office, addressed to Superintendent Augustus Clare at Kemp Hall police station, Oxford, and signed by Commander Atkinson. The message was direct.

Dear Superintendent Clare,
By order of this office I confirm that the original instructions regarding the death of Mr Everett at the Ashmolean Museum are to be complied with. Mr Everett's death is

officially *suicide.* *There* *is* *to* *be* *no*
continuation *of* *any* *investigation* *into* *Mr*
Everett's *death* *by* *your* *force.*
Yours sincerely,
Commander Wilfred Atkinson

'That arrived this morning,' said Clare. 'I had
intended to summon you to make you aware of
this directive, but your request to meet made this
the opportunity.'

'Why did you wait until I'd outlined our case?'
asked Daniel, frustrated. 'Why didn't you tell us
about this letter at the start?'

'I wanted to hear if you had any evidence to
back your claim,' said Clare. 'If you had, I would
have taken it up with the War Office. But you
have no evidence. You have suppositions based
on circumstances. I'm sorry, Mr Wilson, Miss
Fenton, but the involvement of the Oxford police
force in any investigation into the death of Gavin
Everett is now at an end.'

39

There was an air of gloom between them as Inspector Pitt escorted Daniel and Abigail through the police station towards the exit.

'I'm sorry, but there's nothing I can do,' he said ruefully. 'Nor can the superintendent. And it's not his fault. You saw the letter from London.'

'Yes,' said Daniel. 'And fair play to him, he needn't have shown it to us. Many superintendents I've worked with wouldn't have. He's a good man.'

'So, what will you do now? Return to London?'

'There's still the matter of the fakes on display at the Ashmolean,' said Abigail. 'Now we have Goddard's sketchbooks we can identify them and have them removed.'

'Pity the originals have gone.' Pitt sighed.

'Well, we'll see what we might be able to unearth,' said Abigail.

They shook hands, then Daniel and Abigail left the police station and set off for the Ashmolean.

'So that's the end of the case.' Abigail sighed.

'No,' said Daniel.

Abigail looked at him, puzzled. 'But you heard what the superintendent said. And Inspector Pitt. We saw the letter from the War Office.'

'There's to be no official *police* investigation,'

said Daniel. 'But we aren't the police. We've been hired by Gladstone Marriott and the Ashmolean Museum.'

'To do what?' asked Abigail impatiently. 'We have no powers of arrest.'

'I don't like walking away from a case and leaving it unfinished.'

'It's not unfinished,' insisted Abigail. 'We solved the mystery of what happened to Eve Lachelle, and the man who killed her has been brought to justice, to a degree. We've found out who was behind the fakes at the Ashmolean, and there's a very good chance we'll be able to recover some of them, if I was right about what I saw at Lord Chessington's house.'

'But the case we were hired to look into was who killed Gavin Everett.'

'And we know that. If you're right, it was either the Duke of Charlbury or Baron Whichford.'

'*If* I'm right,' stressed Daniel. 'I need to know.'

'But how will you do that?'

'I'm going to have a word with de Witt at the Quill Club,' said Daniel. 'Once we know which of those two is a member, we'll know who the killer is.'

'And do what? It's all still circumstantial.'

'I know,' admitted Daniel unhappily. 'But I need to get the answer.'

'Do you want me to come with you to see de Witt?' asked Abigail.

'No, thank you,' said Daniel. 'I may need to lean on him a bit.'

'I can lean on him,' Abigail pointed out.

Daniel smiled. 'You'd beat him with a shovel. I need to be . . . subtle.'

'Are you saying I'm not subtle?' demanded Abigail.

'Probably 'devious' is the right word,' said Daniel. 'You're too honest to be devious.'

'You make me sound too virtuous,' said Abigail, offended. 'I can be devious.'

'Yes, true.' Daniel sighed, defeated. 'But right now, I need to see de Witt on my own.'

'In that case I'll go to the Ashmolean and go through Goddard's sketchbooks with Gladstone Marriott, and get these fakes identified and out of the museum.'

* * *

As Abigail entered the Ashmolean, she found Esther in an agitated state just inside the entrance.

'There you are!' exclaimed Esther. 'I've been looking all over for you. I tried the Wilton Hotel, but they said they didn't know where you or Mr Wilson had gone.'

'We've been busy,' said Abigail. She hesitated, wondering whether to tell her about Josiah Goddard, but decided against it until she'd spoken to Gladstone Marriott. Instead, she said, 'We may have a story for you.'

'Oh?'

'We discovered the body of a woman who'd gone missing. We believe she was killed, but whether on purpose or accidentally has yet to be determined.'

342

'A murder!' said Esther excitedly.

'It may not turn out to be murder,' said Abigail. 'Whichever it is, we'll let you have details, so you can get your first proper crime report.'

'If Mr Pinker lets me write it,' said Esther unhappily.

'I feel he will,' said Abigail. 'What were you looking for us for?'

'I've done my second interview. Baroness Whichford.'

'How did you get on? What was she like?'

'She was lovely to me, but *so* unhappy!'

'Why?'

'I don't know. I didn't like to ask her. Her husband, the baron, spoke to me before I met her. He was lovely. So caring about her. He wanted me to know some of the troubles she's had lately, so I didn't say anything that might upset her.'

'What sort of troubles?' asked Abigail.

'According to the baron, a cousin whom she was very close to died in a tragic accident just recently. And when I said I'd avoid talking to her about people dying and suggested instead talking about their children, he told me that they didn't have any, and that fact causes her great upset.' Esther scowled. 'I'm so stupid! I should have checked if they had any children before I went out there!'

'So, what did you talk about?'

'The house. The estate. Her husband's family.'

'Did you manage to say anything about famous writers the family might have met?'

'No,' admitted Esther unhappily. 'I tried to, but she seemed so sad I stuck to things that might cheer her up. You know, the decoration of the house, clothes, that sort of thing. But nothing there seemed to interest her. Not that she was unkind; it was as if she wasn't there. Not in spirit. As if she wanted to be alone but was too kind to say as much.'

'Did you get an idea of what the relationship was like between her and the baron?'

'Absolutely lovely! As I said, he was so caring about her before he took me to see her. And when I mentioned him to her, her face softened for the first time and I could see how deeply she felt for him. In fact, she said that he was her salvation.'

'Her salvation?' repeated Abigail, puzzled. 'What an odd thing to say. Salvation from what?'

'Oh, just that he was the right man for her,' said Esther airily. 'It's what women say when they find Mr Right and he takes them out of a life of spinsterhood.'

'I can't imagine myself ever saying anything like that,' said Abigail, being critical.

'Ah, but you're still unmarried, like me,' said Esther. 'Maybe we'd both be saying that if Mr Right turned up and swept us off our feet.'

★   ★   ★

I have found Mr Right, thought Abigail as she headed for their office, *but I'd never call Daniel my salvation.*

She wondered if the fact that she didn't feel

the need of a man to give her an identity made her odd. That certainly seemed to be the opinion of her sister, Bella, who seemed to view her own marriage to Dr Keen as some kind of salvation.

The fact is, I love Daniel for the person he is, and I hope he loves me for the person I am. Short-tempered, belligerent and opinionated, she added slightly ruefully.

She'd promised Esther that she'd be in touch with details of the discovery of Eve Lachelle's body as soon as they had the full facts from the police, so they were able to pass on the details for publication. Right now, sorting out the issue of the forgeries was her main mission.

Abigail collected Goddard's sketchbooks from their office and took them along to Gladstone Marriott.

'Here,' she said, putting the books down on his desk. 'The details of which items from the Ashmolean were copied on the instructions of Everett, then sold and replaced by copies.'

Marriott sat at his desk and watched with a mixture of awe and horror as Abigail flicked over the pages of Goddard's sketchbooks, stopping every now and then to show a particular painted drawing.

'The ones marked 'GE' are the ones that Everett specifically asked Goddard to copy, so those are the ones that we'll find are the fakes. Most of the other sketches are of items that Goddard thought would sell well in his shop, so he made copies, but the originals are still in place.' She passed a sheet of paper to him. 'I've made a list of the items marked 'GE'. There are twelve of them, eight from the ancient Egypt display and four from the Roman. As you know, I'd already identified four of the items on display as fakes, so that leaves eight, which we'll soon identify. I suggest we take these sketchbooks with us to those exhibits and remove the offending items.'

'Twelve!' exclaimed Marriott.

'It could have been a great deal worse,' said Abigail.

'Yes, I suppose you're right.' Marriott sighed. 'But I can't get over the fact that the originals have gone, never to be recovered!' He let out a heartfelt groan. 'If only Everett had left a note of who he'd sold the artefacts to we could try and recover them.'

'He kept his client list in his head, so there was no chance of him being exposed,' said Abigail. 'But there may be a chance to recover some of the items.'

Marriott looked at her in surprise. 'You think so? But how?'

'I can't tell you until I'm sure of something,' said Abigail.

'What?' asked Marriott.

'Again, I think that's best kept secret, just in case I'm wrong and a genuine person is maligned. That would be very unfair.'

'Yes, but . . . ' Marriott hesitated, then gave her a look of almost desperate appeal. 'You think you might be able to locate them?'

'Possibly,' said Abigail.

★　★　★

Vance de Witt looked up as the door of his office opened and Daniel walked in.

'You again,' said de Witt sourly. 'I've got nothing to say to you.'

'That's unfortunate,' said Daniel, 'because I have something to say to you. Piers Stevens has been arrested on a charge of causing the death of Eve Lachelle. The police have his confession. They also have the body of Eve Lachelle. It seems that she was killed here, in your storeroom.'

'I know nothing about this!' snapped de Witt.

'Yes, so you've said before,' said Daniel. 'But when Stevens comes to trial, a few things are going to come out in public, especially when Stevens starts giving evidence. According to him, the trouble began when he came into your storeroom and found Eve Lachelle being raped by three of your members.'

'The charges were dropped,' said de Witt.

'For lack of evidence,' continued Daniel. 'But the confession from Stevens rather changes things. Charges of rape can now be brought, even though the woman is dead. The fact that she is dead will make sure the case gets even bigger publicity in the press. The Quill Club is going to be implicated throughout this case, both from the rape and the killing of Eve Lachelle. It's going to become notorious. *You* are going to become notorious, Mr de Witt.'

'This was nothing to do with me,' said de Witt curtly.

'That will be for the court to decide,' said Daniel. 'I look forward to you giving evidence in a public court and seeing how confident you are then.'

As de Witt glared silently at him, Daniel added, 'And it's not just the trial in court, it's the trial by the press. How much publicity they give it in the newspapers. Believe me, the journalists will be desperate for any juicy details they can get about you, about Stevens, the Quill Club, everything. Now, Inspector Pitt and the police aren't allowed to talk to the press about such things because of their position, but I'm in a different situation. I can talk to them, and I can choose which ones I talk to because I've made many contacts in the world of newspapers. And these will be national newspapers, not just the *Oxford Messenger*, who are easily controllable.'

'How much?' growled de Witt.

Daniel shook his head. 'You misunderstand me, Mr de Witt. I'm not after money, but I would like some information about one of your members. Now, the inspector could get a warrant to confiscate your membership lists, but as we've discussed before, they could well vanish by the time the warrant arrives. I can't promise to keep this story out of the papers, it's going to be too big for that. But I can decide how much I share with certain journalists about the behind the scenes in this case, including you and the Quill Club. In fact, I may choose to say nothing.'

De Witt studied Daniel, then asked, 'What do you want to know?'

Daniel produced the two slips of paper on each of which he'd written a name.

'One of these is a member of your club. Which one?'

Inside, Daniel's heart raced as he worried that de Witt might say both men were members.

De Witt looked at the two slips of paper, then placed his finger on one.

'Him,' he said sullenly.

'Thank you,' said Daniel.

40

'So it's him,' said Abigail.

'I believe it is,' said Daniel.

'I assume we pay him a visit and confront him.'

'No,' said Daniel. 'I think it would be better if it's just me.'

'Why?' asked Abigail.

'Why would this woman hand over such a precious item?'

'According to Marriott it was about revenge on her part.'

'Does that fit with what we know of this particular woman?'

'No,' admitted Abigail.

'With what we know about Everett, it's more likely he had something on her. Something incriminating.'

'An affair?'

'Possibly. And if that was the case I'm sure our man would refuse to talk about it with a woman present.'

Abigail nodded.

'Yes, you could be right. In that case, I'll call on Lord Chessington and confront him about the fakes, and the fact that he has the originals in his house.'

'You're sure of that?' asked Daniel.

'As sure as you are that this man killed Everett. Marriott and I checked Goddard's sketchbooks against the artefacts on display, and we've identified the twelve that Goddard marked as the ones that Everett asked him specifically to copy, eight from the ancient Egypt display and four from the Roman.'

'And those twelve originals have all gone?'

'Yes. I'm convinced I saw one of the missing Egyptian plates in Chessington's secret room, and as he's such an absolute devotee of ancient Egypt, I suspect he'll have the other ancient Egyptian ones. He may even have the Roman items.'

'I'm not sure if it's a good idea for you to confront him on your own,' said Daniel doubtfully. 'As I said, I feel the man is dangerous, despite his outward air of bonhomie. I still have a suspicion he shot Grafton to kill him, not to wound him. And the only reason he'd do that is to protect a secret, such as having the stolen artefacts in his secret room. Go in there and challenge him with what we know and you could be putting yourself at risk.'

'Then I won't challenge him directly,' said Abigail. 'I'll be subtle. I shall phrase what I say that hints at what we know, but without suggesting he is in danger of discovery.'

Daniel looked even more doubtful. 'That sounds like an impossibility to me,' he said. 'I suggest you leave it until we can go and see him together, when I'll make sure I'm armed, just in case.'

'You think he might shoot me?'

'I think he's capable of it,' said Daniel. 'I really

feel there's something about him that's dangerous.'

'In that case, arrange a pistol for me to carry
when I go to see him.'

'No,' said Daniel. 'It would be too dangerous.'

'So it's dangerous if I go unarmed, and
dangerous if I go armed,' said Abigail, annoyed.
'Daniel, I've said before, you have to learn to
trust me. I know what I'm doing.'

'Not with someone like Lord Chessington.'

'I've met plenty of Lord Chessingtons before,'
retorted Abigail. 'And I think I can ensure my
safety.'

'How? By arming yourself with a shovel?'
asked Daniel with gentle irony.

'I thought I might offer to meet him
somewhere public. The Ashmolean, for example.
Or the reception lounge of the Wilton Hotel.'

'Yes.' Daniel nodded. 'Something like that
would be safer. Thank you.'

'That's settled then.' Abigail smiled. 'I can't
have you in a worried state about me when
you're having your all-boys-together chat. You're
going to need your wits about you if you're going
to get a confession out of him.'

⋆ ⋆ ⋆

Keeping her promise to Daniel, Abigail sent a
letter by messenger to Lord Chessington
inviting him to meet her at the Ashmolean 'to
discuss some issues that have arisen over some
of the items on display'. The messenger
returned with a polite reply, offering his

apologies for not being able to accept her kind invitation.

> *As I sincerely hope you may understand and be sympathetic to, my recent dreadful experience has meant that I am reluctant to leave my house. However, I do hope you will do me the honour of coming to my house for the discussion you mention, which sounds most intriguing.*
>
> *I do hope you can come and look forward to seeing you this afternoon.*
> *Yours sincerely,*
> *Chessington*

Well, I tried, Daniel, thought Abigail ruefully.

★ ★ ★

Abigail made her way to Chessington's house, weighing up her options if, as Daniel suspected, his lordship did turn nasty when she told him the reason for her errand. What could he do to her? She was fit and strong and had already overpowered one attacker who'd tried to assault her. Chessington did not seem to be the type suited to physical action. Yes, he'd shot and killed Inspector Grafton, but surely he wouldn't be receiving her with a loaded pistol in his hand. If he did attempt to go for a gun, she was fairly confident she could deal with him before he could aim it at her.

She mounted the steps to Chessington's front door and rang the bell. The door was opened by

William, the butler, who escorted her to the library, where Chessington awaited her. His lordship rose from his chair and came towards her, smiling happily, to shake her hand in greeting.

'Miss Fenton! It was a pleasant surprise to get your note! And thank you so much for agreeing to meet me here, rather than somewhere outside. As I said in my reply, I'm afraid to admit that since the dreadful events of that night when the detective inspector tragically died, I've been reluctant to leave the house. It may sound unnecessarily cautious, but I keep wondering whether other dangers await me. I still don't know why the man had decided to burgle my house, and I'm fearful that others may intend to do the same.' He pointed to a card table, on which lay a pistol. 'But, just in case, this time I will be prepared.'

A pistol, *groaned Abigail inwardly.* And, I expect, fully loaded. I have walked into the lion's den.

'Please, make yourself comfortable,' said Chessington, gesturing at an armchair, and he settled himself down in the chair next to the card table with the pistol within his easy reach.

Abigail sat, wondering how fast she could move if Chessington snatched up the pistol.

'You said you wanted to discuss some issues that have arisen over a few of the items on display,' said Chessington. 'What issues would they be?'

'As you know, Mr Wilson and I were engaged by the Ashmolean to look into the death of Mr

Gavin Everett,' said Abigail.

'Which was suicide, as I understand.'

'The formal inquest has yet to take place, and although it is very likely that suicide will indeed be recorded, there is the reason why he took his own life.'

'And have you discovered any reason why he should have?'

'One situation has come to light that may have an impact on his death. We've discovered that Mr Everett was engaged in a fraud, whereby he had copies made of certain precious artefacts in the Ashmolean collection, and he had these copies put on display while he sold the originals to private collectors. It does suggest that the items that were copied were deliberately chosen to suit the private collectors.'

Chessington fell silent and turned away from Abigail, obviously taking this information in and turning it over in his mind. Finally, he turned back to Abigail and asked, 'How sure are you of this?'

'Very sure,' said Abigail. 'We were able to identify the articles that were copied. I have examined the copies and verified that they are, indeed, fraudulent. We've also effected the arrest of the man who made the copies. He is currently in custody at Kemp Hall police station awaiting a charge of conspiracy to commit fraud.'

Chessington shook his head.

'A terrible situation,' he said. 'I thank you for informing me of it, but I'm not sure that I'm involved in this. Yes, I am a collector, but

I've always made my purchases from bona fide sources.'

Abigail weighed up her next move, and then, with a silent apology to Daniel for her accusation to him of lying to Piers Stevens, she said, 'The other — and most vital — piece of evidence we have is Everett's journal, in which he lists his transactions. The particular item. The date of the sale. The amount. And, most importantly, the name of the person he sold it to.'

Chessington returned her look, but she could see from his eyes and the way a nerve in the side of his face twitched the inner turmoil this last statement caused him.

'You say this man who made the copies is under arrest,' he said hoarsely. 'Does that mean this journal is in the possession of the police?'

'Not yet,' said Abigail. 'Mr Marriott and I decided that this information belonged to the Ashmolean, as the frauds and the sales were committed using their property, and Everett was an employee.'

Chessington fell silent again.

'This is very dangerous news,' he said at last.

'Dangerous, to whom, my lord?' she asked. 'To the people who are named in the journal . . . or to the people who know the information?'

When Chessington didn't reply immediately, Abigail added, 'My partner in this case, Mr Wilson, believes you to be a dangerous person. He believes that perhaps you shot Inspector Grafton to prevent him from revealing what he discovered in your private study, namely that you had the original artefacts there.' When he still didn't respond but kept his face turned away from her, she said, 'Because of that, he advised me against telling you this piece of information. He also has seen the journal, and if anything should happen to me . . . '

'You believe I would harm you?!' said Chessington, suddenly angry and getting to his feet.

'No, but Mr Wilson does,' said Abigail. 'He wonders why, if you had intended to wound Inspector Grafton, as you said, you fired the shot into his chest rather than aiming at a leg or an arm, where there was less likelihood of you killing him.'

Chessington let out a groan, then said, no longer angry, 'Because I do not like guns and I am unused to handling them. Yes, I have one for my protection because, like many successful businessmen, I know I'm a target for burglars, but mostly it is for show. I did not have confidence that a shot aimed at the man's limbs would actually strike home, whereas a shot aimed at the body would.' He sat down, still avoiding her gaze. 'In fact, you are both right. I would not harm you. But I can be, as your partner says, a dangerous man to cross. I would kill to protect what is mine and dear to me.' He paused, then dropped his head before saying, 'Many years ago I killed a man in South Africa. It was not murder, it was self-defence.'

'Just like with Inspector Grafton?'

'No, this was different. This man — his name was Benjamin — thought I had double-crossed him in a business deal. I hadn't, but those were rough times in a rough country, and justice in the goldfields of the Transvaal was equally rough in nature. He came at me with a knife, intending to kill me. There was a struggle, and he died, stabbed with his own knife.

'Benjamin had friends in the Transvaal and I knew they'd be coming after me, so I decided to leave and return to England. But I kept my business interests out there. I appointed a manager to be my contact in the Transvaal, and that's the way it's operated ever since.' Chessington looked directly at Abigail and asked, 'Will Everett's journal be handed to the police?'

'That depends,' said Abigail. 'Mr Marriott and I have discussed the situation and we feel that there is little to be gained by having a public trial of the people involved.'

'And the people who bought these items may have done so in good faith!' said Chessington desperately.

'If these items were copied to order, we feel that would be an unlikely defence,' said Abigail.

Again, Chessington fell into thought, then he said, 'You don't know how lucky you are, Miss Fenton, to have been able to hold these ancient artefacts in your hands, and to have been the first to see them and touch them after they'd lain hidden for thousands of years. It is a feeling I have desired for a long time, much more than my first ambition to make money from the goldfields. To hold something in my hands that was buried with a pharaoh four thousand years ago, to be in touch with that time . . . ' He looked at her appealingly. 'To have such a piece in my own home, to be able to physically savour the reality of that ancient time . . . ' He dried up, lost for words, then took a deep breath before continuing, 'As I said, I would kill to protect what is mine.'

'Those pieces were never yours to own,' said Abigail. 'I know that from my own experiences as an archaeologist. I, too, share your feeling about touching something from that ancient time, and especially when I've been lucky enough to be the first to see something, to bring it out of the darkness where it's lain for so long. But I do not own them. I share in the joy of them, and I pass on that joy and pleasure to others to share. That's why we have places like the Ashmolean, where everyone can experience them.'

'It's not the same as owning a piece,' said Chessington.

'No, it isn't,' agreed Abigail. 'But I've learnt that we never own a piece of history. We are the guardians of it, we take care of it so that we can pass it on to the next generation. History is about always moving on. Today will be history tomorrow.'

Again, Chessington fell silent, and Abigail could see the agony in him.

'You know the pieces I have?' he said at last.

'We do,' said Abigail. 'And I can tell you that both Mr Marriott and I are of the opinion that if the items were to be returned, there would be no need for a police investigation.'

'And the man being held at Kemp Hall?'

'Would undoubtedly be released without charge if the Ashmolean refused to prosecute. Which they would if they had the stolen items back in their charge.'

Once more he fell silent, then said, 'It's not the fact that I will lose the money I paid Everett for them, it's the fact that I have them close, and now I will lose them.'

'You can buy others,' said Abigail. 'There are dealers, genuine dealers, who will sell you genuine articles. You could even fund a dig in Egypt. You are a rich man. You could go out there with the team of archaeologists. You'll be there as they uncover their finds, and — as the sponsor — those finds will be yours. Providing you have made the right arrangements with the Egyptian authorities.'

He weighed this up, then asked, 'Would you go with me?'

She shook her head.

'No,' she said. 'I prefer to work for institutions. But I can recommend some people to you who would be very good, very trustworthy.'

'I'd appreciate that,' said Chessington. He gestured towards his inner room. 'What shall we do about these?' he asked.

'I would suggest we say to Mr Marriott that through an intermediary they came into your possession, and you are delighted to return them to the Ashmolean. There will be no publicity.'

Chessington nodded.

'That sounds eminently acceptable.' He held out his hand to her. 'I thank you, Miss Fenton. I'm glad it ended this way.'

She took his hand and shook it. 'So am I.' She smiled. 'Far better than any alternatives, for all of us.'

★ ★ ★

Whichford Hall, reflected Daniel as he followed the butler to the conservatory where Baron Whichford waited for him, was the ancestral home of the one of the oldest families in England, and now that ancient line could be coming to a tragic end. *My mission is to see that doesn't happen, but at the same time to ensure that justice is served.*

Baron Whichford was standing in the conservatory, looking out through the large windows at the estate, as Daniel was shown in.

'Mr Wilson,' he said, and the two men shook hands. The baron gestured Daniel to a seat. 'I was intrigued to receive your note saying you wished to discuss a recent death in this area. I know of your reputation as a detective with Abberline's squad at Scotland Yard, of course, but I'm puzzled why you feel that I may have any insight into this death. Whose death are we talking about?'

'That of Gavin Everett,' said Daniel. 'The Ashmolean Museum have hired me and my partner, Abigail Fenton, to look into it.'

'Why?' asked Whichford. 'I understand he committed suicide.'

'Yes, that's the official explanation,' said Daniel. 'But there are circumstances that point to him having been shot by someone else.'

'What circumstances?'

'The lack of powder burns around the bullet wound. The fact that the wound entered the centre of his forehead rather than the temple. These, coupled with facts about Mr Everett's life, indicate he did not take his own life.'

Whichford studied Daniel thoughtfully, then asked, 'Are you here in an official capacity?'

'If you mean am I here on behalf of the police, the answer is no. I have been informed that the official verdict is suicide, unless I can gather evidence to prove the contrary.'

'And have you gathered any such evidence?'

'I have,' said Daniel. 'And it has led me to you.'

Whichford studied Daniel again, and then he laughed.

'And how did you arrive at this ludicrous conclusion?' he asked when his laughter had subsided. His manner was apparently cheerful, but Daniel was aware of a wariness in the baron's eyes.

'By a process of elimination,' said Daniel. 'The person who shot Everett had to be someone comfortable with firearms, a good shot with a steady hand.'

'That applies to many people in the area of Oxford,' said Whichford. 'It's hunting country.'

'Someone whose family were here in the sixteenth century.'

'Why the sixteenth century?'

'The Shakespeare play,' said Daniel. 'Commissioned by an ancestor in that time.'

Whichford fell silent at this.

'The Shakespeare play is a rumour,' he said at last. 'A myth.'

'We can always ask someone else to get confirmation that it exists,' said Daniel, adding carefully, 'but I'd rather not involve her. I'm sure you appreciate that.'

Daniel saw that although Whichford's face remained impassive, he swallowed.

'This person also had to be aware of Gavin Everett and his reputation for . . . shall we say . . . deceit,' continued Daniel. 'Which means someone who was in contact with him as a fellow member of the Quill Club. I believe that's where Everett first learnt about the Shakespeare play.'

Whichford sat looking intently at Daniel, as if trying to read his thoughts. Finally, he said, 'When I learnt that the Ashmolean had brought you in to investigate Everett's death, I made enquiries about you and your partner, Miss Fenton. I spoke to high-placed people in London who knew of your work when you were with Scotland Yard. People whose opinion I respect highly told me that you were not only intelligent but more importantly you were honest, with compassion towards the vulnerable and those who suffered injustice through no fault of their own.'

'I hope that's true,' said Daniel.

There was an awkward silence between the two men, then Daniel said, 'It was the play, wasn't it. You found it gone.'

'Yes,' said Whichford.

'And you knew who'd taken it. The only person other than yourself who had access to it.'

'Yes,' said Whichford again. Suddenly his head dropped and his whole body seemed to sag. But it was only for a moment. Then he pulled himself up again.

'It was my fault,' he said. 'I hadn't given Deborah the attention she deserved. And when she went to the various exhibitions and events at the Ashmolean, none of which were my particular interest, so I didn't go with her, she was ready prey for that . . . that leech, Everett. I don't believe they ever actually had an affair! Deborah is too . . . delicate for that. But I can sense that she fell under his spell. He had a silver tongue, full of flattery and charm. She would have been like an infant. As far as I know, they never met anywhere else but at the museum. But it was enough.

'Everett wormed his way into my wife's affections, led her to believe he was — ' Here he choked and also spat the words out: 'That he was in love with her. The lying, deceitful bastard! Of course, there was only one thing he was really after.'

'The play,' said Daniel.

Whichford nodded. 'Again, it was my fault. I remember joking about it at the club with some of my pals, how if I ever fell on hard times this play of Shakespeare's would see me right. Everett must have heard. He did that, you know: eavesdropped. Listened for pearls he could pick up and make use of.

'To be honest, I wasn't really aware of him at first, but then I began to hear about him from Deborah, about what wonderful things he was doing at the Ashmolean, and that set alarm bells ringing. It was the way she spoke about him that did it. You can tell. So I began to pay more attention to him when I was at the club, and I realised what a smarmy, two-timing, deceitful bastard he was.

'I noticed he became like a limpet on another member, that poor Piers Stevens, and I began to become aware he had designs on Deborah, but for what he could get out of her. I realised what that was when I went to check on the play — I was suspicious by then — and found it gone.'

He sat, lost in his own troubled thoughts before he spoke again. 'I confronted Deborah about the play, and she crumpled. She cannot lie. When the truth came out, I discovered just how badly he'd taken advantage of her. Not physically, but of the fact that she had been feeling alone. She'd unfortunately written him a letter in which she expressed her pleasure at his company. As I said, I never went with her to the things she wanted to go to, the new exhibitions at the Ashmolean, things like that. Unfortunately, the wording of the letter could have been interpreted as . . . inappropriate for a married woman. It was written in naive innocence, but to someone who didn't know that, it could have been interpreted . . . badly.

'It was then Everett played his hand and revealed himself for the evil leech he was, and what he was really after. He threatened to publicise the letter unless she gave him the play. He made sure she understood the interpretation people would put on the letter. It would have ruined her. It would also have ruined me, or my reputation as her husband.

'Deborah was trapped. She said she saw no option but to take the play from my study and give it to him. She told me she'd arranged to deliver it to him at the museum. Instead, I went to the museum at the arranged time to confront him. To my surprise, I saw Deborah there, waiting for me, come to beg me not to make a scene with him. She told me she'd made her own way there. I told her to wait for me in the carriage. She left, and then I went up to Everett's office.

'He was shocked when he saw me come in, and even more shocked when I told him why I was there. That he'd been making a fool of my wife, and of me. I told him I knew about the play. He tried blustering, claiming my wife had been the instigator of the plan to steal the play. That made me even angrier. The man had no honour!

'So, I shot him.' He stared questioningly at Daniel. 'What do you intend to do now? Bring in the police?'

'No,' said Daniel. 'I intend to consider this conversation closed. As far as I'm concerned, the police will be happy with the verdict of suicide. There is no need for this to go any further.'

'Then, in God's name, what has all this been about?' exploded Whichford angrily. 'You want some kind of leverage over me, is that it? Some sort of power of blackmail?'

'Absolutely not,' said Daniel firmly. 'You said you had checked my character with people you respect, and you gave no indication that any of them suggested that about me. No, My Lord, it's very simple. Possibly it's vanity on my part, but I pride myself that if I am tasked with an investigation, I follow it through to the end, regardless of what is in my way. In a way, I thought I owed it to you to have this face-to-face meeting and for you to know that I'd arrived at this conclusion. What you've said confirmed that. But this will not go further.'

'I'd been told that you are a fanatic about justice,' said Whichford.

'Yes, I suppose I am,' admitted Daniel. 'And here you've administered your own justice to a confidence trickster and a blackmailer. A man who was going to ruin your family's name, and — even worse — that of your wife. I can understand why you did what you did. But times are changing. You won't be prosecuted because the police have concluded their official investigation and, even if that were not the case, because of who you are, the latest in the long line of a very noble family. A pillar of the English establishment. I feel things will be different in the future.'

'Would you have acted differently if it had happened to the woman you love?'

'No,' admitted Daniel. 'But I would have been ready to take the consequences of my actions if I was found out, because I am not of the aristocracy, not a member of the elite of society, like our senior politicians. Your position has made you secure, and in that you are lucky. Long may your luck continue. But I need to warn you,

Baron, I feel that one day society will have a different attitude. The elite won't be protected any more. And that day may come sooner than you think.'

'You sound like one of these radicals.' Whichford scowled. 'Wanting to overthrow the order of our society and replace it with . . . what?' He shrugged. 'I'm still not sure if I can trust you not to use what you know.'

'You have my word, Baron Whichford,' said Daniel. 'Against my better judgement, this matter ends here. But I would urge you to heed my words. The next time you feel you, or yours, are being wronged, go to the law. It can be done discreetly. But if we all take justice into our own hands, and only the rich and powerful are allowed to get away with it, then there would be no proper society, just the unjust feudalism of the Dark Ages that existed centuries ago.'

'It was an honourable time,' countered Whichford.

'For the few,' said Daniel. He stood up. 'But, I repeat, My Lord, you have nothing to fear from me. This is the end of it. I do believe you are an honourable man. You now have to consider if you are also above the law.'

41

Daniel and Abigail's train journey back to London from Oxford was in the comfort and privacy of a first class compartment, courtesy of Gladstone Marriott and the Ashmolean, which meant they were able to discuss the outcomes of their Oxford experiences.

'Basically, it's unsatisfactory,' said Abigail. 'Baron Whichford murders Gavin Everett and gets away with it. Lord Chessington kills a Special Branch detective and also gets away with it. No culprits have been brought to justice.'

'That's not true,' said Daniel. 'Piers Stevens will stand trial for the death of Eve Lachelle. And we did discover her body. Also, you exposed the fraud that had been perpetrated against the Ashmolean and made sure that most of the stolen artefacts were returned.'

'But again, one of the criminals involved in that, Josiah Goddard, gets away scot free,' protested Abigail.

'Because the Ashmolean didn't want the adverse publicity that would go with a prosecution,' Daniel pointed out.

'It's not justice!' insisted Abigail, frustrated.

'It's justice of a sort,' countered Daniel. 'It's justice for Eve Lachelle. The Ashmolean has got most of its stolen artefacts back.'

'Alright, I believe that Lord. Chessington didn't deliberately mean to kill Inspector

Grafton, but Baron Whichford did mean to shoot Gavin Everett,' Abigail persisted. 'He went to see him armed with a pistol. That's murder! And he's got away with it!'

'I'm afraid it's called living in the real world,' sighed Daniel. 'The British Establishment is very good at protecting its own: senior aristocracy, royalty, cabinet ministers, prime ministers. During our investigation of the Jack the Ripper murders, my guv'nor, Fred Abberline, and I came across evidence that pointed at the possible involvement of Prince Albert Victor, the Duke of Clarence.'

'The Queen's grandson?' said Abigail, stunned.

'The very same.' Daniel nodded. 'In collusion with Sir William Gull, the Queen's physician, who was also the physician of Prince Albert Victor. Although the evidence was circumstantial, there was enough to suggest that we needed to talk to them. You and Inspector Pitt said that I can get people to talk. If that's true, I learnt everything on how to do that from Abberline. He was the master.

'Mary Ann Nichols, Annie Chapman, Elizabeth Stride, Catherine Eddowes and Mary Jane Kelly, all slaughtered during August and September 1888. The newspapers and the public were on our backs to find the killer, and both Abberline and I thought we had a line. Prince Albert Victor and Sir William Gull, in — we were sure — collusion with others.

'It soon became obvious that the idea of talking with Prince Albert Victor was out of the question — we were told so in no uncertain terms. But that still left Sir William Gull. If, as we suspected, Sir William and Prince Albert Victor were working together, and with others, murdering these women, we felt we might have a chance at cracking Sir William and getting a confession from him, in the same way that I got a confession from Baron Whichford about him killing Everett.

'With someone as high up as Sir William, we had to get authority from our superiors to talk to him. He was the Queen's physician, after all. So, just as you and I did when we talked to Superintendent Clare, we presented the evidence we had so far. We were refused permission to take that line of enquiry any further. We were told the evidence we had was only circumstantial with nothing to back it up. We were also told that national security was at risk. The idea that there might even be a suggestion that the Queen's grandson and her physician could be implicated in what was going on was out of the question. So that line of enquiry was dropped.'

'And Jack the Ripper was never caught,' said Abigail.

'No. But there were no more killings. Gull died in 1890. Prince Albert Victor was implicated in the Cleveland Street homosexual brothel scandal in 1889 that Fred and I also investigated, but — as I've mentioned before — none of the top aristocrats involved were ever charged, just the telegraph boys themselves. Like I say, the Establishment looks after its own.'

'Was that why you left the police force?' asked Abigail.

'It may have had something to do with it,' admitted Daniel. 'I'd thought being a private enquiry agent I'd be free of that sort of unfair pressure. But it seems from this case, things don't change.'

Then he smiled and opened the copy of the *Oxford Messenger* they'd bought at the railway station. 'But some things do change for the better. One good thing has come out of it all. Your friend Esther finally has her own byline on a proper story.'

The story was right across the front page.

BODY OF MISSING WOMAN FOUND.
MAN CHARGED WITH HER DEATH.
By Esther Maris.

The body of a young woman, Eve Lachelle, who went missing from her Oxford home three months ago has been found. There is debate on whether her death was deliberate, or an accident, but a local young man, Piers Stevens, has been charged with causing her death.

Then followed details of Eve Lachelle, her time working as a waitress at the Quill Club, which Esther described as 'a secretive club for gentlemen in the heart of Oxford', and a picture of Piers Stevens looking distressed.

'She's on the front page,' said Daniel. 'And that's thanks to you and the stern telling-off you

372

gave her editor. So we have achieved something.' Curious, he asked, 'How did you get Lord Chessington to return all those precious ancient artefacts to the Ashmolean?'

'I suggested to him he set up his own archaeological trip to Egypt and he could find others to replace them.'

'And what did he say?'

'He thought it a good idea. In fact, he asked me to go with him.'

'Oh? And what did you say?'

'I said no.' She turned to Daniel and nestled her head into his chest. 'I think I'm happy with the ancient relic I already have.'

Daniel chuckled and kissed the top of her head.

'Abigail Fenton,' he murmured. 'I love you.'

We do hope that you have enjoyed reading this large print book.

Did you know that all of our titles are available for purchase?

We publish a wide range of high quality large print books including:
Romances, Mysteries, Classics
General Fiction
Non Fiction and Westerns

Special interest titles available in large print are:
The Little Oxford Dictionary
Music Book
Song Book
Hymn Book
Service Book

Also available from us courtesy of Oxford University Press:
Young Readers' Dictionary
(large print edition)
Young Readers' Thesaurus
(large print edition)

For further information or a free brochure, please contact us at:
Ulverscroft Large Print Books Ltd.,
The Green, Bradgate Road, Anstey,
Leicester, LE7 7FU, England.
Tel: **(00 44) 0116 236 4325**
Fax: **(00 44) 0116 234 0205**

Other titles published by Ulverscroft:

MURDER AT THE BRITISH MUSEUM

Jim Eldridge

1894: A well-respected academic is found dead in a gentleman's convenience cubicle at the British Museum, the stall locked from the inside. Professor Lance Pickering had been due to give a talk promoting the museum's new 'Age of King Arthur' exhibition when he was stabbed repeatedly in the chest. Having forged a strong reputation working alongside the inimitable Inspector Abberline on the Jack the Ripper case, Daniel Wilson brings his expertise — and archaeologist Abigail Fenton — with him. But it isn't long before the museum becomes the site of another fatality, and the pair face mounting pressure to deliver results. With enquiries compounded by persistent journalists, local vandals and a fanatical society, Wilson and Fenton must race against time to salvage the reputation of the museum and catch a murderer desperate for revenge.

MURDER AT THE FITZWILLIAM

Jim Eldridge

1894: After rising to prominence for his role in investigating the case of Jack the Ripper alongside the formidable Inspector Abberline, Daniel Wilson has retired from the force and now works as a private enquiry agent. Having built a reputation for intelligence and integrity, Wilson is the natural choice for the Fitzwilliam Museum in Cambridge, which finds itself in need of urgent assistance. The remains of an ancient princess and her entourage are to be unveiled as the centrepiece of the museum's new Egyptian collection, but strange occurrences have followed their arrival in Britain: a dead body is discovered in a previously empty sarcophagus, one of the mummified bodyguards seemingly goes walkabout, and another man is found strangled to death with three-thousand-year-old bandages. Can Wilson unravel the mystery and preserve the museum's reputation?